WHERE WE FOUND OUR
Home

NATASHA BISHOP

WHERE WE FOUND OUR
Home

Prologue

Ciara

I HISS AS THE WARMTH OF MY DRIPPING WET BACK HITS THE COOL FLOOR of my new apartment. Sweat is coming out of places I didn't know sweat could reach. Who told me moving to Texas at the end of May was a good idea?

You could've stayed in Baltimore and waited to die, if that would be better for you.

Okay. I need a snack. Because even my inner voice is being an asshole now.

I search through my purse until I find a granola bar. This'll do for now. I look around at what I hope will be my new safe haven. It's nice. A simple one bedroom. That's all I need. The kitchen is an open floor plan that connects to the living room. The bedroom leads into the bathroom, and the closet is on the other side of the bathroom. I kind of hate that, but I won't complain. I'm lucky to even be here. It doesn't feel like a home but it feels... better. Different.

This will work out. Just fly under the radar, and you won't have to run again.

Ahh okay. The snack is working its magic, I see.

I look around at all my boxes I've brought up so far. I don't have too much stuff but enough that the thought of unpacking right now puts a pain in the pit of my stomach. I decided moving from Baltimore, Maryland to Austin, Texas by myself was enough of a headache with just the small stuff, so I don't have any of the big items yet. No couch, no bed, no table. I have some of that stuff ordered, and they're coming this week, but it'll be an air mattress for me until then.

I should probably take a short rest before I overheat. I might as well take advantage of the slightly less hot air in my apartment and call my mom and friends to let them know I've arrived before going to get the rest of my stuff.

My mom answers on the first ring. "Are you okay? I thought you were going to call when you first got there." She barely takes a breath during that sentence. I feel bad knowing that she's probably barely taken her eyes off her phone since I left.

She tries to grill me on my motivations for moving…again, but I deflect because I don't want to have that conversation. She knows the basics. I was tired of being scared shitless to walk outside. I hated who I had become there. I'm not one to hide in the shadows, afraid to go anywhere or talk to anyone. She doesn't need to know the rest. That she's safer with me gone. I'll do what it takes to protect her and my girls. I fill her in on the ride down here, and she fills me in on everything going on back home before we hang up and my friends invite me to a video chat.

I love my best friends Brittany, Simone, and Sarah, but our conversation is just like the one I just rushed through with my mom. They've been trying to coax more information from me about why I felt the need to move by myself. Anyone else who knew my story would say "ah, that makes sense" and leave it at that, but these girls have been my best friends since elementary school. They know me better than I know myself. They know I'm hiding something. But I'm not telling them the whole story. They'll have to pry the information out of my cold, dead hands.

Which could be sooner rather than later at this point.

I do what I have to do to get them to back off. I lie. I'm becoming concerned with how easily the lies are falling out of my mouth now. The lies are intricate. A simple "I'm fine" won't do. I have to feed them lines about rebuilding myself and needing time to clear my head. They don't need to know that I've sentenced myself to a life of solitude. That I don't plan to let them visit me—ever. That I didn't just come here to put distance between myself and my hometown but between me and them. If I tell them everything, they'll crowd around me and never let me out of their sight. And they'll be rewarded for their efforts with a bullet between the eyes or some other brutal death.

Once the topic is firmly off of me, the conversation flows much better. Brittany gives us the scoop on her latest work drama and last creepy date. The poor thing has the worst track record with dating. Sarah fills us in on her upcoming trip with her longtime boyfriend, Jordan. Simone of course asks me if I've met any attractive guys in the five minutes I've been here, because apparently I need a stress reliever in the form of dick. She's not wrong, but the thought of trusting someone enough to be that vulnerable with them right now? Impossible. The thought of someone seeing and touching my scars? No, thank you. She then gives us the rundown of her quest for good dick and how she thought she found someone to break her four-month drought, but he turned out to be a dud. Her exact words were, "I was trying to get these walls beat up last night, and I had to settle for my vibrator. Again." God, it feels so good to laugh with them. When was the last time I haven't faked a smile or laugh?

After we end our call, I grab my keys and head toward the door. I check the peephole, stand behind the door, and pull it open quickly. Nothing, or no one, charges their way in, so I poke my head out and check the hallway in both directions before stepping out and locking the door behind me. Bringing all my boxes upstairs would be much easier if I didn't have to take the time to unlock the door after every trip, but the last year has bred some healthy paranoia into me.

Okay, maybe not healthy. But I am entitled to do what's needed to feel safe.

Even if you may never be truly safe again.

Do you need another snack? Please shut up.

I grab the last box and lock my car. I start to reach for the building door, but a man opens it before I have a chance. He has a salt-and-pepper beard but no hair on his head. He looks like he's in his forties or fifties, and he's wearing a brown tracksuit that gives me Bernie Mac vibes. But his slow perusal of my body has my guard way up. He holds the door for me but he speaks directly to my chest as he asks, "Need any help with moving in?"

"No thanks, I'm fine." I move past him, careful not to touch him and careful not to look back at him, but I feel him watching me.

"You new in town or you from around here?"

Oh Lord. Please not with the personal questions. When is this elevator getting here?

"I'm from around."

He chuckles. You know—that chuckle men give when they know they're getting the brush-off but don't care.

"Well, if you need anyone to show you around town, let me know. I'm in 4408."

Thank goodness he's not on my floor. Answering my prayers, the elevator opens at that moment.

"Good to know. Nice meeting you," I lie.

I live on the sixth floor, but I'll take the elevator to the seventh floor and walk down a flight. Yeah, I'm that paranoid.

CHAPTER
One

Ciara

AFTER MY NAP YESTERDAY, I SPENT THE REST OF THE DAY UNPACKING. Once I got started, it was easy to get everything put away. It's not like there was much to unpack. Just my clothes, toiletries, kitchen supplies, my laptop, some photos, and my books.

My couch, bed, and TV are all supposed to be delivered tomorrow, so I decided today I would explore my new city. I haven't written anything for my book in two weeks, so hopefully some good old-fashioned people watching will inspire me. I throw on a red T-shirt bodysuit, jean shorts, and my red Chucks. I grab my laptop bag and go through my normal security routine before heading out.

I live in downtown Austin, so there are a lot of places around me, but I don't feel comfortable walking around the city alone so I'm going to drive. I probably won't go far, but I'd rather have my car close to me in case I need to make a getaway. My first stop is 2nd Street District. When I first decided to move here, all my Google searches said that 2nd Street District had everything you could possibly need from retail to restaurants and entertainment. Google was not wrong. This place is incredible. I've already discovered a few restaurants I want to try and a few clothing stores where I know I can get into a lot of trouble.

I'm observing a statue of Willie Nelson when the smell of fresh baked goods draws me to a small coffee shop called Sasha's. My nose tells me I need to go in there. The outside has a modern feel to it, but the inside is bursting with color. The walls, the counter, and the tables are a sleek white, but the chairs are all bright colors. It looks like a rainbow threw up, but... it works. Everything flows together beautifully. I feel immediately relaxed and happy being here.

There are a few people scattered throughout the shop, but none of them are paying me any attention. I like it here. A little girl is perched at one of the hightops coloring, in her own little world.

Behind the counter, there's a gorgeous black woman who eyes me curiously. Her hair is in a big, wild, curly fro that I envy. She has on white jeans with a striped, multicolored shirtdress and large gold hoop earrings. There's a tall white woman working with her. She's wearing her chestnut hair in a messy bun, sporting blue jeans with a bright yellow racerback tank top, and is busy making some sort of latte.

I walk up to the counter, and the black woman greets me with a warm smile. "Hi there, welcome to Sasha's. I'm Sasha." I'm not surprised given that her colorful outfit matches the aesthetic of the whole place. I wonder if wearing bright colors is required for all employees. "What can I get for you?"

I take a quick look at the menu. "Hi, Sasha, can I have a large caramel brûlée macchiato, please?"

"No problem. Is that for here or to go?"

"Here, please." This is as good a place as any to try to get some writing done.

I pay for my drink, and Sasha tells me to pick a seat and she'll bring it over. I decide to sit at one of the booths so I'll have enough room to spread out. I pull out my laptop and bend down to plug it into the outlet. When I come back up, I nearly trip Sasha and then marvel at the fact that the macchiato is in an actual mug instead of a paper cup. That's adorable.

"Sorry, didn't mean to scare you. Here's your macchiato. I'm not sure if you like it or have any allergies, but I brought you over a banana nut muffin too. You looked like you could use an extra pick-me-up."

Holy shit, how did she guess my favorite muffin? And why is she so nice? It unnerves me.

Calm down. Some people are just nice. Don't make it weird.

"Wow, that's so nice of you. I love banana nut. Thanks."

"No problem. You new around here?"

Oh Lord. That question again. It makes me uncomfortable but not in the same way my creepy neighbor did. Sasha seems like one of those women that if you aren't careful, she can get you to spill all your secrets. She's one of those people you just want to share with. I don't need that in my life right now.

"How'd you know?" *What? Why did I say that? Don't engage. See, this is exactly what I mean.*

"You just seem…never mind." Now she has my attention.

"Wait, just seem what?" She looks in my eyes, and I don't see pity, but there's understanding there.

"Lost." Damn. Yeah, definitely can't come back here. She's another Brittany, seeing too much. "Sorry. I shouldn't have said that. I just wanted to make sure you were okay."

I want her to leave me alone, but for some reason I also want to reassure her. "No, it's fine. I am new here. This is my second day in town."

I wait for her to ask where I moved from and try to figure out how I'll deflect that question or what lie I'll tell, but to my surprise and delight that question never comes. "Well, welcome to Austin! I don't know if you live around here. If so, you've probably already seen that there's a lot to do down-town, but even if you go farther away from the city, there's still so much to do and see. I think you'll like it."

My grin grows at the fact that she didn't ask where exactly I live. She seems to pick up that I'm uncomfortable answering personal questions so she doesn't push, but she's still sweet. I didn't even realize my shoulders had tensed up, but they relax the more she speaks.

"Thank you so much. I'm loving it so far." Just then, the little girl I saw coloring walks over to us. Now that I really look at her, I'm positive that she's Sasha's daughter. She has the same curly hair—though hers is lighter than her mom's—the same brown eyes, and the same smile. She looks to be around five, and she makes my ovaries hurt.

Kids are probably not in your future at this rate.

Thank you for the reminder. Jackass.

"Mommy, you making a new friend already?" Oh my goodness, her cuteness goes up three notches right then. Her voice is the epitome of innocence.

Sasha laughs and hugs her daughter. "Let me live, little girl." She turns to me. "She's always inserting herself into my conversations. This is my daughter, Nevaeh. Nevaeh, this is...I'm sorry, I didn't catch your name."

Deep breath. "Ciara."

"This is Ciara."

"Pretty name." Nevaeh smiles.

"Thank you. Yours is pretty too." She beams at the compliment.

"Alright, well, we'll leave you to enjoy your treats and your work. Let me know if you need anything else."

"I really appreciate it, Sasha. Nice meeting you, Nevaeh." Nevaeh waves at me, and Sasha smiles as she leads her daughter back to her table.

I feel immediately comfortable with Sasha and Nevaeh, and that makes me anxious. I can't afford to get close to anyone here. I need to keep to myself. As much as I love the vibe of this coffee shop, I can't come back here.

I'm the worst. The absolute fucking worst. It's been two weeks and my ass has been going to Sasha's shop every single day.

I walk in, catch up with Sasha and Nevaeh, grab a macchiato, sample a different pastry each visit—though the banana nut muffin has remained my favorite—and sit in a booth to write more of my novel. The words come to me easily there.

I write thrillers, which is funny to me when I think about what I've been through, but it's what I've always wanted to write. To put it bluntly, murders fascinate me. I've watched *Unsolved Mysteries* and everything on the ID channel since I was a kid. We've all had someone or something bother us to the point where we thought we would snap, but exploring what pushes a person to the breaking point where they actually take a life is fascinating. Exploring the mindset of a person so cold and calculating that they can take a life without remorse both unnerves and excites me. It's why I've tried, to no avail, to understand what makes the source of my nightmares tick. With everything that's happened in my life in the last couple of years, writing my debut novel feels cathartic. I'm in control of the terror. I control the unease. I know when the bad guy is coming. I control who dies and when. I control the outcome. I need this control. I'm clinging to it with every fiber of my being.

I always wanted to be an author, but working a full-time job stole my spark for writing. I was too tired or annoyed at the end of the day to write. Now that I've received the settlement from my accident, I have more than enough savings so I can take the risk of not working and focus on trying to put my debut novel out there. When I spoke to my mom yesterday, she asked if I'd be trying to get a job soon as she worried I'd go stir-crazy without one. I've always had a job since I was sixteen, so I understand her concern, but right now this is what I need to do for my mental health. The days are starting to blend together for me though. I'll probably end up finding a part-time job to give me something to do and have income coming in— but I don't need to just yet.

"What are you up to for the rest of the day?" Sasha asks, interrupting my thoughts. I really have no idea what I'm thinking about by building a friendship with this woman and her daughter. I guess if I keep it to surface level interactions here at the coffee shop, it's fine. It's not like we've exchanged numbers and are talking outside of my daily visits.

But if they get caught up in your drama and something happens to them, you'll never forgive yourself.

Ugh. Enough already. I can't keep living like this. It's okay to talk to people. I just need to keep my distance.

"Umm, I'm probably just going to go home, honestly," I reply as I start packing up my laptop.

"That's what you say every day."

"Not true. The other day, I went to Randalls when I left here." Yes, Randalls is a grocery store. But it's still going out. If it's not the grocery store or Sasha's, I'm not going. I talked a good game about exploring my new city, but I've done none of that. I haven't even gone out shopping for stuff to put in my apartment. Online shopping is my friend.

Sasha smirks. "The grocery store doesn't count. You need to be exploring more. How old are you?"

Deep breath. "Twenty-eight."

"Yeah, you see. You're younger than I am. You need to be going out to bars or clubs or anything more than going to a coffee shop and then home every day."

She has no idea what she's asking me to do, and she probably never will.

"Yeah, I know, I know. How about this—I'm going to go across the street to that boutique and get myself a cute outfit." It's only around two p.m. I can do this.

"Perfect. A going out outfit maybe."

Going out. Ha. Funny. Yeah, I'll go out. Out of my bedroom to my couch. "Maybe."

Sasha smirks again with those knowing eyes. I grab the rest of my stuff and get out of there before she can dig deeper. I wave bye to Nevaeh and head across the street to the boutique.

I end up buying a cute maxi dress. It's multicolored, so Sasha would probably approve. Walking out of the store, a little girl who has her face buried in a tablet bumps into me.

"Sorry!" the little girl yelps.

"It's okay. No problem, sweetie." I go to move around her when she looks up at me again.

"You're really pretty."

Are all the kids in this city so stinking cute?

"Aww, thank you."

The little girl smiles at me and considers her next words carefully.

"You're welcome. My dad's girlfriend is really pretty too, but my mom doesn't like her because she said my dad cheated with her."

A laugh bursts out of me before I can stop it. Kids are always spilling their parents' tea. "Ohh okay, well, I'm sorry." That's all I can manage without laughing again.

Just then a woman who must be her mother runs over to us. She looks heated and embarrassed, so I'm guessing she heard her daughter's comment. "Candice! What did I tell you about running your mouth to strangers?"

"Sorry, Mommy."

"Girl, just stand here out of people's way and wait for me. I just need to pick up our food real quick." The girl moves over to the bench by the curb and goes back to her tablet while her mom goes back inside the carryout spot.

A minute later, a black Mazda going way too fast comes up the hill racing toward us. The car swerves a few times unnecessarily, and my back stiffens. The thought of an impaired driver gives me chills, and I'm frozen in the past until I realize the car has completely veered to the side and is probably going to jump the curb. Right into Candice.

"Candice!" I scream, but she's so caught up in her tablet she ignores me. I look over to her mom, but she's deep in conversation with the cashier.

Shit.

My feet take off before my mind catches up. I have to get her out of the way. She's just a little girl. She has her whole life ahead of her. I've escaped death a few times already, and maybe I'll be lucky again.

The car's getting closer, and people are finally starting to register what's happening, but nobody has noticed Candice right in the car's path. I reach Candice as the car's headlights momentarily blind me.

This is gonna hurt.

Then everything goes black.

CHAPTER
Two

Lincoln

S HIFT CHANGE WAS JUST TWO HOURS AGO. USUALLY I WOULD SLEEP
for a good eight hours before rejoining society, but my niece, Nevaeh,
called and asked me to visit her at my sister's coffee shop today, and I
can't ever say no to her.

Sasha is talking to a customer behind the counter, and Nevaeh is coloring in a booth, of course. The tiny monster races over to me when she notices me, and I scoop her up in a big bear hug.

I love both of my nieces and my nephew. They own my heart, but
Nevaeh has me completely wrapped around her finger. It's pathetic, really.

"Linky! You're here."

I give her all the side-eye because we both know she's not surprised I
come when she calls.

"I sure did. You better have a good reason for interrupting my slum-
ber, or I'll have to eat a little girl for my snack." I make a growling noise at
her. Nevaeh always calls me a brown bear because I hibernate after work.

She giggles as I tickle her. "Stop it!!" I continue tickling her until she's

"Are you two done acting up in my shop?" Sasha's face is stern, but her voice is full of amusement.

"Nah, not yet." I reach for Nevaeh again, but she dodges my grasp and takes off giggling. I'll give her a head start.

"Hey, little bro," Sasha says as she hugs me.

"Hey, sis. How's business today?"

"Good. Did Mom call you?"

"No, should she have?" I hate being blindsided by my family, so if Mom is calling me to drill me about something, I need Sasha to tell me now.

"I think Reggie wanted her and Dad to babysit the kids this weekend so she and Michael could have a date night, but Mom and Dad are going to Dad's friend's retirement party this weekend, and Carter and I have a date night of our own, so Mom told her she'd ask you."

I chuckle. That's it? "Why wouldn't Reggie just call me herself?"

"You know if Mom offers to take a task off Reggie's hands, she just accepts." My oldest sister, Reggie, is a badass family lawyer and if she isn't dealing with a case, she's busy with her two kids and her husband. She used to refuse help all the time because, in her words, she's goddamn Superwoman, but Mom always insists, worrying about Reggie burning out. So Reggie just started accepting almost anything because it's easier. Reggie may be a lawyer, but no one wins a fight against our mom.

"I'm back on shift on Saturday morning."

"Guess she'll have to call Isaiah then." Even though my schedule is always crazy, my sisters always call me first for babysitting duties before my younger brother. He loves our nieces and nephew as much as I do, but he tends to forget he's actually twenty-eight, not twelve, and ends up needing a babysitter more than they do.

"Guess so."

"Linky, you missed my favorite." Nevaeh nestles into my side.

I feign offense. "Favorite what? Customer?" She nods. "Say it ain't so. I thought I was your favorite."

"No, silly. You're no custard, you're my uncle." She has a point there.

"Customer."

She squints her eyes at me. "That's what I said."

"Right, of course." Duh.

"You don't even pay half the time, so you're definitely not a customer," Sasha adds, unnecessarily I might add. I slap her shoulder, and she punches me in the ribs while laughing.

"Okay, fine, so who is your favorite and what's so special about them?"

"Her name's Ciara. She's so pretty and nice. Her eyes look like yours."

"Ah, gorgeous with a twinkle?" I tease.

"No. Sad." Sasha's eyes widen and she looks away from the both of us.

Sometimes I forget that even though Nevaeh is only five, she's just as intuitive as her mother. She's going to be a force when she's older. I have to work on putting on a better mask with her.

"Well, Ciara seems great. Sorry I missed her."

"You can come again tomorrow! She'll be here." Wait a minute. Is this why Nevaeh wanted me to visit her today? She wanted me to meet this Ciara?

Oh, boy. You know your love life is sad when your five-year-old niece is trying to play matchmaker.

Too bad I have no interest in dating now or ever again. I keep my relationships casual, but I know better than to try to explain that to Nevaeh. Especially with Sasha within earshot. I like my balls where they are, thank you very much.

"Umm, maybe. Here, come with me to the display. You gotta help me pick out my dessert." Distraction is probably my best way out of this, but I have to use food. Otherwise she'll see right through me.

"Can I has half?" Always the negotiator.

"Don't you always?"

Nevaeh beams and runs over to the display case. I look over at Sasha who's watching me with a guilty look on her face.

"Sorry," she mouths.

I shake my head. No apologies necessary. I start to head over to the display case when something outside catches my eye.

I glance over, and the most gorgeous woman I've ever seen is standing outside of a store talking to a little girl.

Her almond-colored skin is flawless. She isn't very tall, but her legs go on for days and they're covered with ripped jeans that fit her like a second skin, accentuating her small waist, thick thighs, and delicious ass. She has on a tight white tank top that's tied in the front so I can make out her toned stomach. I can see she has a full sleeve tattoo on her left arm, but I can't tell what the images are. They're bright and colorful, though, and I want to trace them with my tongue. *What the fuck, Linc?* Her box braids are pulled up into a high ponytail, and it draws my attention to her slender neck that I imagine leaving my mark on. *Woah. You need to relax.* I can't even pull myself away from those thoughts because I'm distracted by her full-bodied, lush lips. She's absolutely stunning. She laughs at something the little girl said and the movement goes straight to my dick. She laughs with her entire body, and it's sexy as hell.

Holy shit, get a grip. Like you've never seen a beautiful woman before. Last thing you need to do is sport wood in the middle of your sister's shop in front of your niece.

"Umm, Linky? Why you looking so hard at Ciara?"

Fuck. Of course she would be the woman Nevaeh was telling me about. Damn, my niece has good taste. I wonder if she'd be down for something casual.

No. Nevaeh said she comes to the coffee shop every day, and she's obviously already developed an attachment to this woman. I can't risk some awkward situation when it ends badly. Which it will.

"I'm not. I thought I saw somebody I know." Nevaeh gives me an incredulous look. Get your too-smart-for-your-age eyes off of me, little girl.

She looks like she's going to say something else, but we both whip around at the sound of screeching tires. A black Mazda is racing down the street. The driver starts swerving, and it's clear they're impaired or distracted. *Idiot. It's the middle of the damn day.*

I pull my cell phone out, prepared to make a call to the police to deal with this guy when I notice Ciara take off running. It takes me a minute to realize she's running toward the little girl she was talking to earlier. I look over and realize the car is heading straight for her. *Shit.*

I turn to the man sitting behind me at one of the hightops watching with his jaw on the ground. "Sir, call 911 now." He snaps to action.

"Sasha! Call Dominic, tell him we're gonna need a unit." She shakes off her worried gaze and grabs her phone.

"Linky, you gotta help her!" I'm already at the door on my way to try to help. Hopefully I won't be too late. Again.

Not now, Linc.

"I got it. Stay here."

I rush across the street, keeping Ciara in my sight the whole time. She reaches Candice in enough time to dodge the car, but when she snatches the girl up she turns her body so she can break the fall for them and slams her head on the concrete as they go down.

The sound of her head hitting the concrete sends chills all the way down my spine, and I feel it in my toes. I spare a glance toward the driver, who has crashed into the light pole a few feet away. *Good, at least he won't be getting away.* A quick scan of the scene tells me everyone else had cleared out of the way without issue.

"See if he's okay. Don't let him leave," I demand of the bystanders closest to his car. They immediately get to work. I love my community.

I reach Ciara and the little girl. Ciara isn't moving, and the little girl is crying.

"Is she okay?" the girl screeches.

"Candice!" A woman runs over to us and scoops the kid off of Ciara.

"Mama, that woman grabbed me. I landed on top of her, so I'm not hurt at all. But she hit her head so hard. Is she okay?"

"It's okay. I'm here to help. She'll be okay." I hope. She'll definitely have a concussion but hopefully that's the worst of it. "Ma'am. Can you hear me? Can you open your eyes?" I ask.

She opens her eyes slowly and her eyes knock me on my ass. She has deep chocolate eyes with a gray ring around the edge of them that completely captivates me.

Focus, Linc. Jesus, she's injured.

I clear my throat and speak again. "There you are. Can you tell me your name?"

"That's some pickup line." She smirks. Good Lord, this woman is trouble. Her plump lips are saying one thing, but her eyes tell a different story. A story packed with vulnerability and rawness. One I'm suddenly desperate to read.

"It works with all the ladies. Why don't we try again?"

She takes a deep breath before answering. "It's Ciara."

"Hi, Ciara. How are you feeling?"

"Like I slammed my head on the ground. How are you?" What a smart-ass. I like it. She isn't slurring her words, so that's a good sign. I feel the back of her head and it's not bleeding, but I can already feel the knot forming.

"I've been better. I wish I didn't have to meet a beautiful woman by getting her to a hospital but such is life."

"Yeah, but this way is more fun, right?" She smiles again, and even though it's clear she's smiling through the pain, it's still the most beautiful smile I've ever seen.

I need to get to safer topics. "Can you tell me what day it is?"

"It's Thursday. I think. I was just complaining that my days are starting to blend together so I could be wrong, but I'm pretty sure it's Thursday."

It is Thursday. I can't tell if her "days blending together" comment is due to her head injury or not, so I probe further.

"Do you feel nauseous or anything?"

She seems to realize that I'm hovering above her at that moment, and she struggles to get up but is too slow.

"No, no nausea. I'm fine. I can walk."

"Okay, let's get up slowly." She seems antsy all of a sudden, so I give her some space to get up but stay close.

"See? I'm fine." She takes two steps and then wobbles. I'm there in half a second to catch her. I want to pick her up and carry her to safety, but that's overkill.

"Let's take it slow. You're going to need to go to the hospital. You probably have a concussion."

"Nah, no need." *Umm, what?*

"Ma'am…"

She cuts me off. "You don't have to call me ma'am. I know it's probably part of the Texas charm, but it makes me feel old."

I chuckle. "Okay, how about Ciara then?"

"I mean, it is my name." Damn, every time she gets smart with me it makes my dick twitch. I need to wrap this up.

The cops and the EMTs arrive at around the same time. Two of the EMTs go over to tend to the driver. I heard one of the bystanders mention that he reeked of booze, so my concern that some sort of medical emergency caused his crash subsides and anger takes root. He'll probably be spending the night in the drunk tank. Hopefully he'll even get a little time for almost killing a child and Ciara. I have no tolerance for that shit.

Two more EMTs head over to us. "Hey, Linc. What we got?" Dominic asks. Dom is one of my best friends, and he's an EMT at my fire station.

"She moved a little girl out of the way of the driver and hit her head on the concrete on the way down. Probable concussion. She needs a hospital."

"No, really, I'm fine," Ciara declares, but her eyes are unfocused.

"Ciara, it's okay. You'll be in and out. I'll ride with you."

"No offense, but I don't even know you so why would that be a selling point? Sexy or not." Dominic's shoulders shake with laughter, and I try to act unaffected, but it's nice to know that she's attracted to me too.

"Stick with me. I'm the best company to have in situations like this."

She starts to roll her eyes but stops, and I curse myself for flirting with this woman when she's in so much pain.

"Can you walk, Miss?" Dominic asks.

"Yes." She stands again but way too fast, and she goes down immediately.

"Shit," I hiss before catching her. I inwardly scold myself for noticing how nice her body feels in my arms.

"You got her?" Dominic eyes me holding Ciara.

I look down at the beautiful woman in my arms and feel a sense of peace, but I don't know why.

"Yeah, I got her."

Dominic leads us over to the ambulance. I have no idea what I'm in for, but it's too late now.

CHAPTER
Three

Lincoln

I NSTEAD OF SEEING CIARA OFF AT THE HOSPITAL LIKE I SHOULD'VE, I back to the exam room with her. I know a few of the nurses and doctors here—that's just the nature of our professions—so I didn't even bother trying to lie about my relation to Ciara. The nurse who admitted her told me to stay quiet and go on back with her.

I can tell Ciara isn't unconscious, but she keeps her eyes closed and stays silent. The bright lights must be bothering her, and her head is probably throbbing, but I feel the need to make sure she's okay. And maybe I just want to hear her voice again.

"You gonna pretend to be asleep the whole time?"

She slowly opens her eyes and curses under her breath. "You're actually here."

Interesting comment. "Did you think I was fake?"

"Actually, yeah. I convinced myself that I made you up somehow."

"Care to elaborate on that?"

"Nope," she says with a pop. "So, why are you back here with me? *How* are you back here with me? Aren't there rules against that?"

"I've got some pull here." She starts fidgeting with her hospital gown, and the need to hold her grows. I want her to be comfortable with me, but that's ridiculous. We don't know each other.

"Actually, I'm a firefighter, and I know some of the nurses and doctors here, so I asked if I could keep you company. I'll step out when the doctor comes in if you don't want me to hear anything. I just didn't want you to be alone."

She looks up at me but doesn't quite meet my eyes. "Thank you. You can stay." I can tell it took a lot for her to let me into her space, and I'm honored she did, which ironically makes me want to run out the door and far away.

"I'm Lincoln, by the way."

"Hi, Lincoln."

"You know, my niece is a pretty big fan of yours. I gotta say, after seeing you jump in front of a speeding car to save a kid, I'm a pretty big fan myself."

She smiles, but it doesn't reach her eyes and her shoulders tense up. Did I say something wrong? "I wasn't aware I had a fan club. Who's your niece?"

"Nevaeh. She said you come to my sister's coffee shop every day." Her eyes widen and she curses under her breath again, but her shoulders relax a bit.

"Sasha is your sister? Well, that's just perfect." She laughs without humor. "They're pretty incredible. Very welcoming. I guess it runs in the family."

I smile. That's one way to say we insert ourselves into people's lives against their will. "Mama managed to instill some manners into us. There are four of us plus she's always reining my dad in from something, so we gave her a run for her money but she still whipped us into shape."

"Four kids, huh? My mom always said never to let your kids outnumber you." She winces, and I can't be sure if she's in pain from adjusting in her seat or if something else is bothering her.

"You okay?"

"Yeah. All good."

I want to probe further, but the doctor comes in and Ciara immediately breaks eye contact with me.

"Hi, Ms. Jeffries, how are you feeling?"

"I feel fine, really." She's obviously in pain. I know most people hate hospitals, but she seems really anxious to get out of here. I have no business speaking on her behalf, but if she keeps downplaying her injury, I will tell the doctor the truth about how she feels.

Why?

Beats the fuck out of me.

"Okay, well, your MRI and CT scans came back clear, so we don't have to worry about any sort of bruising or bleeding on your brain, but you most likely have a concussion." She proceeds to ask Ciara a series of questions, and she answers well for the most part but at times she becomes confused or her reaction time is slow.

"You definitely have a concussion. I'm going to give you some medicine for the pain but otherwise you'll just need to rest." She turns to me. "Will you be the one monitoring her at home tonight?"

Ciara's eyes widen. She looks panicked, and it's a good thing the doctor is facing away from her. I know the doctor is asking because Ciara needs to be on concussion watch. She'll need someone to keep an eye on her symptoms over the next few hours and to check in on her while she sleeps. I don't want to come across as a creep by wanting to be the guy who checks on her while she sleeps, but I don't know if Ciara has anyone to look out for her at home. I doubt it since no one showed up at the hospital and she didn't call anyone. If she doesn't have someone to watch her, they'll keep her overnight at the hospital, and something tells me she would not want that.

So what? Are you going to stay with her?

That'll probably send her into a panic too, but which is worse? I have to hope I'm the lesser of two evils.

"Yes, that's me." Thank God this is not one of the doctors I know, so she doesn't even question it.

"Okay, great. Then if you have no further questions, I'll get your medicine and your discharge papers ready."

Ciara's face transforms to a look of indifference. "Okay, thank you. I don't have any questions."

"Take care, honey." The doctor closes the door behind her and Ciara whirls on me.

"You'll be the one monitoring me tonight?"

"Listen, you seem anxious to not be here anymore, and if I had said no, she would have insisted you stay overnight."

Her eyes soften slightly. "I really appreciate that, and I don't wanna be here, but I'm not comfortable staying with you or you staying with me. I'm sorry."

She's absolutely right. I have no idea how I was thinking that would even be an option. My phone buzzes with a text from Sasha.

Sasha: Hey, Dom said you went back with Ciara. Is she okay? I'm in the waiting room.

Why had I not thought of that before?

Me: How would you feel about two overnight guests tonight?

The reply comes instantly.

Sasha: I'm gonna assume you're talking about Ciara, in which case, I feel great about that. If you're the 2nd guest I'm gonna need more time to consider.

Pain in the ass.

I turn back to Ciara. "Actually, I was thinking you might feel more comfortable staying with Sasha tonight. I'm sure Nevaeh would be excited to have you."

"Oh. Umm, she doesn't have to do that. Really, I'd be fine at home on my own."

"Honestly, you'd probably be doing her a favor. She and Nevaeh seem to really like you, and they watched you hit your head really hard today. My sister is a worrier and she's in the waiting room texting me for updates. If you don't agree now, she'll probably browbeat you down when we get out there. Sooo, would you rather agree now or have a worse headache when you agree later?" I'm really leaning into the guilt trip here, but it's not a lie. Sasha would insist she look out for her. She's always taking someone under her wing, and I don't know if I'm annoyed or grateful that Ciara seems to be the latest target.

She thinks hard for a minute, but then all the fight seems to go out of her. "Okay, fine. But only because my head already hurts enough." I chuckle. Whatever it takes is fine by me.

After she's completely discharged, we head out to the waiting room to find Sasha.

"Hey, thank you for letting me stay with you tonight."

Sasha wraps Ciara up in a hug, and she tenses for a minute before relaxing into it.

"No, thank you. I feel so guilty. If I hadn't gotten on you about getting out more you probably wouldn't have even been there."

"Well, if I hadn't been who knows what would've happened to that little girl, so it all worked out. Please don't feel guilty." My heart jumps at that response. I already admire her for jumping in front of the kid in the first place, but hearing she would willingly do it again gives me a sense of…pride.

I need to get away from this woman. I just met her, and she's seriously fucking with my head. I should go home right now and leave Sasha to take care of Ciara, but I'm apparently a glutton for punishment.

"Let's get you home. Carter called me earlier because Nevaeh is freaking out looking for an update. Linc, Carter and Isaiah went to get your car earlier, so it's at my house."

"Great. Thanks, sis."

On the way to Sasha's house, I take advantage of the fact that Ciara is sitting up front, and I spend the entire car ride stealing glances at her profile. I study her tattoo. It's an intricate image of a phoenix rising from flames. It's mesmerizing, but when I look closer, I can tell the tattoo is covering some extensive scarring. *What happened to you, Ciara?* I wonder if whatever caused the scars is the reason she was so anxious in the hospital.

When we get to Sasha's house, I hop out quickly so I can help Ciara down. She hesitates but takes my hand anyway, and a shock shoots up my spine when our hands touch. I look over to Sasha, and she's eyeing me curiously but doesn't say anything.

"We're here!" Sasha yells when we get inside. Nevaeh runs downstairs and hugs Ciara first, then me. Carter strolls down behind her.

"Are you okay? That looked like it hurted."

Ciara chuckles, and the sound goes straight to my dick again. "Yeah, I'm okay. Just a bump on the head. I just need to take it easy."

"Hi, Ciara, it's nice to finally meet my daughter's favorite customer. I wish it was under better circumstances."

"Nice to meet you too, Carter." She turns to Nevaeh. "Am I really your favorite customer, or do you say that to all the people with head injuries?"

Nevaeh giggles. "You're my favorite! That's why my Linky was there to save you today. I wanted yous to meet."

I start to intervene before Nevaeh can say anything else embarrassing like how I was drooling over her in the window before the incident, but Ciara surprises me with her next comment.

"Well, I'm sure that's not exactly the meeting you had in mind, but I'm glad we did meet."

She looks up at me, and I'm once again lost in those eyes.

"Alright, Ciara, we have you set up in the guest room upstairs. Linc, the couch is all yours, my guy."

Ciara side-eyes me. "I didn't realize you were staying too."

"Yeah, Linc, why are you here again?" Sasha asks, trying to hide her amusement. *Asshole.*

"I just figured it would be best for me to check on you tonight. Sasha sleeps like a log, so there's no way she's getting up to look in on you." All the adults look at me like I've grown three heads.

The rest of the day flies by with easy conversation. Carter and Sasha give Ciara recommendations for places to visit outside of the city. Nevaeh shows off her toys. I encourage Ciara to take a nap but she refuses, though she does pop her pain medicine so I know her head is still bothering her.

Sasha yawns. "Alright, well, we're gonna head up. Ciara, I'll put some clothes in your room to sleep in and towels for your shower. Just let me know if you need anything else."

"Thank you both, really," Ciara responds.

"Can I stay with Linky for a little bit?" Nevaeh asks. Sasha looks to me, and I nod in silent permission. Nevaeh pumps her fists in victory.

"Fine, little girl. But behave." Sasha and Carter head upstairs.

Nevaeh nudges me in the side. "Can we watch a movie?" Nevaeh looks between Ciara and me with that puppy dog look she's perfected.

"We should let Ciara rest, Short Stack. She shouldn't watch TV anyway with her concussion."

"Actually, I'm not quite ready for bed yet. I'll close my eyes during the movie, but I'd love to sit with you guys while you watch. Just let me take a shower first."

I swat the image of Ciara naked in the shower out of my head.

"Yeah, okay, great. We'll get it set up. Take your time."

Ciara bites her bottom lip and nods.

I'm vaguely aware of Nevaeh going to the kitchen to get snacks, but I watch Ciara the whole way up the stairs.

CHAPTER
Four

Ciara

WHAT IN THE ENTIRE FUCK AM I THINKING? "I'D LOVE TO SIT WITH guys while you watch"? Have I lost my mind?

A long time ago, yes.

I roll my eyes at myself. The correct thing to do would've been to say, "Yeah, your uncle's right. I shouldn't watch TV with a concussion, so I'll just go to bed. I'm sorry. See you in the morning." But no. The cuteness of a five-year-old and the damn queen downstairs that zeroed in on Lincoln's fine ass had me opening my big mouth.

And the worst part is that I actually am tired and I do have a headache.

This is not what I'm supposed to be doing. I left my family behind to start fresh somewhere else in the hopes that if he found me again I'd be alone and my loved ones would be out of danger.

How did I go from casually making small talk with Sasha and her daughter to staying at her house after a near death accident? And why in the hell did her brother have to be so gorgeous?

When I first opened my eyes and saw him looking at me, I was convinced I was dreaming.

When I got a good look at him in the hospital, I couldn't take my eyes off of him. I'm five feet seven and he stands a good seven inches taller than I do. His chocolate skin stood out against his white T-shirt that was molded to his bulging biceps. He has a full beard and mustache, but I could still make out the dimple on his left cheek. His eyes are a warm, deep brown, and I swear they can see through to my soul. Even his damn bushy eyebrows are sexy. He was wearing jeans that hugged his muscular thighs but weren't too tight, and all I could think about was wrapping my legs around them while he fucked me senseless. Honestly, the more I think about it, the more I'm convinced that my head injury didn't cause my confusion during Dr. Lewis's questions. I think I kept getting flustered by Lincoln's presence.

That damn man.

It has been too long since I've been interested in a man. I've been too busy focused on my survival, but Lincoln wakes up every sexual yearning in me.

I can't go there. I should just go to sleep, but I promised Nevaeh I would come back down. I just need to get through this movie, then I can escape to the guest room, and tomorrow morning I'm getting the hell out of this house.

When I get downstairs, I find Nevaeh cuddled up with Lincoln on the couch, and the sight makes my chest ache. He's adorable with her.

He's got to have a flaw somewhere. He's a man. Find it and hold on to it. It's the only way you'll get out of this unscathed.

Right. Flaws. I can do that.

"Hey there."

Lincoln and Nevaeh swivel around to look at me. "Hey there, we weren't sure if you'd want salty or sweet, so we have popcorn and we have M&M's," Lincoln declares, holding out a bowl of popcorn and a bag of M&M's.

I flop down next to Nevaeh. "Oh, the answer is always both. Have you ever mixed your M&M's with your popcorn?"

Nevaeh gasps. "Ooh, that sounds yummy! Do it, Linky. Dump them!"

He laughs, showing those perfectly white teeth of his. "Yes, ma'am." He throws a piece of popcorn at Nevaeh's nose then dumps the bag of M&M's in. He dives right in to try the mixture and moans as he chews. Lordt. Strike me down now. I push my thighs together and hope he doesn't notice. "I think you're onto something here."

"This is really good! How come I've never had it like this?" Nevaeh ponders.

"I'm kind of the queen of snack combinations." I shrug.

"What else do you mix together?" Nevaeh gives me her full attention, anticipating the discovery of new food combos, and fuck, this kid is going to be my undoing.

"Peanut butter and maple syrup sandwiches. Potato chips and chocolate sauce. Ice cream and french fries. I'm a big fan of salty and sweet together."

Nevaeh wrinkles her nose. "Okay, okay. Tato chips and chocolate sounds nasty, but I trust you." Lincoln's shoulders shake with laughter. Nevaeh is five going on twenty-five.

"Well, I'm honored to have your trust. You're gonna like it, I know it."

"We can try it next time you come over."

Shit.

There can't be a next time. I have to keep all interactions to the coffee shop.

Deflect. "So did you guys decide on a movie to watch while I was gone? Or in my case, listen to?"

Nevaeh claps her hands in excitement. "I wanna watch *Coco* but Linky wants to watch *Good Burger,* so you get to be the tiebreaker."

"Ooh, both excellent choices. How am I to decide?" I pause for dramatic effect. "I'm going to say *Coco*."

"Ha! I win, Linky."

"Alright, the better person won this go-round, I concede." He winks at me, and I feel it in my core. This is going to be a long night.

He cues up the movie, and I do everything in my power to focus on it. At one point, Nevaeh lays her head on my shoulder, and my heart melts.

When it's over, Nevaeh is dead asleep in my lap.

"I'll take her up to bed and be right back." Lincoln scoops Nevaeh up with ease and carries her up the stairs.

Now would be a perfect time to escape to my room, but I make no effort to get up. I shake my head at my foolishness and chuckle to myself.

"You okay?"

Damn, for a muscular man he has quiet footsteps.

Well, say something before he thinks you're a crazy bitch.

I am literally having a conversation with myself in my head so…he may not be far off.

"Yeah, just thinking." Lincoln takes a seat next to me on the couch, closer than he was before, and I lose all focus. He smells like sandalwood and something else that I can't quite put my finger on, but it's intoxicating.

"So I'm sure this isn't how you saw your Thursday night going."

"Definitely not."

"I'm really glad you're okay." I look at him and the sincerity I see in his eyes threatens to undo me.

"Me too. Thank you for being there."

"No thanks necessary. I didn't do anything. I couldn't get to you in time to stop it." He tries to brush that off as a casual statement, but I can hear the pain in his voice. "So, do you have any family in the area? I'm just wondering if there's anybody we should've called for you."

My hackles rise. I should've known the personal questions were coming. What's crazy is that a part of me wants to share with him, and that should alarm me. I guess I can tell him a little about myself, but nothing about the past two years.

"No, no family here. I moved here from Baltimore. I should call them and let them know, but it can wait until tomorrow. I don't need them worrying tonight."

"What made you move here?"

A deranged asshole.

Hush. "I needed a change. To be honest, I chose this city at random. I made a top five list of cities I wanted to visit and picked one out of a bowl."

"Really? That's kind of awesome. What cities did we beat out?"

"Memphis, Houston, Portland, and San Francisco."

"Well, I happen to think Austin is the best of those options, but I'm biased. I'm happy our city won out."

"Yeah. I am too, so far."

But if I let you get too close, I may be going to one of those other cities anyway.

Do you have an off button?

I shake off my thoughts and immediately ask another question. "So were you guys born and raised in Austin?"

"Yeah. My dad is from here. My mom was raised in California but came here for college. She met my dad, and they never left."

"That's sweet. So tell me about your other siblings." Ugh, what is wrong with me? Asking Lincoln questions only opens myself up for him to return the favor. But I want to know more about him.

He smiles and runs his hands down his beard. "Well, you know Sasha already. She gets under your skin in the best way and just stays there. She's a firecracker. My oldest sister, Regina, she's tough. She has the biggest heart but she will also cut anyone down who tries to fuck with her. My younger brother, Isaiah, is a fool but so damn lovable. My sisters won't even ask him to babysit because he acts like a big kid himself half the time. He's always been like that, but a few years ago he moved to Arizona for awhile, and when he came back he was a little bit lost. Since then he's amped up the big kid routine."

"What happened in Arizona?"

"He doesn't talk about it." I nod. I understand that better than anyone. He rolls right into another question. "What about you? Any siblings? I know your mom said never to let your kids outnumber you so I'm willing to bet you're either an only child or only one sibling."

31

I chuckle even though I cringed when I told him that earlier because I couldn't believe I let a personal anecdote fly out my mouth so easily. "Only child here. My dad wasn't in our lives so she was a one and done."

"I'm sorry to hear that."

"Don't be. I didn't miss anything." He smiles at that.

We go back and forth asking each other questions, and I give him more information than I'd given anyone in a long time. He makes me feel comfortable, safe. I know that's a problem, but I can't stop spilling my guts.

"Wait, what? You're a firefighter, like that's been what you wanted to be since you were a kid. So you've always wanted to run into burning buildings and save lives and yet you're afraid of…zombies?"

"Hey! I am not afraid of zombies per se, just the idea of a zombie apocalypse. That shit is scary! Haven't you ever seen *The Walking Dead*? No, fuck that. The people are bigger monsters than the zombies on that show. Haven't you ever seen *28 Days Later*? Those fuckers were not only undead, they were fast! Terrified the ever loving fuck out of me. I used to beg my parents to let me make a bug-out bag."

"Like with med-kits, weapons, and food?"

"Yeah, I wanted to have it packed so if anything happened I could take off. I told them we should each have one, but they said no."

Oh my God, is this a flaw? No. Dammit, it's adorable.

"Wait, wait. I'm sorry. Let's back up. I thought we were talking about you as a kid."

"We were."

"But *28 Days Later* came out in like 2007. How old were you then?"

He rolls his eyes. "Seventeen." I burst out laughing. I did the best I could to hold it in, but I can't take it anymore. "You laugh, but that shit is no joke. I was always afraid of them. The bug-out bag phase was when I was a kid, but when I saw *28 Days Later* that just made me feel justified in my fear. I'd like to see you not be scared if one of those fuckers came at you."

"No…you're…so right. I'm sorry…" I croak out in between laughs.

"Yuck it up, Ci. If a zombie apocalypse were to happen now I'd be so ready. I'd make Rick Grimes look like a pussy, so you better be nice to me if you want me to allow you to travel in my group."

"Oh, well excuuuuse me. And by the way, I was and will forever be #TeamShane."

"Oh shit. A woman after my own heart."

A moment of comfortable silence passes before I check the time on my phone.

"Wow, it's late. I should probably head up to bed."

"Yeah, you're supposed to be resting, and I'm monopolizing your time."

"Exactly, you monster."

"As punishment, I banish myself to this lumpy couch while you go enjoy the plush bed in the guest room."

"Hey, I earned that plush bed today. What'd you do today? Put out some fires, save some lives? Psh, child's play." I wink. A surprised laugh bursts out of him, and I want to hear more of it.

"I bow down to you." He feigns a bowing motion.

"As you should." I get up from the couch, and Lincoln rises as well. "Well, good night."

"Good night, Ciara, sleep well. I set some alarms on my phone so I can wake up every few hours and come in to check on you."

The thought of Lincoln coming to my room—to my bedside—tonight has me clenching my thighs again. "You know it's funny, doctors tell you to rest for a concussion but also make sure you get no rest at all the first twenty-four hours." He looks at me in confusion so I continue. "It's just that I'm such a light sleeper so there's no way I'll sleep through you coming in to check on me." I'm not really that much of a light sleeper, but that sounds better than "the thought of your fine ass being that close to me when I'm in bed is gonna keep me up all night so I'll be up when you come in anyway."

"You got a point there. It's a conspiracy."

"Definitely, we should make a subReddit about this."

"Way ahead of you."

"Goodnight, Linc."

"Goodnight."

I walk over to the steps then turn around again. "Hey, Linc?"

"Yeah?"

"Thank you."

His lips turn up in a grin. "You're welcome."

As I close the bedroom door behind me and slide under the covers, I wonder how the hell I'm going to shake my attraction to this man.

CHAPTER
Five

Ciara

I FEEL HIS MUSCULAR ARMS ON ME, AND I WANT TO BITE HIM. NOT IN A sexual way. I want to cause him pain so he'll leave me the fuck alone.

"Nooo, not again. No more, Linc. My name is Ciara Jeffries. I'm twenty-eight years old. The year is 2020. We are in Austin, Texas. A cheese puff is president. See? I'm fine."

I open my eyes to find Lincoln sipping from a "World's Bestest Uncle" mug, eyeing me with all the amusement. "You know, to be fair, I tried to be quiet every time I came to check on you so that you wouldn't wake up, but you really are a light sleeper. I just figured since you were up I'd have a little fun and quiz you. I came in here this time to let you know that breakfast is ready. Sasha said feel free to sleep in if you want, but the food is there."

"Oh. Umm, yeah, I'll come down."

"Take your time, slugger." He smirks.

"Slugger?"

"Ha! Yeah, you punched me in the arm when you woke up during my four a.m. check-in." He rubs his arm, looking for sympathy, as if I could ever make a dent in that piece of steel he calls an arm.

"I did not!"

"Oh, but you did. It's okay. It'll heal, I'm sure."

"Great, I was so worried." Cue the sarcasm.

He flashes that panty-melting smile at me again. "See you soon."

I take a moment to really appreciate the gloriousness that is Sasha's home. I realize I was so caught up in Lincoln and Nevaeh last night that I didn't really notice my surroundings. The guest room I stayed in is hotel level quality. It's considerably more neutral compared to the rest of the house.

When I was a kid, my mom took me to North Carolina for a week on vacation. She never wanted me to miss out on experiences she didn't get as a child, so she worked her ass off to give me once-in-a-lifetime moments. In North Carolina, we had an entire rental house to ourselves. It was gorgeous. The place was painted slate gray and white, but it still felt warm and inviting inside. I'd help my mom cook dinner every night, and she'd ask me about all my hopes and dreams while we ate. We'd go for walks every day, and she'd tell me stories on the balcony every night. Those days were some of the best days of my life. This room takes me back there. I can practically feel my mom's loving embrace in this room, and that makes me grab my stuff quickly and head downstairs.

Heavenly scents pull me into the kitchen. It smells like bacon and cinnamon, and I can feel myself salivating. The kitchen is mostly gray, but every accent is a sunshine yellow that catches my eye. I wonder if Carter had any say in the decorating for the house or if Sasha just ran point. This house screams family and happiness, unlike my cold apartment. My place screams hiding in plain sight.

Sasha is buzzing around the kitchen in full-on Mom mode. Carter is pouring coffee into a mug for her—surprise, it's yellow. Lincoln is pretending to steal bacon off of Nevaeh's plate, but she's not paying him any mind because her pancakes are demanding her full attention. She catches a glimpse of me standing in the entryway and waves to me. "Good Morning, Ciara!" she says, then goes right back to stuffing her face.

"Good Morning, Nevaeh. Good Morning, Sasha. Good Morning, Carter."

36

"Good Morning, Jim Bob," Lincoln mocks.

"Shut up before I sic a zombie on you."

Lincoln smacks his hands to his chest. "You wouldn't."

I only offer him a smirk in return. "Everything smells delicious, Sasha."

"Aww, thank you."

"Who is Jim Bob?" Nevaeh asks.

"It's from an old TV show called *The Waltons*, Munchkin," Carter responds.

"Oh. Well if it's old, why'd you say it, Linky?"

"I was teasing Ciara, that's all, Short Stack."

"He was trying to be funny, but it fell flat," I tease.

Lincoln sticks his tongue out at me. This is all feeling very…domestic. I don't like it.

"Stop being a whole man-child, Linc. Ciara, I've got pancakes, bacon, eggs, sausage, and fresh fruit. What would you like?"

"Oh, you've done enough. You don't have to fix my plate."

She waves me off. "Oh girl, please. This is your first time in my home, plus you have a head injury so I'm being the hostess with the mostest. But best believe next time we hang out here, you'll be serving your damn self," Sasha says with a smile.

"You said a bad word, Mommy."

"I told you to stop trying to get me to start a swear jar, little girl. I'm too old to change!" Sasha protests. "What's the rule?"

Nevaeh giggles. "Do as you say, not as you do."

"Lord knows if we did start a swear jar, Nevaeh would be rich by now," Carter chimes in.

God, this family is cute. It makes me miss my own family.

After breakfast, Lincoln and Nevaeh wash and dry the dishes while Carter sweeps the kitchen floor and Sasha watches over her minions with a cup of coffee in her hands. She's got a well-oiled machine going here, and I'm not mad at it.

"Alrighty, I am off to work. Nevaeh, you've got a five-minute countdown to grab your stuff before this train leaves the station," Carter says while boop-ing Nevaeh on the nose.

"On it, Cap'n." She takes off upstairs.

"I've gotta head out too. You gonna be okay?" Lincoln asks me, and I bite my bottom lip then curse myself for being so pitiful.

"I'm good."

"You can ride with me to the coffee shop since your car is still there," Sasha offers.

"I can't drive yet because of my concussion, but I'll grab an Uber from there and get my car later."

"That works for me!" Sasha replies.

"Have a good day, family!" He turns to me. "See you around, Jim Bob."

I roll my eyes, and I hear Lincoln's laugh long after he shuts the door.

I've been avoiding Sasha's gaze all morning. Those knowing eyes are trying to trap me, and I won't have it.

She fakes a cough, and I brace myself. "I mean it's the chumminess be-tween you and my brother for me."

"Oh my God."

"Don't get me wrong, I am here for it. I just was not expecting that. I can't believe Nevaeh felt the vibes before I did. I must be losing my touch."

"There are no vibes."

"Right."

"I'm serious. He swooped in and did his fireman thing after I busted my head, and we were being nice. That is all. Periodt."

"I don't recall asking a follow-up question. You're offering a lot of de-tails I didn't ask for."

Send help.

I roll my eyes. "So anyway, I'm going to start looking for a part-time job. I need some income coming in while I'm working on this book. Any suggestions?"

"Mhmm. I see your deflection and I could call it, but I'm gonna fold for now because it's what you need."

Get me out of here! "I didn't realize I was dealing with a card shark."

"THE card shark so be thankful for my generosity."

"Oh, I'm incredibly grateful." I smile.

"Good. So how do you feel about bartending?"

"I did it all throughout college, so I'm good with it."

Without another word, Sasha makes a call. "Hey, Nina, what are you up to?"

I can make out a female voice on the other end of the line but can't hear what she's saying.

"Can I bring a friend over to talk about a job real quick? Yes, I'll bring donuts. How gluttonous you trying to be today? Yeah, it's a real question, smart-ass. A dozen it is. Be there soon. Bye."

Sasha instructs me to follow her, and I try to piece together what the hell just happened.

Neon Nights is a bar not too far from Sasha's coffee shop. It definitely has a college town feel to it. There are TVs lining the walls. Most of them are playing sports, but one of them is set to Bravo where *Real Housewives of Dallas* is currently playing, and another is set to TNT showing *The Fast and the Furious*. It's the middle of the day right now, so it's bright and quiet in here, but I can imagine the whole place being lined with bodies at the bar and the neighboring dance floor once night falls.

Nina Williams is what they call a fucking powerhouse. She's the manager of Neon Nights and the one Sasha called before we walked over. She's wearing a simple pair of jeans with a Poetic Justice T-shirt and Jordans, and she's rocking the hell out of it. She commands a room, but she also puts everyone at ease. Two vendors, her bouncer, and two of her bartenders have come in since we've been here talking, and you can tell they trust and respect her implicitly.

"Okay, where were we? Oh yeah, so when you can start?" Nina asks.

Umm, what? Is she kidding me? "Don't you wanna ask me more questions first? To see if I'd be a fit?"

"Oh honey, I decided to hire you the moment you walked in."

My head jerks at that. "Really? Why?"

"You trying to talk me out of it?"

"Just trying to see if I'm signing up to work for a crazy woman is all."

She barks a laugh. "Fair. Okay, well, one, Sasha vouched for you and I know she wouldn't vouch for anyone who won't stack up. Two, when you walked in, my bartender Lindsay was struggling to carry a few cases, and you immediately jumped in to help her. Three, you greeted everyone who came in here with a smile, but you also weren't afraid to give Frank's dumb ass shit when he flirted with you. And four, the first thing you said to me was a compliment about my shirt. I've seen all I needed to see. So I'll ask again, when can you start?" She leans forward on her elbows, waiting on my response.

Well, okay then.

"Friday?"

"Perfect." She grabs a maple bacon donut and goes to town. "You can come back any day before then to fill out your new-hire paperwork."

"Well, shit, this is the best job interview I've ever had. Thank you."

We spend a little more time shooting the shit before Sasha heads back to the shop and I grab an Uber home.

Walking into my building, I get the overwhelming sense that I'm being watched. My eyes scan every inch of the lobby, but I don't see anyone. I jam the call button for the elevator. My eyes never stop darting around while I wait.

I once again take the elevator up to the seventh floor and walk down a flight. I wonder if anyone actually watches the cameras in the stairway. They probably think I'm crazy.

I scan my hallway one more time before rushing to my door and slamming it closed behind me and sagging against it in relief.

I just need more sleep. I didn't get much with Lincoln slipping into my room every few hours. He hasn't found me. I'm here, I'm alive, I'm okay.

I flick both the locks on my door, move my end table so it blocks the door a bit, grab the chef's knife, and check all the rooms before settling on the couch to do the breathing exercises Dr. Goodwin taught me.

I want to sleep, but I know if I wait any longer to make this call, the girls will flame my ass.

I start the video chat and wait for Brittany, Simone, and Sarah to hop on.

All of their jaws are on the floor when I finish filling them in on the last twenty-four hours.

"Umm, I'll go first. Why the hell didn't you call us sooner?" Sarah shrieks.

"I mean, what would you have done? Hopped on a plane?"

"Yes!" they all scream in unison. I sigh. I don't know why I said it. I know they wouldn't hesitate to hop on a plane for me. They're my ride or die girls. Each one of us would go to the ends of the Earth for each other. It's why I left home. I recognize that I'm not giving them the chance to do something I wouldn't hesitate to do for them, but I just can't. I can't be the reason they end up in danger.

"Alright, alright. I'm sorry, okay?"

"It's absolutely not okay. Did you tell Ms. Angela about this?" Simone asks, folding her arms across her chest.

"No, I did not tell my mother, and I don't need to. I'm a grown-ass woman."

"Ha! Okay. Well, I think I'll fill her in then. Since you're a grown-ass woman and all, it shouldn't matter if she knows." I've left sweet little Brittany alone with Simone and Sarah too long. They're corrupting her.

I fold my arms in defiance. Brittany picks up her phone and starts typing a text. Simone and Sarah wait anxiously.

"Okay, you're not actually gonna tell her, are you? Please don't. You know she'll be on my ass!" I relent.

"This bitch," Simone cackles.

We all burst into laughter. I may be a grown-ass woman, but I know better than to play games with my mom. Mama ain't raise no fool.

"Well, don't keep secrets from us then." Sarah pokes her tongue out.

Oh, if you only knew.

"Alright, so let's address the other part of this story." Simone licks her lips, and I know what's coming. "Is this Lincoln sexy? That name is sexy. Let's get some more Lincoln details."

"I don't wanna talk about Lincoln." I absolutely do want to talk about Lincoln. The man has me dickmatized and I haven't even seen the dick.

"Oh shit, he must be sexy," Sarah chimes in.

Irritatingly so. He's like a sexy combination of both Lawrence and Daniel from *Insecure,* but I know if I tell them that they'll never leave me alone about it. I refrain from biting my lip at the thought of him.

"There's nothing to tell. Yes, he's good-looking. But nothing is going to happen."

Simone looks as though I've slapped her. "And why not?"

"Because I told you—I'm not dating right now."

And now she looks like she's ready to slap me. "There you go again thinking I'm telling you to date someone. You don't need to date him to let him dick you down."

"Jesus, Simone."

"Girl, you're damn near a virgin again. You need to use it before you lose it."

"One, it has not been that long. Two, that's not even possible. How the fuck would I lose it?"

"I'm dying, and it's been four months. After two years, I'm surprised your pussy has not turned into a shriveled up desert."

Brittany chokes on her water, and Sarah just shakes her head.

"Jesus. I can assure you it's not a damn shriveled up desert. I've been a little busy being tormented these last two years." Her eyes soften, but I know she's not done with me.

"Yes, which is exactly why you deserve a good dicking after what you've been through. Look, what I know is that you need your wet-ass pussy serviced before it develops cobwebs, and a sexy fireman has literally fallen into your lap to do the job."

"Ugh, okay, Megan. Or would you prefer Cardi?"

"Either. Both are queens. "WAP" is my anthem, and I feel no shame about that."

Please remind me why I've been friends with these women for eighteen years.

I can't breathe. Paranoia has its claws wrapped around my throat so tightly I'm gasping for air. I can't do this. I'm safe within these four walls, so that's where I should stay.

In that moment, frustration takes over. The nerve endings that were frayed with fear are now coated in anger. Dammit, I am not this person. I've allowed this man to reduce me to a shell of myself. Scared to walk out of my own mother's house to check the mail?! I can't let this happen. It's three feet. I can walk three feet to the mailbox, no problem.

Do it.

Just fucking do it.

Tunnel vision takes over, and all I can see is the bright white door in front of me. My breath is labored as I reach for the door. The doorknob scorches my skin, and I nearly fall back but then I chastise myself for imagining its heat and press on.

The door is open for a single moment before I realize he's standing before me. His breath reeks of cigarettes. His eyes are cold. Hard. Void of all emotion. I'm frozen in place, his stare dragging my soul with him down to the pits of hell.

I see the glint of a blade seconds before he plunges it into my abdomen. Hot, searing pain spreads throughout my entire body, and I fall to my knees, the force of the drop vibrating in my bones. I hold on long enough to watch his back fade into the night as he leaves me for dead on my mother's doorstep. My last thought before my head hits the cold floor is regret that those eyes are the last thing I'll ever see.

My eyes adjust as I'm flipped over, but it's not my body I'm looking at. I'm now the one looking down at what should be my bloody corpse, but instead I find Lincoln. His beautiful brown eyes are cold and glazed over, and my heart constricts at the loss of their warmth. I look down, and his blood is literally on my hands. They start to tremble as my attention is forced back to his face when I hear him choking on his own blood. His eyes beg me to put him out of his misery.

I jerk awake in a cold sweat. *Fuck.* I've had this nightmare before. I'm always transported back to that day at my mom's house, and I have to live that horror over and over again, but then it always turns into an out-of-body experience where I have to look at my own body but it's never me. It's always Mom, Simone, Brittany, or Sarah. This vision of Lincoln, though? Far more graphic than I've ever experienced before. He was literally begging me to finish him off so he wouldn't have to suffer anymore. If I didn't know I needed to stay far away from Lincoln before, I sure know now. But I'm so deep in with this family already, I don't know if it's even possible to disentangle.

Double fuck.

CHAPTER
Six

Eddie

O h, Ciara. If you really wanted to keep me out, you would've
moved into a place with a doorman. It's like you didn't even try.

You like our little game, don't you?

You little devil.

You did a decent job evading me on your way here. Or you tried at least.
You got a new car just before moving so I'd be on the lookout for your old
car. Too bad I was with you at the dealership when you bought it. You paid
cash in all the hotels you stayed in on the way here. Did you know that we
shared a wall in the hotel in Tennessee? So close yet so far.

Don't you see? You're only here because I allowed it.

This is my favorite part of the game. The part where you think you're
free of me and you build up that happiness again only for me to rip it away
piece by piece. You'll never be free of me, doll.

You never learn your lesson. I've seen you in that coffee shop with the
owner and that little girl. How pathetic. Are they your new bodyguards?
Meant to replace those obnoxious girls back home? If you think I won't

kill them too, you haven't been paying attention. We'll have to fix that, now won't we?

Or how about that man from yesterday? Is he supposed to save you? Yeah, I saw your heroics yesterday. Pft. You never knew how to mind your own fucking business. Always stepping in where you're not wanted. Does it make you feel good to ruin other people? You just can't help yourself.

Before this is over, I will teach you the error of your ways.

Enjoy your so-called freedom...for now.

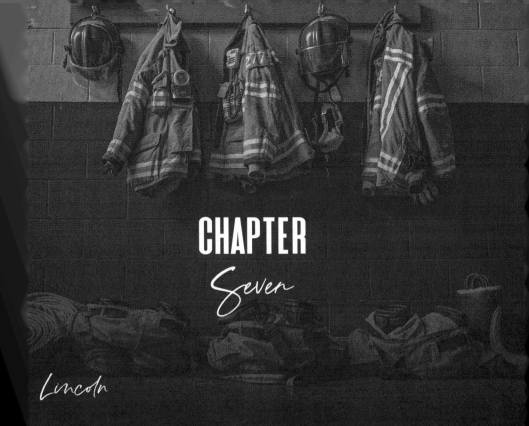

CHAPTER
Seven

Lincoln

I'M TRYING TO SLEEP, BUT MY BRAIN IS ON OVERDRIVE. I CAN'T STOP thinking about Ciara. I have no idea why she has such a strong effect on me. I'm finally able to lull myself into sleep, but the dream I'm pulled into isn't the sexy one of Ciara I imagined. Even though I'm confused about my feelings for her, I would've much preferred that dream over this one I've had too many times before.

I take a deep breath, look up at my condo, and for the first time in three years, I am dreading coming home.

Yesterday was a long shift, and all I want to do is come home, take another shower, order a pizza, and watch movies with my girl. But I know we have to have this talk…again.

Erica has been relentless since I was let off desk duty two weeks ago. I know she's just scared, but shit, this is part of the job. I thought she understood that. It's not the first time I almost died on the job, and it won't be the last, but I will never stop because it's my calling. This city needs people who will sacrifice for

I love Erica with every fiber of my being, but I love this city, too, and I won't turn my back on it.

It'll be okay. We'll be okay. I just need to remind her how good we are together. I need her to see how much she means to me.

I take one more deep breath and turn the doorknob. I go to call out for Erica, but I stop short when I see the suitcase in the living room. I scan the room and see a duffle bag by the door and Erica's work tote on top of it.

This can't be fucking happening.

"Erica!" I yell, heading straight for the bedroom. When I open the bedroom door, Erica has her back to me. She's packing, but I know she heard me come in because her back is stiff as a board. "Erica." As if my voice jolted her back to reality, her posture relaxes, but she continues packing without acknowledging me. I move closer to her and reach out to touch her arm, but she shrugs away from me. Fuck, that hurts. "Erica, come on. Please. Talk to me."

"I think we've done enough talking, Linc," she rasps. She's trying to keep her voice calm, but I can hear the emotion behind her words. Maybe I haven't lost the fight yet.

"We haven't finished talking, babe. This isn't fair and you know it."

She turns and glares at me, and I know that was the wrong thing to say.

"No. What isn't fair is that you love your job more than you love me."

"That's not true."

She scoffs. "Isn't it? Jesus, Linc. You almost died five weeks ago. Do you know how terrifying that was for me?"

For her? I know it was terrifying for her, but I was the one it happened to. I know I made the choice to do this for a living, but did she think it was easy for me to run into danger and think I may never see her again?

"I'm a fucking firefighter. It's not the first time I've almost died and it won't be the last." I take a deep breath because I know I shouldn't be irritated with her.

"Exactly! You want us to get married and start a family, but you really expect me to want to do that when I have to wonder every time you walk out that door if it will be your last time?"

Fuck.

"This job is all I've ever wanted to do. I've been on the crew since I was

eighteen, and you knew this when you met me and now what? You want me to quit and find a desk job somewhere?"

She rolls her eyes, but a tear falls out too. I reach out to wipe it off her cheek, but she moves away from me again. I am really losing her.

"Don't be so dramatic. I'm not saying a desk job. I know you'd go crazy with that." I absolutely would. "But damn, Linc. I mean, would it be so bad to go work in construction with your dad? Something that's not life or death all the time?"

"It's not life or death all the time."

"Are you fucking kidding me right now? I'm sitting here telling you I'm unhappy, and you're just worried about defending your job?" I mean she's right. I should be groveling, telling her I know being with a man in my profession isn't easy but begging her to love me anyway.

But I just...can't. The words are not coming. Everything is coming out wrong.

"So you're unhappy with me in general now? It's not just the job?" See? Wrong. All wrong.

Erica crosses her arms, and the look she levels me with cuts me to the quick. "Unbelievable. I just want you to choose me."

Turn this around, Linc. Open your damn mouth and fix this. "I love you. I chose you the day I met you. I want to marry you. I want to watch you walk toward me in your white dress. I want to buy the house we love and fill it with little Ericas and Lincolns." Her gaze softens a bit but it still looks guarded, and I pray that what I'm about to say won't send the wall sky high. "It's just...I want to have all that and my dream job too. Erica, I'd never ask you to give up your dream job for me. I would support you no matter what. And I know you've been supporting me all this time, but I'm begging you to just stick by me. I'll put my hat in the ring for a promotion. Eventually, when I get to be Chief I won't be out in the field as much. I'll hate that. But I'll do that. For you. But I cannot leave the force. I can't, babe. These guys are my family. AFD is my home."

Erica looks away from me, and when her eyes find me again I know it's over. She looks...defeated.

"That's the problem, Linc. They're your family. I'm nothing."

"You are not nothing. You're everything."

"I can't do this anymore." My chest aches. My heart is about to walk out the

door, and I can't bring myself to say the one thing that will make her stay. What does that say about me?

"Don't do this. Please."

"I'm tired, Linc. Go. Have your family. But you can count me out. I won't stick around and wait for you to die some hero's death. Fuck that." She puts one more shirt in her suitcase and then zips it shut. "You say you love me and that may be true, but you love being a hero even more. I hope when you look back at your life you're happy with the choices you made. I hope your uniform keeps you warm at night because you will never love any woman enough to truly put her first, and no woman will ever love coming second to a goddamn engine."

If her goal was to completely destroy me, she's doing a bang-up job.

My heart tells me to try one more time, but is she right? I thought I could have it all. The woman of my dreams and my dream job. But I was too damn blind to see it was all falling apart right in front of me.

"Don't do this to us. Please don't make me choose."

"You already chose." She slips her engagement ring off and leaves it on the dresser. I don't remember moving, but next thing I know I am behind her at the front door.

"Goodbye, Linc," she says barely above a whisper, so quiet I think I imagined it. She spares me one last glance and then she's gone.

I stumble back to the bedroom, but when I get there a woman is standing by the window with her back to me. Her box braids fall to the middle of her back. Her body is like a siren song. She turns to face me, and I'm stunned. Ciara.

"What's going on? How are you here?" I ask her.

She gives me a sad smile and then grabs a suitcase that I swear wasn't there before. She walks up to me and gently places her hand on my cheek. "She's right, you know."

"Who? What?"

"We'll never work. I'm not your second chance at love."

I shudder under her touch. What the fuck is happening right now?

I try to stammer out a sentence, but all that comes out is incoherent nonsense. She clicks her tongue and carries on like I never spoke. "I've got secrets, Lincoln. You've got skeletons. Do you really think we can fight them together?" She moves *her hand from my cheek, and it feels cold without her. She grabs the suitcase and starts walking toward the door. I snap out of my haze and chase after her. I'm reaching for her, but no matter how close we are she's always just out of reach.*

"Ciara, wait!" I yell right as she gets to the door. She stops with a sigh and turns to face me. Those chocolate eyes and their gray ring mesmerize me once again.

"Make a choice, Lincoln."

"A choice between what?"

"Your past and your future." And with that, a second woman walks out on me.

My eyes slowly flutter open, and I look at the clock on my phone. Four a.m. Shit. What the fuck was that? I've been forced to relive the moment Erica left me in my dreams countless times, but Ciara being there threw me for a loop.

Make a choice between my past and my future? I don't even know what to say to that. Was she trying to say that she's my future if I let her be? No. I need to get it together. There's no future for me and Ciara or anyone else for that matter.

But as I drift off again with Ciara's lips on my mind, I wonder who exactly I'm trying to fool.

CHAPTER
Eight

Lincoln

NO, NO. DON'T EVEN THINK ABOUT IT. YOU DON'T NEED TO GO TO SASHA'S. *There's absolutely no damn reason to go there.*

In the past two weeks, I've been to Sasha's at least once after every shift. The gorgeous, sassy, incredibly witty woman who has been haunting my dreams has been in the shop every day, and I'm drawn to her like a moth to a flame. Our interactions have mostly consisted of her waving in my general direction. No banter back and forth like we had that first night.

To top it off, Sasha and Dom opened their big-ass mouths to the rest of my dickhead friends about the incident with Ciara, so they've been giving me shit nonstop. I open my group chat with the guys to find them still at it.

Isaiah: Hey hero boy, seen your lady love lately?

Kai: He's probably drooling over her through Sasha's window

Shane: *inserts gif of Homer Simpson drooling and wiggling his fingers*

Dom: That's exactly how he looked at her when he was carrying her to the ambulance

Me: There was no drool, asshole

Dom: Little bit of drool

Isaiah: Stop being a creep and shoot your shot

Kai: *inserts gif of Blake Griffin shooting a hey into someone's DMs*

Me: Damn don't y'all have better stuff to do?

Shane: I don't have anything. How bout you guys?

Kai: Nah. I'm free til six p.m.

Dom: My schedule's clear

Isaiah: Same

Me: Dickheads

Me: I don't wanna shoot my shot

Me: *inserts gif of Red M&M saying no thanks*

Isaiah: Weak

Me: You know I'm not destitute? If I want to sleep with a woman, I can find a woman to sleep with. It just won't be her

Kai: *crying laughing emoji* he's pulling out the SAT words. Got his ass

Shane: *inserts got eem gif*

I delete myself from the group chat because fuck those guys.
But of course my phone pings with another text.

Isaiah has added you to a group chat

Isaiah: Where you going? The bell don't dismiss you, I do

Shane: *three crying laughing emojis*

Me: *inserts a gif of a sad cat*

Dom: Yeah that's you alright. A sad pussy.

Isaiah: *three crying laughing emojis*

Me: Dom, you ain't shit. Isaiah, I guess you don't need my help later then?

Isaiah: Lmao iight iight we're cool for now

The guys have no idea what they're talking about. Yes, Ciara is drop-dead gorgeous and yes, I would love nothing more than to spend a night between her luscious thighs. But that's it. I'm not some lovesick puppy trying to get her to fall for me. Love isn't in the cards for me. That's just a fact of life. If the dreams I've been having lately are any indication, then I definitely need to let go of any hope of anything happening with her. And yet...

Fuck it. I head over to Sasha's because I want a goddamn muffin and I'm entitled to it.

"Oh look, if it isn't my little brother. I'm shocked to see you today," Sasha mocks.

"You're a pain in my ass. I come in here to see my favorite sister and this is how you treat me?"

"I'm one hundred percent telling Reggie you said that."

"Go ahead. She's my favorite sister when I'm with her, so she won't believe you."

"So who's your favorite sister when we're all together?"

I shrug. "You'll never know."

She rolls her eyes and continues wiping down the counter. "Whatever. Anyway, Ciara isn't here right now. Just putting that out there."

"Good thing I'm not looking for her then. Now get me a chocolate chip muffin, woman." I give her my best impression of a toxic asshole voice, and it works. She looks like she wants to kill me.

She scowls but grabs a chocolate chip muffin out of the case and goes to warm it up for me.

Before Sasha gets back, the door flies open and the woman I've been avoiding—yet so desperate to see—strolls in. Today she has on gray bike shorts that make my mouth water, a baggy graphic T-shirt, and Jordans. She looks adorable, and I don't want to look away.

She startles when she sees me. Do I affect her as much as she affects me?

"Here's your muffin, creep." Sasha nudges me with the plate.

I grab it and start to head over to a hightop, but at the last second I detour over to Ciara's booth.

"Mind if I sit?" She looks up at me for a split second but darts her eyes right back to her laptop screen.

"It's all yours." She bites her bottom lip as I sit directly across from her.

"How are you feeling?"

"Much better, thanks."

"How's the book coming along?"

"It's really good. I'm about a quarter way through."

"That's really great. Congratulations."

She looks at me with those chocolate eyes and smiles. "Thank you. Ooh, hold on." Her fingers start flying across her keyboard, and I've lost her to the world she's created in her head. I take a moment to admire her dedication. I recognize that dedication. It's the same look I've had since I was five years old and witnessed a firefighter carrying a teenage girl away from a house fire that her dad was badly burned in. That was it for me. The moment I decided I wanted that to be my future. I see that same passion burning in her. It's sexy as fuck. Her eyes are laser focused on her screen, and she doesn't look at her keyboard once. She pauses and wraps a finger around one of her box braids in concentration, and I imagine her hands wrapping around something else much harder. She bites that bottom lip again that I want to suck into my own mouth. I have to have a conversation with the Big Guy to not embarrass me here. She goes back to typing ferociously for another two minutes before her eyes train their focus back on me. "Sorry, an idea for a scene came to me. I had to get it down before I lost it."

Fuck, she's cute.

"It's no problem. I probably should let you get back to it anyway."

"I'll see you around, Linc."

"Hey, when you become a best-selling author, will you include a dedication to me in your book?"

She giggles, and I have to hold back my groan. "Yeah, sure. It'll say 'to the cocky ass firefighter who saved my ass that one time, I hope your arm has healed by now and I expect you to drop me a pin to the meet-up spot when the zombie apocalypse hits.'"

I bark out a laugh. "That's perfect."

I wave good-bye to Sasha and ignore her sly grin.

"Pass me the reciprocating saw." Isaiah motions to the saw on his workbench. I came over awhile ago to help Isaiah with the clubhouse we're building for Reggie's kids, Denise and Malcolm, and Nevaeh. Isaiah is an architect, so of course this clubhouse is more involved than I originally planned for, but they're going to love it. This is where Isaiah shines. I pass him the reciprocating saw then go back to nailing the pieces of already cut plywood together.

"So now that you're here doing the work and I know you won't walk out on a project we're doing for our nieces and nephew, I'm gonna ask you one more time. When are you going to stop being a pussy and ask Ciara out?"

I groan and nearly drop my damn hammer. "Fuck, why are you so invested in this?"

"Because from what Sasha and Dom said, you didn't look at her like she was just another potential hookup. You looked at her the way you used to look at—"

No. "Don't. Don't go there." I don't want to talk about Erica. I thought I was doing better. That the hold she had on me had loosened to a dull ache, but spending time with Ciara has that ache increasing until it's impossible to ignore.

He sighs in exasperation. "I mean what's wrong with that? You're not me, bro. This whole meaningless hookups thing is my ministry, not yours. I know she broke your heart and then the unthinkable happened, but you're meant to have the real deal, Linc. It's out there for you."

"Meaningless hookups didn't used to be your ministry either, hypocrite," I spit out.

He points his finger in my face. "You're fucked-up for bringing that up."

I sigh. He's right. I don't want to throw his past in his face just because he's doing it to me. "Just drop it, Zay. My head can't process this shit right now."

"Fine." A beat passes. "So, how hot is she? Dom said she's a ten."

My head snaps up. "Dom said what?"

"Ha! Knew it, you got it bad," Isaiah says. I scowl, and Isaiah raises his hands in surrender. "You know you should just go visit her at work. It's not too crazy so you can talk to her but loud enough that you can get lost in a distraction if you want."

"What work?" I'd never seen her anywhere but the coffee shop. I assumed writing was her career.

"Sasha didn't tell you? Ciara got a job bartending at Neon Nights."

Interesting. "Nah, I didn't know that."

His lips turn up in a grin. "I know where we're going tonight."

"One, what do you get out of going with me? Two, that's stalkerish."

"Of going with you to a bar? Umm, drinks and women, idiot. The manager of that place, Sasha's friend Nina? She's hot as fuck. I'd love to go home with her. And it's not stalkerish. Sasha's basically declared her part of the family now, so you better swoop in there before she gets our parents to adopt her. You'd be really scarred for life if you fuck your own sister."

Are the rest of our minds this warped? I'm convinced he was dropped on his head multiple times as a baby. "What is wrong with you?"

He shrugs. My brother may be a damn weirdo, but I know I'm a liar if I say I'm not seriously considering going to Neon Nights tonight.

"So?" He stares at me, waiting for my answer.

"I guess we're going out tonight."

Isaiah raises his fist in celebration. My dick twitches, and I know the Big Guy is happy about my decision even if I'm still confused.

Later that night, Neon Nights is crowded as all hell, but my eyes immediately find Ciara. She's wearing the Neon uniform of tight blue jeans with a white button-up tucked in. Her hair is pulled up in a bun with a few strands falling down in her face. Her lush lips are painted a deep purple, and it makes her teeth look even whiter. I want to kiss her until the purple fades from her lips.

She looks around as if she's looking for someone and then her eyes find me. She blushes as much as her almond skin will allow and looks away. *Yeah, I feel it too, Angel.* Angel? Where the hell did that come from?

Isaiah pats me on the back, and we make our way over to the bar. There are a bunch of college students grinding all over the dance floor. I'm pretty sure one of the couples is just straight fucking, but the lights are dim in here so more power to them. The Carters' "Apeshit" blasts through the speakers. The bar itself is completely full. There's a group of young women downing shots at the far end letting out ear-piercing hollers with each one. A group of frat guys hang around them, watching with hungry eyes.

A guy who looks exactly like Chris Evans in *Infinity War* is shamelessly flirting with Nina. I don't know her well. Sasha's brought her for Thanksgiving dinner a few times, and she seems cool but I do know enough to know that she's actually enjoying his flirting. Isaiah better get in there quick if he wants a chance. There's a couple who appear to be my age sitting on the middle stools completely wrapped up in each other. I think I could yank their stools from underneath them and they wouldn't even notice. I might have to test out that theory if a seat doesn't open up by the time I get to the bar.

I continue staring at Ciara as I make my way to the stools. She's a force behind the bar. Men and women alike are drawn to her and not just because she's pouring their drinks. The men linger, hoping to get a sliver of her attention, and she shoots them all down with grace, which makes me feel good even though I don't deserve it. The women all hang on to her every word like she's the coolest person they've ever met. They admire her. She's everything they wish they were. On the surface, she's got an unmatched confidence that's contagious. Underneath that, she's got a vulnerability that makes you want to protect her at all costs. That's the side I want to dive into. As if the universe is smiling down on me, an older man stands up from his stool and throws a few bills on the bar before walking out. I'm quick to grab the seat and smile at Ciara who smirks as she walks over to me.

I raise my voice so she can hear me above the music. "I heard you were slinging drinks like a badass, so I had to get a front row seat."

"Well, welcome to the show. Don't expect special treatment unless you leave a big tip."

"I can definitely leave you a big tip," I reply with a wink. She rolls her eyes, and I can't help but smile. Isaiah finally pushes past the last of the crowd to stand by my side. "Ciara, this is my younger brother, Isaiah."

She turns to him. "Ahh, you're the brother. He talks a lot of shit about you, you know?"

"Most of it's justified I'm sure. Nice to meet you. It's no wonder my brother can't stop dreaming of you."

"Alright, fuck off." I say as I shove his shoulder, but he just comes right back to his original spot.

Isaiah laughs, talks to Ciara for another moment, before beelining for Nina. The Cap lookalike scowls at him and then grabs his drink and heads over to the dance floor. Nina laughs at something Isaiah says. I hope she knows what she's in for.

"I like him," Ciara says.

"That makes one of us."

"Oh, please. Your whole damn family is likeable, much to my dismay." She says the last part so low I'm not sure she meant for me to hear it.

"We're alright. My dad is really laid-back and cool—you can't help but to like him. My mom is the best woman I know and the queen of our family. You'll like Reggie too, she's got that whole—in her words—'boss bitch' thing going on."

She clears her throat and looks away for a moment. *I see you, Ciara.* She gets fidgety every time someone mentions bringing her into their circle or getting to know her better. The girl's got walls as tall as a castle. Lord knows I've got my own walls surrounding my heart, but something makes me want to tear hers down. Dreams be damned.

"So, what can I get you to drink?"

"Surprise me."

"Hmm, a challenge. Okay, I see you. Liquor or beer?"

I think I'm going to need some liquid courage to get through tonight. "Let's go with liquor."

Ciara saunters off, and I can't help but watch the gentle sway of her hips as she goes.

Isaiah is caught up in flirting with Nina. He's always a flirt, but I've never seen him so enraptured in just one woman. A woman whose breasts are spilling out of her shirt and who is wearing shorts that barely cover her ass purposely brushes up against him, but he doesn't spare her a single glance. Interesting.

My thoughts jump back to the sexy siren, Ciara, when she returns with my drink. "Cheers," she says.

I smile as I raise the glass to my lips. "A whiskey, neat. How'd you guess?"

Her eyes travel slowly down my body, and I'm five seconds from hopping over the bar and taking her mouth when she answers. "Well, you decided you wanted to be a firefighter when you were five years old and never gave up on that dream until you became the Fire Lieutenant sitting in front of me. That's a man who knows what he wants and doesn't need to put on airs about it. You don't crave attention, but you can capture the focus of a room easily. You're comfortable with yourself, and you're a simple man who enjoys simple pleasures. Enough said."

Okay, looks like I'm not the only one doing the seeing here.

"Damn, girl. Color me impressed." She takes a bow and saunters away again. She grabs her water from behind the counter and raises it to me in a silent cheers.

Cheers. I lift my glass in solidarity and maintain eye contact with her as I take a long swig.

Ciara

This man is killing me, and I'm in desperate need of a new pair of panties at this point. He's been sitting at the bar all night, staring at me. I can feel his eyes on me no matter where I am, and instead of feeling uncomfortable, I'm feeling an overwhelming sense of…want. I can't take much more of this tonight. There's no denying the desire in his eyes, and I'm sure that same desire is reflected in mine every time I look his way. He is downright mouth-watering in his Air Max's, black jeans that look like they were tailored to his muscular thighs, white T-shirt, and denim jacket. I want to lick him from head to toe.

He walked in here with his brother, Isaiah, who reminds me a little of Bryson Tiller. Isaiah's been laying the charm on Nina all night which doesn't surprise me. What does surprise me is the full toothy laugh she gives him. Oh, he's good. It's actually ridiculous how good-looking the Cole family is, but my eyes are planted on the anomaly that is Lincoln Cole. Holy shit, Simone may not have been wrong about needing my lady bits serviced because they're starting to do all the thinking for me at this point.

He gives me the rundown of how much I'll like the rest of his family when I meet them. Though I have no doubts about that, the thought makes me nervous. I can't seem to distance myself from the people in this city, and what's worse is I don't think I want to. Knowing the danger I could be putting them in by doing so, what does that say about me?

After I serve him his whiskey, I take the opportunity to run to the other side of the bar for some much needed space. I make the mistake of looking over at him again, and he winks at me. He fucking winks! I'm concerned that I've soaked through my panties to my jeans now. I just need a second to breathe away from his lustful eyes. I tell Nina I'll be back, and she nods before calling Julie over from the tables.

I step inside the back room to fan myself and take a deep breath.

A minute later, Nina steps into the room with me and closes the door behind her, taking in my flushed appearance.

"You okay?" she asks.

"Yep. Just needed a moment."

She gives me a knowing smile. "That Lincoln is hot as hell. Honestly, I thought I was gonna spontaneously combust from the vibes he was throwing your way."

You and me both.

I fan myself again, and Nina takes pity on me and changes the subject. "Hey, are you sure you're okay closing with Lindsay tomorrow? It'll be your first time shadowing a closing shift, but if you're not comfortable yet I can have Julie switch with you."

I'm grateful in this moment for Nina knowing I need a distraction to bring my body temperature back to normal and grateful to Julie and Lindsay for covering the bar while Nina babies my ass back here. I've never had a man make me feel so off-kilter before.

"Yeah, I'm fine. Where are your parents off to again?" Nina is taking the night off tomorrow to babysit her younger brother and sister while her parents go on vacation.

"Honestly, I don't remember," she sighs. "I can't keep up with their many adventures or trips, which sucks for my brother and sister, but that's what happens when your parents wait sixteen years between their first two kids and then eight years between the last two."

I let out a whistle. "No offense, but what were your parents thinking?"

"I don't think they were. I think they were panicking that my teen years were flying by and they didn't want to be empty-nesters so they had my brother. I'm pretty sure my sister was an oops baby, but she was the best oops. I don't know what I'd do without Logan and Jada. I just wish they didn't have to get the short end of the stick because my parents are in retirement age and want to embrace that."

"What do you have planned for them tomorrow night?"

"Jada will most definitely have our asses playing every board game known to man, so that will probably take up a good portion of the night. Logan will probably have his face buried in a book for the rest of the night, so it'll be low-key."

"That's the best kind of night in my opinion."

"You would think that, Loner Girl."

I throw a rag at her head. "I'm not a loner."

"You're kind of a loner. Nothing wrong with that. It just means when you do allow people into your circle, they've truly earned their place there. Except me—I just steamrolled my way in because that's what I do. You have no choice but to stan for me."

I had to come to this city and befriend the pushiest bitches in existence. Then again, look at the friends I left behind. This is very on-brand for me.

"You have steamrolled me, one graphic tee at a time."

"That's the name of the game. You ready to get back out there?" she asks.

One deep breath. Two deep breaths. Three deep breaths. Let's do this. "Let's go."

I spend the rest of my shift channeling the sexual energy from Lincoln into my work. I am Ciara, queen of the taps and bottles, and these booze-hounds need their queen to sit on her throne.

Usually at the end of my shift, I ask Frankie to walk me to my car so that I'm not alone, but tonight my lady parts have me doing something very stupid.

I tap him on the shoulder before I lose my nerve. Lincoln spins around, and I speak before he can trap me in his gaze. "Hey there, so since you've done nothing but watch my ass all night, I'm willing to bet I'm the reason you came tonight, which means the least you can do is walk me to my car." I crook my fingers, say good night to Isaiah, and walk away without waiting to see if he follows. I know he will.

I have no idea who this bold woman is who says shit like that to men. Actually, I do. She's me. The me I used to be before these last two years stripped me of my very essence. I've been finding her again slowly—piece by piece—since being in this city and especially since spending time with Lincoln, his family, and Nina. I know it's incredibly stupid and reckless to trust it, but I have missed this version of myself, and I'm not quite ready to let her go again.

"You are trouble." He does a quick jog to catch up to me.

"Oh, you have no idea."

"Okay, quick question. Don't think about it, just answer. Would you rather be magical but live on Earth or live in a magical land but be normal?"

A surprised laugh falls from my lips because I was not expecting that to be his question, but I'm relieved. "Hmmm. Well, no one wants to be the Argus Filch surrounded by the magic that is Hogwarts, so I'm gonna say magical but live on Earth."

"Okay. I like it."

"Okay, my turn. Would you rather have an abnormally big toe or an abnormally big ear?"

He doesn't hesitate. "Oh, that's easy. An abnormally big ear. I already got big-ass feet. I don't need to size up to a damn size fifteen shoe trying to fit my big-ass toe in there. I'm cool with a big-ass ear; it would give me character."

Size fifteen shoes. Gulp.

Before long, we've reached my car, and Lincoln holds the door open for me after I unlock it.

"Thank you, Linc." I get in the driver's seat but make no moves to shut the door. Lincoln places one hand on the roof of my car then lightly grabs my wrist and rubs his thumb over my pulse point.

"One more question. Don't think, just answer."

"Okay."

"Will you go out on a date with me?"

Fuck. Everything in me wants to say yes. I want to go on a date with him. I want more than a date. I want him to touch me…everywhere. But there's only so much recklessness I can allow. It's one thing to hang out with him as a friend and exchange flirty banter, but crossing that line puts him in more danger.

I take a deep breath and give him the only answer I can.

"No."

I close my door and drive off while trying to ignore the pang in my chest.

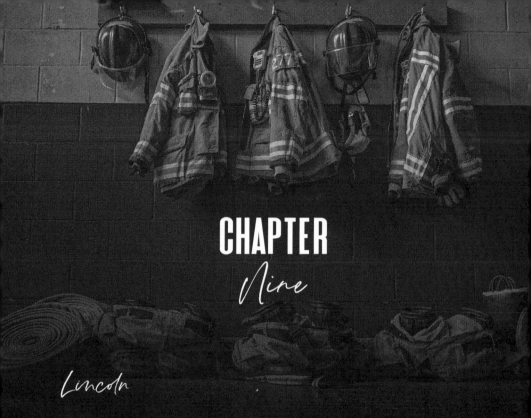

CHAPTER
Nine

Lincoln

WELL. *SHIT.* I WAS NOT EXPECTING HER TO SAY NO. NOT BECAUSE I think I'm God's gift to women or anything like that, but because the chemistry between us can't be ignored.

Except apparently she can ignore it.

Right. There's that. I watch her tail lights turn out of the parking lot and wonder where I go from here. I actually should have seen this coming. Those walls of hers are still firmly in place.

I won't ask again. I can't offer her a serious relationship anyway, and that's what she deserves. But I will make it my mission to bring those walls of hers tumbling down. Ciara is a beautiful person inside and out. The world would be knocked on its ass if she allowed one hundred percent of her essence to shine through. I want to be the one to coax that beauty out of its cage.

I grab my phone and hesitate before making my next move. Sasha gave me Ciara's phone number a while ago but I never used it because how fucking creepy is that? In this case, I think I need to be the one to smooth things over before Ciara runs and hides again.

Me: Hey, it's Lincoln. Sasha gave me your phone number a while ago, I hope that's okay. I just want to make sure you got home safe.

I send it before I can change my mind.

Walking back inside Neon, it seems like it's even more crowded than it was moments ago, but everyone feels like they're moving in slow motion for me. I walk over to Isaiah and tap him on the shoulder. "Hey, you ready to go?"

"Damn, I thought for sure I was gonna be riding home solo tonight. What happened? You puss out again?"

I clap Isaiah on the shoulder. "Not even close. You ready or not?" Zay glances at Nina one more time before following me out.

I'm inside my condo for two minutes when I hear the ping of a text message, and I race to check it like a damn teenage boy.

Ciara: Other than the fact that your sister has no fucking boundaries, yeah no problem lol

Ciara: Yes, I'm home safe

I grin at the screen like she can see me. *That's a start.*

"Anyone need a beer while I'm up?" Shane asks the group. I'm spending the afternoon with the guys today, and I'm regretting it because I'm once again the topic of conversation.

"So she said no, huh?" This from Dom.

"Yep."

"And you're okay with that?" Kai questions.

"Yep."

"I call bullshit." Dom and Kai nod their heads in agreement with Isaiah.

Shane comes back and hands out the beers. "I call bullshit too, man. Your ego's gotta be wounded."

"See, that's where you fuckers are wrong. My ego's not wounded because

I never let my ego enter the conversation. She's not ready. I respect that. Nothing more, nothing less."

"And are you ready?" Kai takes a long pull from his beer.

"I mean I'm not saying I wanna head down the aisle or anything. I don't think I'll ever be ready for that. But I'm ready for more than she is and that's fine." I've come to terms with the fact that I want something with Ciara. A date. A kiss. Anything she's willing to give me.

"Okay, and what if she's never ready?" Dom is really trying my patience today. He needs to go back to being the grumpy, quiet guy in the corner.

"Then I guess we'll just be friends."

Shane cackles but stops when I don't join in.

"Oh, you're serious. Okay."

"Right. So we're all on the same page then. I'm gonna bide my time until she's ready, and if she never gets there, that's fine too. Okay? Okay. Let's move the fuck on. What's going on at work, Shane? You still fighting with that woman in the office? What's her name?"

A growl escapes his throat. "Lauren. We're not talking about that Devil woman. Yes, I'm still fighting with her. No, I don't wanna talk about it."

"Sounds like you two just need to fuck and get it out of your systems," Kai pipes in with a shrug.

Shane startles. "Bro, didn't you hear me? I said she's the Devil. I'm not going there."

"We'll see."

"No the fuck we won't see."

I tune the guys out when I see her message come through.

Ciara: Hey, I just wanted to apologize for last night. You're Sasha's brother so I don't want things to be awkward.

Me: Hmm is that the reason you said no to my question?

The dots appear and disappear a few times, and I begin to think I made a mistake asking.

Ciara: No, believe me I'm doing you a favor by saying no

Me: I highly doubt that but don't worry you don't owe me

any explanations. My fragile heart can take any beatings you throw at me

Ciara: Well that's comforting

Ciara: *inserts a gif of Fox from Fox and the Hound with the words 'we're...we're still friends, aren't we?'*

Me: *inserts a gif of Hound from Fox and the Hound with the words 'best friends'*

Over the next week, Ciara and I take the term best friends to a whole new level. We're in constant contact. I sit with her at Sasha's while she writes. We sometimes meet up for lunch, which feels like a date but I don't want to spook her so I don't say that. We text and FaceTime all the time. I can feel her opening up to me, and I love every minute of it. She still holds a lot of things close to her chest. Most of her recent history leading up to her move she skips right over, but I'm like a dog looking for table scraps, so I'll take whatever I can get.

We're on yet another lunch "not" date today, talking about everything and nothing. "I gotta say when I asked what your stress reliever was, I wasn't expecting you to say rock climbing."

She smirks. "And what were you expecting?"

"I don't know. Yoga, shopping, listening to music, baking, sex. Anything that's not actually a strenuous activity. How is that a stress reliever?" The server arrives at that moment to drop off our food.

"Leave your toxic masculinity at the door, Linc. Damn, I expect better."

I throw a fry at her, and the little minx catches it in her mouth.

"That was pretty sexist, huh? I didn't mean it to be. I just meant rock climbing is really strenuous. I've seen people take forty minutes plus to climb a wall, and the frustration on their faces screams anything but relaxed."

"No, you're right. I think that's what I love about it, though. I have to be so focused on what I'm doing I don't have room for all the other bullshit in my head. Plus, I'm up there and I'm in complete control of my safety. Well, myself and my belayer. It's a feeling of complete contentment. Whatever I'm feeling, I leave it on the ropes. Simple as that."

I zero in on the part where she said she's in complete control of her safety. Something tells me that's her main draw to rock climbing. *What have you been through, Ciara? Let me protect you.*

"Well, that's pretty badass."

"Thank you. And by the way, sex is a strenuous activity, is it not?"

Calm down, Big Guy.

"Ci, sex can be a religious experience when done right."

She clenches her thighs ever so slightly, but I catch it. She clears her throat and reaches her dainty hands over to steal a fry off my plate, and I grab her little finger.

"Ciara," I warn. "I told you the garlic fries here were not to be missed, and you insisted on getting sweet potato fries, and now look at you, over here in my space."

She jokingly tries to pull her finger from my grasp, but she barely puts up any fight so I know she doesn't mind. "Okay, but the sweet potato fries were speaking to me at the time, and you didn't sell the garlic fries correctly! When you said they were really good and I should get them, you neglected to say they were like an orgasm in my mouth. You can't possibly deny me now."

"Oh, I think I can." Especially when you talk about orgasms in your mouth and my dick is fighting against the seams of my jeans.

"Lincoln, I'm gonna get a fry. That's just the bottom line. So we can do this the easy way, or we can do this the hard way. Your choice."

"I gotta say I'm tempted to find out what this hard way is."

"Impossible man," she says with a shake of her head.

I shove my fry basket in her direction because I would gladly give her all my fries, and that thought is fucking wild.

The next day, she's still on my mind when I'm on shift. We just got back from putting out a structure fire, and I'm bone tired but seeing her text perks me right up.

Ciara: Drums or flats?

Me: You take me for some kind of amateur? Drums all day baby

Ciara: *inserts a gif of James Hardin rolling his eyes and walking away*

Ciara: Welp it was nice knowing you buddy

Me: lol WHO THE FUCK LIKES THE FLATS BEST??

Ciara: I do, Linc. I do. It's the only correct answer. You heathen. At least tell me what you dip your wings in

Me: A wing that's made correctly needs no dipping sauce. But I can fuck with some lemon pepper or hot sauce.

Ciara: Okay you have my attention again

Me: Let's be real I never lost it

Ciara: Impossible man

Me: That's me. This works though, if we ever get wings I'll eat the drums like a proper American and you can have my pitiful flats

Ciara: *eye roll emoji* Trash

Ciara: Don't you have fires to put out? Go back to work sir

Me: Yes ma'am

I try to wipe the smile off my face, but it's impossible.

CHAPTER
Ten

Eddie

YOUR PLACE IS PITIFUL. YOU BARELY HAVE ANY FURNITURE. ARE YOU trying to live modestly now? How cute.

Your house back East, before you stupidly moved in with your mother, had a lot more stuff, so if you tell me you're a minimalist you're a liar. Your mom's house was full of pictures of you. There was one on the wall above the TV in the living room that always caught my eye. It was you and her on a balcony with trees behind you. You looked happy, whole, and blissfully unaware. But that's not how I like you. I much prefer you battered and broken.

I bet when you took that picture you never imagined you'd go on to ruin my life one day. So selfish.

These security measures, if you want to call them that, that you put in place were a valiant effort. But really, a coffee table in front of the door? Was I supposed to bump into it to alert you to my presence? I'm nothing if not patient, Ciara. You should know this by now, and it's really pathetic that you don't. It was nothing to slide that shitty ass coffee table backward from the small slit in your door. Child's play.

Your bedroom is slightly better than the rest of this place. Not much though. And look at you. You look uncomfortable. Your brow is furrowed. Your face is turned up in a scowl. You're shivering. Is it me you're dreaming about? You can't even escape me when you sleep. How fitting.

The urge to reach out and touch you is strong. Just a whisper. But I resist. I can't let you know I'm in town just yet. The games have just begun.

I'll see you around, doll. Don't worry—I'll make sure to put the coffee table back where I found it.

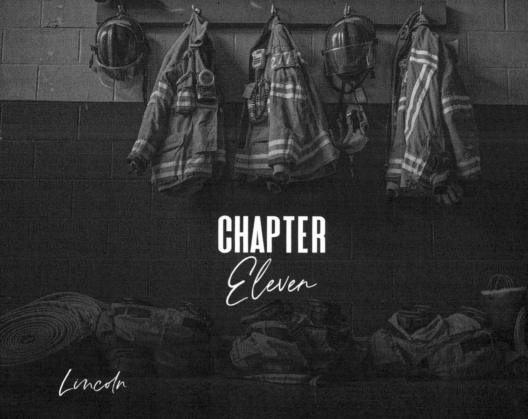

CHAPTER
Eleven

Lincoln

THE OBNOXIOUS RING ON MY PHONE STARTLES ME OUT OF MY SLEEP. I'm shocked to see Ciara's name on my screen. We may talk all hours of the day, but she never calls me at three a.m.

"Ciara, are you okay?"

"I'm so sorry. I'm so stupid for calling." I can practically hear her heart pounding over the phone, and I'm already out of bed stumbling around for clothes.

"You're not stupid. Tell me what's going on."

"Nothing. I just had a…nightmare. And then when I woke up I swore someone was inside my place. But I just did a full sweep, and there's no one here and nothing's out of place. I thought my coffee table was moved a little, but I honestly think that's my mind playing tricks on me. It's not possible. I just…I don't know. I was already calling you before I realized what I was doing, and I figured you'd be more concerned about a missed call at three a.m. than if I just told you what happened so I stayed on the line. I'm sorry. Go back to sleep. I'm okay." I've never heard her sound so scared, and all I want to do is run to her.

"Ciara."

"Yes?"

"Don't ever apologize for calling me when you're scared. What kind of best friend would I be if I said 'call me anytime, except for when you're scared'? I'll tell you. A shitty one." She chuckles, and it settles right in my chest. "I'm here, okay? Do you want me to come over?"

"N-n-no!" she stutters. "That would just make me feel guilty as hell. I'm fine, really."

I sit on the edge of my bed and debate if I should demand she give me her address so I can check in on her. I don't want to scare her even more. We've made a lot of progress, but if I push her too much right now she'll shut down. "Okay, fine. How about you talk to me for a little bit?"

"What? Linc, you don't have to do this. I'm the jackass that woke you up. You can go back to sleep."

"Psh, do you have spies on me or something? How would you know I was asleep?"

"It's three a.m. and you're boring. What else would you be doing?" There's the Ciara I know and...*woah, umm what? Don't finish that sentence. That would be crazy talk.*

"Angel, I'm far from boring. But because you called me that, you'll never know."

"Angel. What's that about?" she asks.

"It's your nickname now. Deal with it." I don't know why that nickname speaks to me when it comes to her. I'm sure if I really took the time to analyze it, the reason would be clear as day, but I'm not going to do that. Just let it be.

She hums her approval of the nickname. "Okay, fine. I'll take it. Ugh, fine. What do you want to talk about?"

"Tell me about your book. How's it coming along? You never told me the plot of your book, just that it's a thriller." We've talked about her book a few times before. It's her happy place, so it's the perfect subject change to get her mind off of the nightmare she had.

She takes a deep breath. "I'm a little more than halfway through, so it's good. I'm happy with it so far. You know I'm obsessed with all things true crime. I listen to all the podcasts, read all the books, and watch the ID channel all the time. It will be about a serial killer, but that's all I'm telling you." The smile in her voice is the balm to my soul. I love how passionate she is about her writing. Her passion is contagious too. Last week, she had me on the phone while she watched *Dateline*, and before I knew it I had on that channel and was asking a bunch of questions.

"No spoilers at all? So I'm just common folk now? That's cruel."

"You get what you get. Besides, you can't have a dedication and get spoilers. It's one or the other."

"Oh, in that case, I definitely want my dedication. Well, give me something. How does your villain kill the victims?"

"I'm not telling you that either. But I've looked up so many ways to kill a person that I'm pretty sure whatever FBI agent is tracing my search history thinks I'm a psycho. I found myself typing 'I'm an author, please don't arrest me' into my search bar the other day just to be safe."

I chuckle. "So what you're saying is you could kill me and dispose of my body without a trace."

"Exactly. So you better mind your Ps and Qs with me."

"Well I can't when you say shit like mind your Ps and Qs."

Every laugh I draw from her resonates in my spirit. I strip my shirt back off and settle back into bed now that I'm more confident she doesn't need me to run over there.

"Whatever. How was work today? Or yesterday, I should say."

"It was good. We responded to a structure fire that was a bitch to put out, but there were no injuries or casualties so I'd call that a job well done. The rest of the night we had some medical calls and a few other small things. Pretty quiet shift."

She chuckles. "I love how my idea of a quiet night on the job is not spilling a drink or no one throwing up and yours is you only put out one major fire and helped a few people with medical emergencies. We have two very different ideas of slow, my friend."

I laugh, but it falls short. I know my job is a lot to take in, and this is my reminder to not get my hopes up with Ciara.

"Hey, Linc?"

"Yeah?"

"What's your greatest fear?"

Now that gets a real laugh out of me. "Diving deep in the wee hours of the morning, huh?"

"I'm just curious. What makes the great Lincoln Cole tick."

"Letting the people I love down." I wasn't planning on going that deep, but here we are.

"In what way?"

"Just disappointing them." *Leave it at that.* "Or being too late to save them from some sort of danger or emergency." *Jesus. I need to go back to sleep. My guard is not up high enough for this conversation.*

The silence between us borders on uncomfortable before she puts me out of my misery. "I get that. More than you know."

"What about you? What's your greatest fear?"

"Death." There's a short pause. "Or being the cause of someone I love's death, I guess."

"Aren't we a pair?"

"Ha! Something like that. Wanna hear a joke?"

I want to hear everything from her lips. "Bring it on."

"Why did the golfer bring two pairs of pants?"

"Why?"

"In case he got a hole in one."

I'm too tired not to think that dumb shit was funny so I laugh. "I'm only laughing at how bad that was, Ci. You want dad jokes? I got you. Ready for this?"

"I was born ready."

"What do you call a crayon dressed in a sexy outfit?"

"I don't know, what?"

"Foxy brown."

A laugh escapes her, and I can tell it's against her will. "That was better than mine? I think the hell not."

"It was way better than yours."

"Okay, I will admit it was funnier than mine. Still trash though."

"You know what, I'm taking that as a W. So thank you."

"Yes, get your flowers now."

We spend another fifteen minutes telling corny jokes and talking about our hopes and dreams. Her voice is my lullaby. The more time I spend with her the more I want from her. She brings this light to my life that I never thought I'd have again.

"Hey, Linc?"

"Yeah?"

"I'm kind of tired now."

"Then it's time for you to go to sleep."

"I'm really sorry I woke you up."

"I told you you'll never know if I was sleeping or not." That earns me another chuckle.

"Good night, Linc."

"Good night, Jim Bob."

She chuckles again as she hangs up, and I let the memory of the sound lull me back to sleep.

CHAPTER
Twelve

Ciara

I THOUGHT LINCOLN COLE WAS SEXY BECAUSE HE'S GOT THE BODY OF a god, saves lives for a living, is good with his niece, and makes me laugh.

Those reasons are still valid, but I was not prepared for the version of Lincoln that talks me back to sleep after I had a nightmare and convinced myself my worst nightmare had made it inside my apartment. That's some romance novel level shit, and I am not equipped to deal with that. This session with Dr. Goodwin could not be coming at a better time.

"So how are you settling into your new city?"

"I'm good. Things are good." I mindlessly wrap a braid around my index finger. When I finally realize I'm doing it, I pray Dr. Goodwin hasn't noticed, but her eyes tell me she has.

"Have you been exploring the city? Meeting new people?"

"Against my better judgment, yes."

"Why do you say against your better judgment?"

"Because why would I want to drag anyone into the drama that is my life?"

"Are you feeling unsafe there?"

I've actually felt safer here than I have for a long time. I know the reason for that is a certain six-foot-two firefighter. He has cast his shield around me, allowing my breaths to come easier. It's a false sense of security though. He's not indestructible, no matter if he seems that way. I shouldn't ask so much of him. Especially when he's not aware of the shitstorm swimming around me. "I mean, I've had feelings of being watched or like someone is in my apartment, but I've been careful and there doesn't seem to be anything to it, so I think it's leftover paranoia."

She makes a note in that god-awful notebook. I hate that fucking notebook. It holds my darkest moments. My greatest fears. My biggest regrets. When we first started therapy, every time her pen would move toward that notebook, I'd clam up. Now I'm used to the rush of anxiety that flows through me every time she writes down another judgment. "And you still feel that not telling your friends and your mom about the threats Eddie made against them is the best decision?"

"Yes. If I had told them they would have done everything in their power to stop me from moving."

"And why do you think moving was your only option?"

I'm so incredibly tired of reliving this. I grab my laptop and move from my living room to my bedroom. I need the comfort of my bed for this conversation. "He was everywhere. Everywhere I went, all I could see was his face. I had to leave for my own sanity. It just wasn't home anymore. It was my own personal hell."

"And the threats don't play a factor?"

"Of course they do!" Ugh, she's too good. All she does is ask a question with that tone and I'm spilling my guts. "He said he'd kill them all. He said if they tried to protect me, he'd tear them limb from limb to get to me. How could I stay after that? I will not have their deaths on my hands."

She takes a pregnant pause before asking, "Do you feel you deserve to die, Ciara?"

I try to wipe my tear before it falls, but it's too late. "No."

She's silent, and I know her game. She's staying silent waiting for me to keep going, but I won't do it.

"It's not that I think I deserve to die." Damn, I'm weak. "I just…I escaped death three times. I feel like I used up all my lifelines. Somewhere along the way I accepted the fact that I would die at his hands and that's okay. I mean, it's not okay but you know what I mean. I just would rather I be the only one he takes. I cannot accept the deaths of my loved ones because I brought this man into our lives."

"You didn't bring him into your life, though. This all started as a random accident. And even if you had known Eddie on a personal level before this all started, you in no way deserved for any of this to happen."

"He chose me for a reason. I just wish I knew what it was."

She shakes her head vehemently. "You can't dive into the mental psyche of someone else. You can only focus on yourself." That's exactly what I need to do though. I dive into the psyche of murderers and criminals for the sake of entertainment. Yet I can't see into the psyche of my own tormentor.

"Yeah, you're right."

"Tell me about the nightmares. Are you still having them?"

"Not as frequently," I lie. Why did I lie? I told myself I wouldn't do that during my sessions since I'm lying to everyone else, but here I am. "They um, actually changed a bit."

"How so?"

"Well, it still starts with the morning of the stabbing. And sometimes I still see my mom, or Brittany, or Sarah, or Simone staring back at me when I turn the body over, but now sometimes it'll be Lincoln I see. Sometimes it's his sister Sasha, or his niece Nevaeh, or my friend/boss, Nina, too. But Lincoln's always the worst. It's always the most gruesome when I see him."

"I see. Who is Lincoln?"

I dive into the mystery that is Lincoln and tell her all about him and the circle of friends I've reluctantly built here.

"So why do you think Lincoln's is the most brutal?"

Because my feelings for him are on a level I am in no way prepared for. Shut up. "I really don't know. I actually called him after the nightmare I had last night."

"Seeking comfort?"

"I guess. And also I thought someone was in my apartment after I woke up, but I confirmed there wasn't on my own."

"And what did Lincoln say or do?"

He became the hero I needed and refused to have all in the same breath. "He offered to come over but when I insisted I was fine, he stayed on the phone with me until I went back to sleep."

"Do your feelings for Lincoln make you uncomfortable?"

Get out of my head, Dr. Goodwin. I mean, I know I literally pay you to get inside my head, but I want you out right now.

"Who said I have feelings for him?"

"Do you?"

"Ugh, yes."

"But you're not ready to explore them."

"You said that like a statement, not a question, so should I answer?"

Her lips purse into a line, and I feel bad for snapping, but I know she doesn't take it personally. "You have to do what feels right to you, but I would encourage you not to put yourself in isolation, because that's what Eddie wants you to do. You've built a circle of friends in your new city that seem to genuinely care about you, and your friends and family back here are in your corner. I know you want to protect everyone but your head and your heart are in battle over it, and you need your full strength to conquer the real battle."

She's got that right. My head and my heart are in full out war with each other, and my soul is losing because of it.

I'm in a funk after today's therapy session, and I don't want to talk to anyone, but Sasha's name flashes on my screen and I force myself to answer.

"Hello."

"Ciara, it's Nevaeh!" My smile immediately grows tenfold. I guess the universe sensed I needed a pick-me-up in the form of a tiny caramel diva.

"Well, hello, cutie. What are you doing with your mommy's phone?"

"I borrowed it to watch YouTube."

"Ahh, of course."

"Are you busy today?"

"For you? Never. What'd you have in mind?"

"Could you come to my mommy's shop and visit us?" I was planning on writing from home today, but with the mood I'm in all of my characters are going to end up getting picked off so it's best I take a break. Plus, I need a Nevaeh hug. She gives the best hugs.

"I would love to. Give me twenty minutes and I'll be right over, okay?"

"Okay!" Her excitement is so contagious.

I head over to my closet, suddenly happy to get the rest of my day started.

That little girl is nothing but trouble. Lesson learned. When little Nevaeh asks you to do something, ask for details because chances are she's playing you.

I was prepared to spend my day with the little brat and Sasha. I was not prepared to see the man I cannot get out of my head, in reality and in my dreams, in full uncle mode with Reggie's kids, Malcolm and Denise.

"Hey, what are you up to today?" Lincoln asks when he puts his niece back on the ground after spinning her around for what seemed like forever. He's not even remotely winded. He could definitely toss me around.

And I am going straight to hell for having that thought with children present. Oh well. Insert Kanye shrug here.

"I don't know, Nevaeh, what am I up to today?"

"Oh Lord. What did you do, little girl?" Sasha asks her daughter.

"I just wanted Ciara to hang out with us." Oh damn, she's already mastered the art of choosing your words carefully. Sasha is in for an adventure with this one.

"This is true. I just didn't know who 'us' was." Nevaeh smiles proudly, and I don't think I've ever wanted to shake a child until this very moment. She's so damn cute though.

Lincoln's eyes twinkle with amusement, and he wiggles those bushy eyebrows at me before motioning to the other two kids. "Ahh, she got you with the wordplay I see. Welp, you're here now. Ciara, this is my nephew, Malcolm, and this is my niece Denise. We just call her Niecy though. Guys, this is our friend, Ciara."

Malcolm throws me a head nod and Niecy gives me a small wave. "Hi," they say in unison.

"Hey, guys. Thanks for letting me hang with you today."

"No problem. Nevaeh never shuts up about you," Malcolm says.

"We're going to the park and then we're going to the arcade and then Uncle Linc's house." Niecy lays out the agenda.

"Oh, well I've definitely picked the right day to tag along then. Lead the way." Except to Lincoln's house. I don't want to step foot inside the place where that hunk of man gets naked every night. Nope. No, thank you.

"Good luck!" Sasha calls out, and I can't even process what she may mean by that.

We're at the park when a chocolate lab runs by dragging his owner along with him. "Ooh, look at that puppy. I want a puppy so bad. Linky, will you tell my mommy to get me a puppy?" Nevaeh begs.

"Absolutely not. I like my balls, and I'd like to keep them where they are." Lincoln shakes his head as he speaks. Malcolm laughs, and Niecy makes a disgusted face.

"What are balls?" I laugh at Nevaeh's question and throw my hands up in surrender. *You're on your own here, buddy.*

"Ummm. Woah, look at that puppy!" He points to a French bulldog running around with its owner.

"Ooh, where?" Nevaeh turns and awws at the puppy cuteness.

I look at Lincoln, and we have a whole conversation with our eyes.

Nice save.

Thanks. That was a close one.

You might want to watch your mouth next time.
Smart-ass.

"I want to play a game," Nevaeh declares.

"What should we play?" Lincoln asks.

"Tag?" Nevaeh says, her voice full of hope.

"Tag is boring," Malcolm whines.

"Yeah, it's just we're older than she is, so her little legs won't let her catch us," Niecy offers.

Malcolm is nine and Niecy is twelve, so I can imagine it's hard to have to include a five-year-old in your games, and they're nearing the age where they won't want to include her, but Nevaeh worships the ground they walk on. I want them to find a common ground.

"What if we make it more challenging for everybody?" I ask.

"How do we do that?"

"We'll play TV Tag instead of regular tag."

"What's TV Tag?" Niecy asks, but her voice goes up a little bit. I might be onto something here.

"It's still Tag but there's no safe spot. The only way to not get tagged is to stop and shout out the name of a TV show before the It person gets you. And you can't repeat the show the last person said or you get tagged anyway."

"Ooh, I know a lot of TV shows." Nevaeh is pumped. I know when she's at Sasha's if she's not coloring she's usually watching a show on Sasha's tablet, so I figured this would be a good twist for her. I used to love TV tag when I was a kid.

"And Nevaeh gets three cheats. She can call on me or Uncle Linc three times to carry her if she's It." I gotta give the munchkin an advantage somewhere.

"Okay, I like it." Malcolm is on board now too.

"But how does someone win?" Niecy asks, and right there I'm convinced she's going to grow up to be a lawyer just like her mom.

"In the last round, the It person has to tag everyone before the players untag each other and they win. Otherwise, the players win." All the kids nod their head in agreement.

I look up to find Lincoln watching me, and I squirm under his gaze. *Take that heat elsewhere, sir. There will be none of that today.*

We play rock, paper, scissors to figure out who's It first, and of course it's Lincoln. Then it's off to the races.

We've been playing way past the point of this being entertaining for me, but I'm glad they're having fun. These kids are fast as hell. I need to up my cardio game. I may be strong but I am slow. Good Lord. Honestly, I'm praying for a full-blown asthma attack to give me an excuse to take a break, and I don't even have asthma. Whose idea was this?

Don't answer, I know.

Malcolm has picked up on my weakness, and he's beelining straight for me.

"*Golden Girls!*" I yelp at the last second. Malcolm stops and looks at me in full-blown confusion.

"What's *Golden Girls*? You can't make shows up."

Gasp! "What's *Golden Girls*? That question is blasphemous."

"I don't know what that means."

"Good point. Anyway, it's a real show, I swear. It came out in the eighties." I cross my heart.

"That's old!"

Ouch. I'm not sure why that hurts my pride, considering I wasn't even born in the eighties, but still, how dare he disrespect the ladies. "I'm going to trip you, kid."

He chuckles. "Uncle Linc, is *Golden Girls* a real show?"

He cackles. Once again, he's not even slightly winded. *Okay, Linc. I'm picking up what you're putting down.*

No, stop!

"Yeah, it's a real show. Blanche was my first girlfriend in my head."

Oh my God. "Wait, are you serious?" The man winks at me again.

"Okay, fine. You're safe for now," Malcolm decides then leaves me behind in pursuit of Niecy.

Malcolm and Niecy may be faster than Nevaeh, but it's impossible to tag her because her knowledge of TV shows is unmatched.

"*PAW Patrol!*"

"*PJ Masks!*"

"*Doc McStuffins!*"

"*Boss Baby!*"

"*Bunk'd!*"

"*Magic School Bus!*" The kid is a machine. Niecy finally catches her after she accidentally repeats "*Carmen Sandiego,*" but she is ever the strategist.

"Linky! I wanna use my cheat. Carry me!" I crack up as Lincoln rushes over and swoops her up.

"Last round!" he declares right before going after Malcolm. He's on Malcolm before he can even form one word. One down. Niecy is next, and she gives it her all but she's too winded to even say anything, so she's down too. I'm the last one, and I pretend to run away, but really I'm grateful my lungs will be able to draw air again, so I can't wait to be tagged.

Lincoln catches up to me in seconds, and he whispers in my ear right before Nevaeh tags me. "Don't run from me, Angel." My pussy clenches at his words, and I am a fucking goner. I feign a dramatic fall as Nevaeh tags me to hide the fact that I desperately need friction between my thighs.

"Good game, Nevaeh!"

"Yeah, you were so good!"

I love that Niecy and Malcolm are celebrating Nevaeh's win right now instead of being sore losers, and it's enough to get my sinful-ass vagina in check. She may be the queen, but I can't bow down to her with children present.

Nevaeh's glee at her win lasts the rest of the day. She's all smiles at the arcade, and Niecy and Malcolm are all too happy to let her play with them at all the games. She's in heaven, and I love that for her.

"You're great with them," Lincoln says as he sips his water.

"Aww, they're great kids. Today was a lot of fun."

We've been at the arcade for an hour and the kids show no signs of slowing down, so Lincoln and I have claimed a table at the connected restaurant where we can watch them but also relax.

"Well, thanks for coming with us."

"I don't think I had much of a choice, but it was my pleasure."

"Yeah, what Nevaeh wants she gets most of the time."

"Like niece, like uncle, I guess."

"I don't get everything I want, Ciara."

Fuck. I'm in dangerous waters here, and yet here I am. Throwing my paddles overboard.

"What is it you want that you don't have, Lincoln?"

"I don't think you're ready for that answer." His eyes drink me in slowly.

Gulp. "You're probably right about that."

"You're getting close though."

"Oh really? You can sense that?"

"Yep. You're so close I can taste it." He licks his lips.

Oh, shit. Where are those paddles? Can I get them back, please?

"Lincoln," I rasp. I've got to get us back to calm waters.

"Can I ask you a question?"

"Anything." *Unless that question is "can I take you the nearest bathroom and fuck you." In which case the answer will be "yes, but I don't want to end up on some sort of list so please don't ask."*

"What are your thoughts on dating someone with a dangerous job?"

Huh. "That is not where I thought you were going with that."

"Oh, I already know the answer to my other question, but this is the one I'm really curious about."

"What other question?"

He flashes that goddamn smirk at me again. "Answer the question that was asked, Angel. Please."

There's a desperation in his voice. He needs this. "Let me guess. We're talking about a dangerous profession like a firefighter, correct?"

"Any job where safety is constantly at risk. Firefighter, cop, military. Any of it."

"So you're asking if I'd have a problem dating someone who did that for a living?"

"Yes. And would you ask him to quit?"

"I wouldn't have a problem with it, and I would never ask him to quit."

He arches his eyebrows. "Never? You really think you can say never?"

"Without a doubt."

"How so?"

Lincoln and I are entering dangerous territory here. We're obviously not talking in general terms and yet I don't want to shy away from the question. I feel like this is a make-or-break moment for us, and even though I'm not ready to address the feelings I have for him, I do want to be clear in my feelings on this. He needs my complete and total honesty.

"Dating someone who puts their life on the line every time they walk out the door is not for the faint of heart. It takes a special person to accept that. But high risk brings high rewards, and being loved and cherished by someone whose heart is big enough to be willing to sacrifice for others every single day is an honor. And to ask a person who has made it their purpose in life to save lives and change the world to step away before they're ready is a cruel injustice."

His eyes widen, and he looks away for a moment. When his beautiful eyes meet mine again, I see a whole host of emotions swimming in them. Appreciation. Respect. Doubt. Fear. Anxiety. Hope.

My gut reaction is to reach for his hand, and I do. "Are you okay?"

"Yeah. I just…I wasn't expecting that answer, and I don't know what to do with it, to be honest."

"I'm missing part of the story here, aren't I?"

He nods. "I was in a serious relationship three years ago. Her name was Erica. We had been together for three years, and we were gonna get married. I always knew my job was hard on her—it's hard on all significant others—but she kept it to herself for the most part. I didn't even know she was hurting. Until I got hurt on the job really bad once. I got trapped in a bad fire, evacuating the family out, and I almost didn't make it. After that, she begged me to quit because she couldn't handle it anymore. But that's just not me. I was put on this Earth to do this. I believe that with my whole soul, and I couldn't give it up. She told me I didn't love her enough, and she left me."

I watch as the painful words spill out of him. He looks like a weight has been lifted off of his shoulders after sharing that and yet I can tell that weight he lifted was barely a drop in the bucket.

"I'm sorry, Linc."

"That's not the worst part. She umm, died." I gasp. It's quiet but he notices. I stay silent hoping he continues and am grateful when he does. "One week after breaking up with me, she was on her way to her parents' house in San Antonio, and she was in a really bad car accident." I wince at his words as a certain memory threatens to overtake me, but I won't let that overshadow Lincoln's needs right now. "I was called to the scene, but I was too late. I couldn't save her."

"Jesus. I'm so sorry, Linc. I know that doesn't mean shit in the grand scheme of things, but I am truly sorry."

"I just feel like if I couldn't save her life, the least I could've done was not waste the last three years of her life. She could've been happy elsewhere. But she stuck with me hoping I would choose her over my job, and I didn't. Who knows, maybe she wouldn't have even been on that road at that time if it weren't for what happened between us."

Shit. The pain radiating off of Lincoln right now is unbearable. I want to take it all away from him. I realize in this moment how much I've really grown to care for this man. It's terrifying. How did I let this happen?

"Listen to me. She didn't deserve to die, but if I can be honest, she didn't deserve you either. You didn't steal her happiness, Linc. She gave it to you because you were worth it. You are worth it. Her issues with your job were more about her than you. It was wrong of her to ask you to stop. She put you in an impossible position, and if you had given it up for her you would've grown to resent her because you are absolutely right that you were meant to do this. You can't blame yourself for what happened after the break-up. It's okay to mourn her, but do not take that guilt on or it'll eat you alive." *I would know.*

He squeezes my hand in thanks and then promptly changes the subject. This day is nothing like I expected. I got an impromptu play date with Lincoln's whole family and a heart-to-heart with him in the middle of a crowded-ass arcade. This is a whole new brand of crazy, but it feels like a brand that's imperfectly ours. I'm honored that he chose to open up to me today. I feel ten times closer to him now that he shared his history and ten times guiltier that I didn't share mine with him.

Can I really bring him into my shit? Definitely not today. Today has been heavy enough. But shit, maybe. Just maybe.

"What are you doing next Friday?" Lincoln asks, bringing me out of my trance.

"Umm, I've learned to be very skeptical with this family, so I'll say it depends. What's up?"

His shoulders shake with laughter, and it feels so good to hear that laugh again. "It's my birthday. I'm going to have a cookout at my parents' house with my siblings and a few friends. Very low-key. Will you come?"

His birthday? I wonder why he never told me before that his birthday was coming up. The crazy thing is there's not a doubt in my mind that I'll go to his birthday cookout. I can hear it in his voice how badly he wants me there, and I don't want to disappoint him. I'm about to agree to meet Lincoln's parents, the last sibling I haven't met, and his friends. Shit is getting real.

"In that case, it's my first Friday off in forever so yes, I'd love to come." And the smile on his face is worth the pain I feel in the pit of my stomach right now.

CHAPTER
Thirteen

Eddie

HOW DARE YOU?

You spent the entire afternoon with that man and those fucking kids. Looking like you didn't have a care in the world. I'm beginning to think you don't take me seriously and that pisses me off.

I know you haven't forgotten about me, though, because you talked about me in your last therapy session. Again. That's good to know, but it's not good enough. Your every waking thought should be about me. Maybe I've given you too much freedom. You seem to be under the impression that you're safe now.

Is it because of him?

Lincoln Cole. I've learned a lot about your precious firefighter over the past few days. He's a Fire Lieutenant at the Austin Fire Department. A real hero. Give me a fucking break. He cannot save you from me, doll. You're my toy to play with. I don't share.

He's also the brother of that coffee shop owner you seem so enamored with, Sasha. You're just blending right in with this little family, aren't you? We'll see how much they love you when you're the reason every single one of them dies.

Their blood is on your hands.

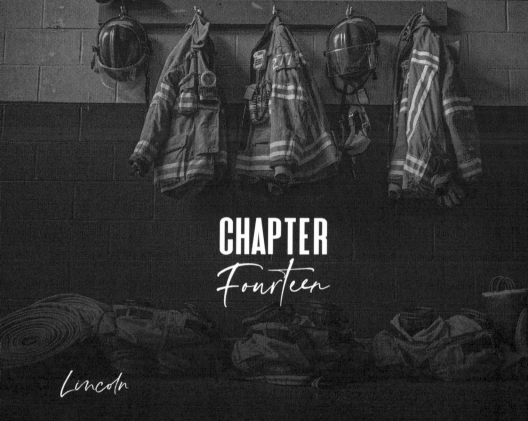

CHAPTER
Fourteen

Lincoln

I WANT HER.

There is no denying that anymore. I've long accepted that I want her in my bed, but I'm starting to get hopes of the real deal with this woman. I want it all with her.

I don't know if I can fully trust the things she was saying about dating someone in my line of work, because Erica used to swear it didn't bother her at all in the beginning—but God, the conviction in her words and the sincerity in her eyes hit me square in the chest.

I just have to convince her to take a chance on me. I know she's still fighting her own demons, and she still hasn't given me every part of herself, but I'm willing to fight for it.

"All the smoke alarms are in good shape, Mrs. Townsend. Jenny said your blood pressure is much better than last time we visited. I'm impressed," I say to my favorite woman outside of my family and a certain Angel.

Today I'm visiting a few people in the community on my Red Angels shift. Red Angels is a program comprised of a few of us AFD firefighters and some licensed nurses. We go door-to-door offering free in-home safety and wellness checks. We do this every few weeks. It's one of my favorite things the station does because I get to be a part of my community and connect with them without an emergency taking priority.

Mrs. Townsend is one of my favorite people to visit during these shifts. She's an elderly white woman with hair so platinum it looks like a White Walker from *Game of Thrones*. Every time I come here, I'm guaranteed to leave with a batch of freshly baked cookies, new sweet stories about her late husband, complaints about her son Billy, and at least one pinch on my ass for having such a "cute butt."

I checked all of her smoke alarms and conducted a general home hazard assessment, and Jenny, the nurse working with me on today's shift, just finished checking Mrs. Townsend's blood pressure, glucose, and pulse.

"Yes, well, Billy has been up my ass since the doctor said my blood pressure was high last time. He cleaned out all the good stuff from my house and ordered that damn Hello Fresh service to come weekly. Like I can't prepare my own meals."

"Well pasta Bolognese, meatball subs, and hushpuppies are not meals you should be preparing every day."

"Bleh, you sound just like Billy."

I shake my head trying to hold in my laughter. "You gotta give Billy a break."

"Oh, you know he's the apple of my eye, but he treats me like an invalid now. I am not too old to put him over my knee, you know."

"Oh, you'll never be too old for that."

"Damn right. You know how in all the old movies the wives would say 'wait until I tell your father'? Not me. My Harold used to say 'wait until I tell your mother.' I'd lay down the law, and he'd hand out the candy behind my back."

I smile. I wish I would've met Harold. He seemed to be a good man, a great husband, and a fantastic father. Everything I once wanted to be. Everything I find myself imagining more these days. "Sounds like you two were the perfect team."

"We sure were. Come on with me to the kitchen before you go. I got a fresh batch of cookies for you."

I raise my eyebrows at that. "I thought Billy cleaned all the good stuff out of the house."

"Ha. I have my ways. You think I wouldn't have cookies ready for my favorite fireman? The day I don't have cookies ready for guests will be the day I go to reunite with my Harold."

"You sneaky woman. Lead the way."

"Alrighty, dear. I've got chocolate chip and oatmeal raisin this time. A dozen each."

"You're too good to me, Mrs. Townsend." I'm probably going to eat at least one in the car. No one makes cookies like she does. I'll bring the rest to the fire station for the guys, so I don't have to be the only one putting in work at the gym.

"Maybe you can share some of these with your lady friend," she says as she wiggles her eyebrows.

"Who said anything about a lady friend?"

"Oh, please. You don't get to be my age without learning a few things. Before my Harold I'd been around the block a few times, ya know." She puts her hand on her hip, and I bite the inside of my cheek.

"Your smile was a little extra perfect today, and you whistled while checking the smoke detectors. I know the look of a smitten man, and you, my friend, are as smitten as they come. Now are you gonna share these cookies with your lady friend or am I taking a batch back?"

I can admit when I've lost. "I'll make sure she gets some."

"I knew it." She smiles as she walks me to the door. "Thanks for visiting an old hag, Lincoln. Tell that lady friend I said hello, and keep that butt nice and tight. She'll appreciate it too," she says with a pinch on my ass. It never fails.

I've just gotten back to the station when I see my siblings have blown my phone up.

Reggie: Please tell me you invited Ciara to your birthday

cookout on Friday? I'm the last one to meet her! Btw Malcolm said to tell you his favorite Golden Girl is Sophia

Sasha: Sophia will forever be that bitch

Isaiah: Blanche can get it

Sasha: *eye roll emoji* perv

Reggie: You do know Blanche is dead, right? #LongLiveBettyWhite

Isaiah: I said what I said

Reggie: So is Ciara coming or not?

Sasha: She said she'd be there

Reggie: Okay good. At least someone has the decency to answer me

Isaiah: If you wanna have a chance to talk to her you better grab her fast. You know Mom will be pulling her aside teaching her how to make jollof rice by the end of the night

Reggie: *crying laughing emoji* So true

Sasha: Did you tell Ciara that Mom will probably beg you guys to pick Nigerian middle names for your future kids?

Isaiah: Yeah let's not repeat the NiecyGate drama of 2008.

Reggie: *insert middle finger emoji*

Sasha: Sasha's a great name for a girl, just saying

Isaiah: No one wants name suggestions from you, sis, that's how we end up with hippie dippy-ass names like Nevaeh

Sasha: *inserts gif of Tracy Morgan gasping*

Reggie: Oh shit

Isaiah: *three crying laughing emojis* You know I love my short stack but heaven backwards, really? That's what happens when you marry a white man

Sasha: Oh this bitch

Isaiah: I'm kidding!! LOL I love Carter. Lowkey I love him more than I love you sometimes

Sasha: *inserts gif of Zendaya rolling her eyes*

Sasha: Lincoln get your brother

Reggie: He's too busy for us

Isaiah: Probably jerking off to Ciara's picture

These fuckers.

Me: I was doing what some people call working. Don't y'all have jobs?

Me: Yes, Ciara is coming on Friday. Mom is not teaching her how to make jollof rice and THERE'S NO BABY! Happy??

Reggie: Who are you yelling at?

Sasha: Well I for one hope Ciara is coming in more ways than one on Friday. My girl needs a stress reliever

Isaiah: *crying laughing emoji*

Me: *inserts a gif of Sam from Netflix's GLOW with the words 'you're a fucking nightmare'*

Jokes aside, I am slightly nervous about my half-Nigerian mother scaring Ciara away with talks of future kids' names. She allowed my father to name all of us whatever he wanted so long as she got to give us each a Nigerian middle name, and when Reggie and Sasha started having kids she forced them to do the same. Reggie wanted Denise's middle name to be Raquel, and all hell broke loose. We call that period of time "Niecygate" now and Denise Raquel ended up being Denise Oviereya at the end of it. She didn't even attempt to do something different for Malcolm, and Sasha definitely didn't try when Nevaeh was born.

As for making sure Ciara comes in more ways than one, what can I say? I want that too. I've jerked off so many times in the past couple of months, I feel like a teenager again. All I can hope is that Ciara's self-control is on the verge of snapping as much as mine.

Kai hands me my second beer of the day on the afternoon of the cookout. Dad is manning the grill. Mom is sipping her sangria, keeping him company. Isaiah and Shane are chasing the kids around. Sasha is stealing potato salad off of Carter's plate. Michael is fixing a plate for Reggie. Dom is talking to a few of the guys from the station. All that's missing is my Angel.

Right on cue, the energy in the yard shifts, and I know she's here. I turn around to be once again stunned by her beauty. She's wearing orange high-waisted pants that complement her skin tone perfectly and make her ass look even sexier, a tight white V-neck T-shirt that stops right at the dips of her breasts, and sandals. Her braids are pulled into a half-up, half-down style, and those lips I'm dying to taste are painted a nude color.

"Hey, you made it."

"Of course I did. I wouldn't miss your birthday celebration. How's it feel to officially be the dirty thirty?"

"Not nearly as dirty as it could be," I say, allowing my eyes to travel down her body before snapping back up to those chocolate eyes. She shivers and I smirk.

"Where should I put your gift?" She holds a box I honestly didn't even notice before.

"Oh, you didn't have to get me anything."

She shoots me an incredulous look. "Did you think I would show up here empty-handed? Please. I brought wine for your parents too."

"Trying to score brownie points, I see."

"It's your birthday, so I would hate to have to pop you in your arm again, but I will."

"Oh shit, slugger's back. Okay, save your strength. You may need it for later."

"You are trouble."

"Only for you, Angel."

"Can we say hi to her now, or do you want to hog her all to yourself?" I turn around to find Sasha watching us with Reggie right on her heels.

"No respect for the birthday boy."

"No one cares past the age of twenty-one. You're lucky you got this cookout." She turns to Ciara. "Hi, I'm Lincoln's sister Reggie. I've heard a lot about you. Mostly from my kids. Lincoln's very tight-lipped."

Ciara chuckles. "Nice to finally meet you, Reggie. Your kids are great. Although, Malcolm made me feel like an old-ass woman for my TV shows."

"Yeah, he's a little shit like that. But I have you to thank for his new obsession with *Golden Girls*. Excellent choice."

"Oh, and who's his favorite?"

"Sophia."

"I knew I liked that kid."

Reggie beams at Ciara, and I know she's been won over.

I escort Ciara over to the grill, and my mom immediately perks up.

"Mom, Dad. This is Ciara. Ciara, these are my parents, Trinity and David."

"Nice to meet you, Mr. and Mrs. Cole. What I've seen of your home is beautiful."

"Aww, thank you, sweetie. We don't need formalities here, though. You can just call us Trinity and David."

"Okay, thank you. I brought you a bottle of wine." She holds out a bottle of merlot.

"Ooh, perfect timing. I'm all out of sangria, and I need a refill. Here, come with me to the kitchen." Mom practically drags Ciara in the house, and I'm left saying a silent prayer that she won't send Ciara running for the hills.

"It's out of your hands now, son. She can handle it though. I can tell," Dad offers.

"Yeah, you're right."

"Cheers to the love of a good woman." He holds out his beer waiting for me to return the cheers.

"Dad, we're not—" He cuts me off and clinks my bottle with his before winking and turning back to the grill. *Alright, old man.*

After Mom spends way too long in the kitchen with Ciara, she still looks happy and not looking for the exits so I guess we're okay. Although, I consider asking her if my mom shared any recipes with her while they were in there. She catches my eye and walks over to me. I try to keep eye contact with her, but I fail miserably and continue to trace her curves the entire way over.

I gesture toward the assholes in front of me. Might as well get this introduction over with. "These are my dickhead friends, Dom, Kai, and Shane. Ninety-eight percent of what they say is complete bullshit, so feel free to just tune them out."

"But it's that two percent you really don't wanna miss," Dom says.

"Nice to meet you, Ciara. I'm Shane. Also known as the handsome one of these ugly motherfuckers."

"I mean I'd say you're definitely in the top five of this group," Ciara retorts, and I love that she immediately jumped in to give these guys shit.

"Ha! I bet you're number five too. You dumbass," Isaiah laughs.

"I'll never share my rankings." She turns to Dom. "I never got a chance to thank you for your help that day, but thank you and nice to officially meet you."

Dom blushes. *Yeah she has that effect on people.* "No thanks necessary, I was just doing my job. I'm glad you're okay, even though I think you may have some residual effects if you're hanging with this guy by choice." He points to me.

"Oh yeah, the doctor told me poor life choices were a side effect of the head injury."

"Very funny, you assholes," I joke.

This cookout is exactly what I needed. Time to just relax with the people

I care most about in this world. Nevaeh is sitting on Ciara's lap whispering secrets in her ear. I imagine Ciara's belly swollen with our child, and the thought is not so scary. Would our child have her eyes, her cheekbones, her giving spirit? I'm getting way ahead of myself, but it doesn't feel so wrong.

Nevaeh demands I open presents, so I get down to business. When I get to Ciara's gift, I lock eyes with her, and she shoots me a sneaky smile.

Oh shit.

"What is that, Uncle Linc?" Malcolm asks.

"It's a bug-out bag." A zombie apocalypse bug-out bag just like the one I told her I wanted as a kid. It's packed with dried food, a first aid kit, an extra pair of clothes, and a bunch of other essentials. On top of the bag is a book titled *The Zombie Survival Guide* by Max Brooks.

"I figured you should be all set with this. I still expect a pin with the meet-up spot, by the way," she teases. I laugh, but all I really want to do is pick her up, carry her inside, kiss that smart-ass mouth senseless, right before sinking inside her.

You're playing with fire, Angel.

The guys suggest we continue the night by heading over to Neon Nights, and I'm excited Ciara agrees to join.

"I'm too old to go drinking with you fools, so I'm heading home," Reggie declares, which earns an eye roll from all of us.

"You're thirty-six. Stop it." Sasha scowls.

"Okay, fine. I'm not too old but I've had four drinks which is more than my tolerance will allow these days, so I'm gonna go put my kids to bed and then fuck my husband if that's okay with you."

I blanch at that. I do not want to hear about my sister's sex life. "Oh. Well, you should've just said that then. Carry on." Sasha blows her a kiss.

"I could've done without that," Carter says and wrinkles his nose.

"Aww, babe, well, you'll get the same treatment if Nevaeh is in bed when I get home," Sasha promises him with a wink.

Carter throws me a quick good night and grabs Nevaeh to find and catch a ride with Reggie and Michael. *This family really needs some fucking boundaries.*

Sasha turns to Ciara. "Ciara, I'll follow you back to your place. That way we can just drive one car to the bar."

"Sounds good." Ciara throws me one more look over her shoulder as she walks out with Sasha, and the look I give her is a promise of things to come.

The energy between Ciara and me could set this place on fire, and this time she can't hide behind the bar.

I notice Isaiah and Nina arguing. She walks away from him, and he wipes his hand down his face in frustration. I make a note to ask him about that when I'm not so focused on the temptress in front of me.

We keep finding reasons to touch each other. I place my hand on the small of her back when she speaks to me. She grazes my arm with hers when she walks by. She puts her hands on my neck when she asks me a question. Her touch sets my soul ablaze, and I'm ready to burn.

At the end of the night, Sasha offers Ciara a ride back to her place, but I'm not ready to pour water on our flames just yet.

"I'll drive her home." I'm speaking to Sasha, but I never take my eyes off Ciara.

"Riiiight. Okay, good night, you two. Happy birthday, Linc!" Sasha scurries away. I don't even say good night to everyone else. I just rest my hand on the small of Ciara's back and lead her out.

Ciara clenches her thighs three times during the ride home, and I can imagine how wet she is for me, but I have to let her lead things with us. I can see she's still hesitant to let me all the way in, so the ball has to be in her court. The sound of Snoh Aalegra's melodic voice fills the car. The tension in the air is palpable. My hand aches to reach out and graze her thigh. To drive her as crazy as she's driving me.

I manage to keep my hands to myself, and soon I pull up in front of her apartment building. "I'll walk you up." She doesn't argue as I run around the front of the car and help her out. She's quiet on the elevator ride up to her floor, and I'm pretty sure our flames are about to be put out.

"Thanks for tonight, Linc. I had fun."

"Thanks for coming. And for the gift. Can't tell me shit now."

She shakes her head and laughs. "Look out, Rick. There's a new sheriff in town."

She's so fucking cute. "You had to make it sound corny." She laughs with her whole body, and I drown in the sound.

"Good night, Linc. Get home safe."

"Good night, Angel. Sleep well." I lean in to kiss her on the cheek, and her breath hitches.

I wait until I hear the click of her lock to turn for the elevator. My self-control is hanging on by a thread. I know she wants me, but I don't know if that's enough.

Take a chance with me, Angel. Let's burn together.

Fuck it. I head back toward her door.

CHAPTER
Fifteen

Ciara

WHAT IS WRONG WITH ME?

I'm about to come out of my skin with want. This war between my head and my heart is about to split me in half, and I don't think I'll survive the aftermath.

I'm about to force my legs to carry me through my routine when there's a knock on my door.

Is he…?

I stop to check the peephole because I will never blindly open a door again, and there he is. He's too gorgeous for his own good. I want to rip his shirt off and lick each one of his abs.

"I can hear your heart pounding, Angel." He groans, and I bite my lip at the sound.

I open the door, and he's standing with both arms up against my doorway, eyes staring into my soul.

"Lincoln."

"Question time. Don't think, just answer."

I nod.

"Am I crazy? For feeling this heat between us?" he rasps.

"No." I waste no time answering. He looks up at me with a look that flays me wide open. It's a look of danger and unbridled passion, but also a look of relief. I've made him doubt that I want him as much as he wants me. I shouldn't feel bad about that since it was my plan all along, but I do. I want him—no, I need him—more than I need my next breath, and I feel like shit that I've made him feel like he's alone in this.

"Do you want me to kiss you, Ciara?"

"Yes." The word has been out of my mouth for half a second before his lips crash into mine. There's nothing gentle about this kiss. It's almost punishing, and it's gloriously painful. He traces his tongue against my bottom lip, and I immediately open for him. I'm matching his intensity stroke for stroke, we're taking turns giving and taking control, and I swear I could come right here from this kiss alone. I bite his bottom lip, and he groans before pulling away.

"Tell me no, Angel. Tell me to stop, and I'll leave right now. We can forget it ever happened or we can slow it down. But if you tell me yes— if you tell me you want me—I'm going to carry you to your bedroom and worship your body from head to toe until you scream my name and then I'm going to bury myself so deep inside you, you'll still feel me there tomorrow."

Did I say I almost came from that kiss? No, it was right now. This moment.

I'm not strong enough to deny this heat anymore. I want to get lost in him.

"Don't stop, Linc. I want you."

He growls, and next thing I know my legs are wrapped around his waist and he's carrying me through my living room, never taking his lips off of mine.

The locks. He sucks on my neck.

The end table. He squeezes my ass.

The knife. He runs his hand through my hair.

The room checks. He nibbles on my ear.

My head is too loud, and I can't ignore the pounding in my chest anymore. My breath catches, and Lincoln pulls away from me, eyes wide with concern.

"Ciara? Are you okay?" He slowly lowers me down, and the feel of my body sliding down his has me cursing myself for my paranoia.

"I'm sorry, it's not you. I just…have these security checks I do for myself every time I come home, and I didn't get to do them yet. I tried to ignore it because I want you so badly, but I'm kind of freaking out, honestly." I can't believe I just admitted that out loud. I look away from him, not wanting to see the confusion and pity that I'm sure will be in his eyes. He doesn't give me a chance, though, before he lifts his finger beneath my chin and tips my head up to meet his gaze.

His eyes soften but it's with adoration, not pity. He grabs my hand. "Show me."

"What?"

"Show me the routine. I'll do it with you."

"You're serious?"

He glares at me like he can't believe I would ask him such a thing. "Angel. Nothing is more important to me than your safety. If you need this to feel comfortable, let me give it to you. I wanna be the only thought on your brain when I sink inside you."

This man.

He never lets my hand go as I walk him through my routine of double-checking both locks on the door, sliding the end table in front of the door, grabbing the chef's knife from the kitchen, and checking every room and door for anything out of order. I don't even feel self-conscious doing it. I feel…safe. Lincoln makes me feel safe. And cherished. He doesn't even ask to take the knife from me. I think he senses that I need the control.

"That's it."

"Okay. How do you feel?"

Like I might die if you don't fuck me. Soon. "Good. Really good." He smiles, and the heat is right back in his gaze. "Do you want to ask me about that?" I absolutely do not want to talk about it. What I want is for him to fuck me senseless until I forget any of that just happened, but if he wants to ask I won't shy away from it. I owe him that much.

"Do you want to tell me about that?"

Never, but definitely not tonight. Talk about a mood killer. "Not tonight."

"Then I don't want to ask tonight. When you're ready." Relief washes through me at his statement. I need his hands on me.

"Linc?"

"Yeah, Ci?"

"Take me to bed."

"Thank fuck."

His lips crash against mine again, and he carries me the final feet to my bedroom, tossing me onto the bed. He rips his shirt over his head and peels my shirt off of me in seconds. I unclasp my bra, and he immediately takes a nipple in his mouth. He's licking and sucking with so much intensity while massaging and pinching the other one. I moan right in his ear.

He unbuckles my pants and slides them down my legs, then takes a pause to admire my near naked body.

"Fuck, you are gorgeous."

I squirm under his appreciation. I've never been shy about my body, but I haven't been with anyone since my life turned upside down. No one has seen the raised scar on my torso up close. No one has touched the scarring beneath my tattoos in such an intimate way. I'm completely exposed to him, and he looks like he's just unwrapped an amazing gift. Fuck, it feels good to be wanted like this. I needed this reminder that I am more than what that asshole did to me. "Lincoln, please."

He slides my panties off my ass, and I kick them off, giving him full access. He traces his hands down my body before sliding a finger into my heat, and my back arches off of the bed.

"So beautiful. You're so wet already."

He removes his finger, and I mourn the loss. He crawls up the bed toward my headboard and lies on his back. "Climb up, Angel."

Wait, what?

"Umm, what?"

"I need to taste you. Come here."

"You want me to...sit on your face?"

He chuckles. *This is not a laughing matter, sir.* "Yes."

"Have you seen my thighs? I'm not exactly light." My thighs are the product of good eating and strength training. I've always been strong because I rock climb for fun, but after everything happened to me I dove into self-defense training too. To strengthen my mind and my body. I also have a very passionate relationship with food, so my thighs, though they are strong, they are not light. Not in the slightest.

"Believe me, Ci. I've seen your thighs, and there's nothing I want more than to have them on both sides of my ears."

"I might suffocate you!"

He sticks his tongue out to wet his bottom lip. His eyes are locked onto said thighs for a long, torturous moment before he looks up and pins me with his unwavering stare. "If I die between your thighs, I'd die a happy man. Put it on my headstone: he died worshipping a goddess."

Well, when you put it like that. I climb up his body and settle my thighs on either side of his ears.

"Grab the headboard," he orders.

I do as he says right as he puts his hands under my ass and slides his tongue between my folds.

"Oh, shit," I cry out. He laps at me like a starving man, sending shivers up my spine. My hips start moving on their own, riding his tongue like it's my job. His tongue dives so deep I feel like I'm floating. He squeezes my ass and presses a finger against my hole as he sucks on my clit, and a deep guttural moan escapes my body. I never thought that would be something I'd be into, but he's driving me crazy in the best way. I arch myself harder against his finger. He rewards me with even more pressure. I never knew it could be like this. I'm far from inexperienced, but he's manipulating my body in delicious ways. He's reading my body like a book and giving me what I need before I even know what that is. I'm gripping the headboard so hard, my knuckles have turned white. I'm pretty sure

I'm about to crush his skull between my thighs with how hard I'm squeezing, but that only seems to spur him to suck harder so I can't bring myself to care.

"Fuck!" I scream, and suddenly I'm in the air. In a split second I've gone from on my knees to flat on my back with Lincoln towering above me. I knew he could toss me around.

"You taste better than I imagined. I need more. I want you to rain down on my tongue." He lifts my legs over his shoulders and brings his mouth right back to my clit. He slips two fingers inside me along with his tongue. My back arches, and my hands fly into his hair. I leave one hand in his hair and trace the other one up to my puckered nipple. I'm biting my lip so hard I think I draw blood.

"Come for me, Ciara." This is not a request. This is a demand by a man on a mission, and my soul wants to give him his every desire. To deliver to him his every desire on a silver platter created from my own body. I come with his name on my lips. He peppers kisses and gentle bites against my thighs as I come down from my orgasm.

I can see his erection pressing against his jeans, and I lick my lips at the thought of finally seeing his shaft.

"I need you inside me. Now," I pant, reaching for his jeans and flicking the button open.

He pushes his jeans and briefs down his legs, letting his erection spring free, and my eyes bulge out of my head as he tears open the condom he grabbed out of his pocket. My first thought is "that thang is thangin," and I have to fight to hold back my laugh at that stupid thought because I'm sure he wouldn't appreciate laughter after he whips his dick out. But goddamn…that thang is thangin!

Fuck, I laughed!

He sheaths his third leg in the condom and strokes himself twice as he settles between my thighs. "Something funny, Ci?"

Just trying to figure out how the fuck that thing is fitting inside me. I'm going to have fun finding out though. "Nope, nothing."

He traces his length through my folds, teasing me. "You sure about that? I like to laugh."

"Jesus."

"Nope. Just me, Lincoln." A laugh bursts from my lips, but it quickly turns into a moan when he traces my folds again. I'm aching for him. I reach for his erection, but he grabs my wrists and pins them above my head. His cock, thick with need, pokes me in the stomach.

"I don't know if it's gonna fit," I pant.

He smiles down at me.

"It'll fit, baby." He raises two fingers to my lips, and without a second thought, I suck them into my mouth until he groans. He slips those fingers inside me, and I'm rising high once again. Right before my second orgasm hits, he pulls his fingers out and then slips them into his own mouth. "I just prepped you for it."

Oh. My. God. I'm basically dripping at this point. "Fuck, Lincoln. Please."

"Please what? Tell me what you want, Ciara."

Fuck it. Call me TLC because I ain't too proud to beg. This commanding side of him has me craving him in ways I never imagined. "Please fuck me!" That's all it takes. He thrusts home and I see stars. Fucking stars. He stills, giving me a chance to get used to the feel of him.

"Fuck, you feel so good. Your pussy is choking my dick. I love it." My hips start moving and he springs into action, pulling almost completely out before thrusting in again. Our moans and groans fill the room, and I'm meeting him thrust for thrust. Giving and taking control.

He runs his tongue from the base of my ear down the column of my neck and between the dip of my breasts. Each trace permanently marks me. There should be a study done on the things he can do with that tongue. It's a work of art, and I'm his canvas. I moan his name when that talented tool circles my nipple before sucking it into his mouth. My arms fly around his neck when he bites down on it. It's so deliciously painful I need more. I look down to where our bodies are connected, and I'm mesmerized by the sight. That push and pull between us. My body making room for him to fill me completely. When I look back up at him, the heat that I see there sets me on fire. He loves that I love watching.

My nails scratch their way down his back, and his eyes roll in the back of his head. I'm leaving my mark on him too. What's happening between us right now is more than sex. It's a possession. We own each other. The marks we're leaving will fade physically, but we've embedded a piece of our souls within each other, and I know already that it can never be undone.

The heels of my feet press into his ass forcing him to go so deep I can't tell where he ends and I begin. My nails dig into his lower back and an ass cheek, and a low groan rumbles from his chest as he latches his mouth onto my neck. He's everywhere. I feel him everywhere. My senses are overwhelmed, and I let them drag me under.

He presses his thumb against my clit, and I shatter around him as he swallows my cry with his kiss. He pumps three more times before I feel him let go of his release. "Fuck, Ciara!" He slumps against me but catches himself before his full weight lands on top of me.

He rolls over to the side and pulls me against his chest before laying a sweet kiss on the top of my head.

"Holy. Fucking…"

"Shit." He finishes my sentence.

"That was amazing. No. Amazing doesn't do that justice."

"That was life-changing," he murmurs on an exhale.

"Exactly."

He gets up to dispose of the condom, then comes back and pulls me under the covers with him.

Life-changing.

That's a perfect word for what we just did, because there's no way we can ever come back from this. And I can only hope that when I tell him about my past he doesn't regret it.

I wake to find an empty bed. I stretch and smile when I still feel him between my legs. I'm bone tired. There was not a lot of sleeping done last night. I woke Lincoln up with his dick deep down my throat, and he thanked me by flipping me on my stomach and sinking into my heat from behind.

I find the button-down shirt he wore last night and slip it on with nothing else and head out to the kitchen. I lean against the entryway and admire the sight in front of me. He's scrambling eggs and frying up sausage, and he looks so right in my kitchen. So at home. It feels domestic as fuck, but the thought doesn't scare me like it did that morning at Sasha's house. I don't want to walk through life with everyone at arm's length. I want to lean into Lincoln and hold each other up.

"Good morning."

He turns around with a smile, but his eyes darken the minute he sees what I'm wearing.

"Good morning, gorgeous. Come eat breakfast." I saunter into the kitchen as the bagels pop out of the toaster.

"Can I help with anything?"

He shakes his head, pointing to the chair he's already pulled out for me. "You can sit that pretty ass down and let me serve you."

"Oh, you served me plenty last night."

"And that's just the beginning." He slides a plate in front of me and grabs a mug of coffee for each of us before sitting down. I pour a healthy serving of cream and sugar in my coffee, and he wrinkles his nose. "Do you want any coffee with your cream?"

I playfully roll my eyes. "Yes, I like cream and sugar in my coffee because I love myself. I can't help it that you weren't hugged enough as a child and started drinking straight bean juice."

He throws his head back in laughter then plants a soft kiss on my lips. I bite his bottom lip in response, and he growls.

"Fuck, Angel. I was trying to provide us with some sustenance, but I might just eat you for breakfast instead."

"You'll hear no complaints from me." His eyes darken, and he pulls me onto his lap. His eyes widen when his fingers reach my core.

"Where the fuck are your panties?"

"I guess I forgot them," I tease with a shrug.

Play time is over. He spreads my folds and dives inside, and the laugh that was on the tip of my tongue fades into a deep moan. His fingers curl inside me, and my head tips back in ecstasy. My hips start rocking forward, chasing my release. He takes his other hand and rips open the shirt, exposing my breasts. Buttons fly everywhere. I'm pretty sure one just landed in my coffee, but I couldn't care less right now.

He pulls me in for a heated kiss, and I can't help but moan into his mouth.

"Fuck, you're so responsive," he breathes out as his lips make their way to my needy breasts. My hips start moving faster as I grab the back of his head and hold it tight against my nipple. He takes my cue and bites down right where I need him. Fuck, why does everything about this man set me on fire?

He looks me in the eyes as his thumb presses against my clit, and my pussy clenches his hand as my eyes slam shut. "Look at me when you come on my hand, Ciara." Oh my God. I shatter and slouch into his chest. He sucks his fingers into his mouth, and if I wasn't already spent I'd come again.

Breakfast is a little cold when we get back to it, but it was so worth it.

Hours later I walk into Sasha's and spot Nina sitting in our usual booth. I'm not even fully seated before I'm accosted. "Oh shit, you and Lincoln fucked!" Nina shouts, and I look around nervously.

"Shit. You wanna shout out more of my business? I don't think the kids in the back heard you."

"I mean I can. Oh shit…" She gears up to shout again, and I kick her right in the shin. She doubles over in pain, and I feel no sympathy.

114

"You definitely have the 'thoroughly fucked' glow going on." Sasha smirks as she slides my caramel brulee macchiato in front of me.

"Isn't this weird to talk about considering he's your brother?" I ask.

"Oh, I definitely don't want the nitty-gritty details, but I know he's not a virgin. And you guys were sucking all the air out of the room with your sexual tension last night, so I'm glad it finally happened."

"Well, I definitely do want the nitty-gritty details, so you'll have to tell me at work tonight."

Just thinking about last night and this morning has a smile threatening to take over my entire face. But if Nina thinks she can dish the heat and not take it, she is sorely mistaken. "Ugh, nosey bitches. Anyway, since I'm not sharing details right now, let's talk about another Cole brother, shall we? You and Isaiah seemed to be having a heated discussion last night. What was that about?"

Nina's eyebrows shoot up to her hairline. "Oh. Nothing." Mm-hmm. Right.

"Oh shit. Are both of my friends dating my brothers?" Sasha leans forward, ready to pounce on this nugget of tea.

Nina scoffs. "Definitely not. Isaiah and I are not dating and we never will be. He's cute, and he's funny, and sure, I'd love to jump his bones, but he doesn't take shit seriously, and I just don't have time or patience for games. So no dice."

"Damn." Sasha actually looks disappointed at that, and I love her for it. She loves us so much she wants us to be with her brothers for the chance that we'll eventually become her official family.

Nina's phone rings, and she answers it right away.

"Hey, Logan, what's up? ... No, I haven't heard from Mom and Dad, why? What's wrong?" She lets out a frustrated sigh at his response. "Okay, you okay to pack a bag for you and Jada? ... Okay. ... No you don't have to walk, I'll come get you in a minute. ... See you soon. ... Love you too."

She hangs up and lowers her head into her hands. Sasha rubs her back, and I grab her hand.

"Your parents left on another trip?" Sasha asks.

"Apparently. They just forgot to give any of us a heads-up this time. They left a note by the door that Logan didn't see until he called."

Poor Logan and Jada. I get that their parents had them later in life and now want to enjoy their retirement years, but Logan and Jada didn't ask to be born. They shouldn't have to suffer. And Nina shouldn't have to take on the responsibility her parents rejected.

I feel a chill down my spine, and my eyes jerk around. I don't see anyone in the shop looking at me. I look out the window and don't notice anyone out in the street watching me either.

When will I stop feeling like this?

CHAPTER
Sixteen

Lincoln

T HANK GOD IT'S BEEN A QUIET SHIFT SO FAR, BECAUSE MY MIND refuses to venture far from Ciara.

She already had me hooked with her smile, sense of humor, and vulnerability, and now I'm just a full-blown goner. Sinking inside her was like coming home. I'll never get enough of her.

I already created the schedule for next month's shifts and did a bunch of other administrative stuff, so I might as well have some fun. I pull out my phone and send a text to Ciara.

Me: Miss me yet?

I'm excited when I see she starts typing back immediately.

Ciara: *eye roll emoji* You've been gone for four hours. Don't get a big head just because you've got a big head *wink emoji*

Me: *crying laughing emoji* Oh come on can't you stroke my

Ciara: I can stroke something else though *2 wink emojis*

Me: It's gonna be real awkward when the Big Guy jumps up in front of everyone at the station

Ciara: OMG, do you call your dick The Big Guy? Really?

Me: Hey you said yourself he's big, why fight it?

Ciara: So unoriginal

Me: You got something better??

Ciara: It'll take some research but I'm sure I can come up with something

Me: Oh I'm happy to sacrifice my body in the name of research

Ciara: I thought you would be

Ciara: I'm thinking Jay or Khal Drogo but I'll refrain from making my final choice until I do more research

Me: LOL ummm do I even wanna know why those are your top 2 contenders?

Ciara: To match me, of course

Umm, what?

Me: Do you...do you call your pussy Beyoncé and/or Khaleesi?

Ciara: Sure do! I switch off whichever one I'm feeling in the moment

Me: But...why?

Ciara: Because she's a goddamn queen and she should be treated as such

This woman. She's going to be the death of me, and I'm loving every minute of it.

Me: *crying laughing emoji* I can't argue with that

Ciara: Of course you can't it's perfect logic

Ciara: I gotta go, Nina is begging me for details about your dick

Ciara: *inserts gif of Larry from Curb Your Enthusiasm with the words 'I knew that big penis was nothing but trouble'*

Me: Make sure you tell her about that thing I do with my tongue too

Ciara: Impossible man. Stay safe, okay?

Me: Yes ma'am

Ciara: Told you about that ma'am shit

I send her a gif of Beyoncé in full queen attire right as the alarm goes off. Time to get to work. I have to push Ciara aside for now.

My unit arrives to the scene of an apartment fire, and I take command. The crew gets the pipe hooked up to the apparatus and gets to work. I'm giving an order to a probie when a tiny voice yells in my direction.

"Excuse me!" A girl who looks to be no older than twelve calls out to me. I wave my hand to keep her from coming any closer and jog to see what she needs.

"There was a man over there. He said he saw someone run inside the building!" She's winded from running over to me, so I'm piecing together her words.

"Woah, slow down. Sorry, did you say someone ran inside the building?"

"Yeah! I overheard a man say he saw a guy run in there after you guys came out because his daughter was crying about her cat still being inside. I turned around to tell him to tell you guys but he was gone."

"Okay, okay. Did he say where he saw the man run in?"

"He pointed over there." She points to the north side of the building.

"Okay, thank you. We got it. Stay here, okay?" She nods, and I run off to my crew.

While my crew and I have contained the flames enough that we aren't concerned about it spreading to other buildings, the blaze is still going strong. We were told the entire building was evacuated, and we did a primary search and found no one, but if a man ran in after we came out, we could've missed him. It seems odd to me that he would do that instead of just telling us about the cat, but I can't risk shrugging it off. I'd never forgive myself if someone died in a fire and I could've prevented it.

I make the decision to be the one to go inside the building with two other guys from the crew to look for the man while the rest of the crew focuses on getting the fire under control. We need to be quick and efficient.

"First floor clear!"

"Second floor clear!"

We continue to radio to each other through the five floors of the building and have turned up no signs of other life in the building. I start to head back down to meet my guys when I hear a deep voice call for help. I rush into the room where I heard the voice, but before I can radio to the guys that I located our target on the fifth floor, something slams me in the back. The wind is knocked out of me momentarily, but I scramble to turn over on my back just in time to see a figure dressed in all black throw a two by four on the floor and then throw a burning rag on top of a pile of clothes and curtains that are drenched in what I assume to be gasoline. I can't see his face at all, but his stature tells me it's a man. The only part of his body showing is the hand he used to toss the rag. I can see he's got scars covering it. I commit that to memory as he runs out of the room and slams the door behind him. The flames from the pile of clothes spread quickly. I run over to the door, but the man somehow locked it from the outside. *What the fuck is going on?*

"This is Lieutenant Cole. I'm trapped in a room on the fifth floor on the north side of the building. The fire is spreading quickly, and the door is locked from the outside. Need RIC ASAP."

"We need RIC to the north side of the building now. Fifth floor." I hear my command echoed through the radio, and I take a minute to observe my situation. The flames are spreading fast, but they aren't blocking the window yet, so I should be able to get out when my crew arrives.

Who the fuck was that man and why did he do this? Was he targeting me? Was the man lying about what he saw? Was the girl who came to me lying? So many questions are swirling around in my head.

"Lieutenant!" Peters, a member of the Rapid Intervention Crew sent to retrieve me, calls for me. I grab his hand, and he pulls me onto the ladder back to safety.

"PAR!" I call over the radio. I need to make sure my other crew members made it out of the building and there were no other run-ins with the man.

"Engine 1 has PAR," they call back. We're all accounted for. Time to get some answers.

The fire is under control now, and a secondary search was completed, but no one saw the man I mentioned run in or out. I've given the Austin Police Department my statement about what happened so they can investigate, and I've been cleared by the medical team to leave the scene, so we head back to the station.

Ciara.

Images of Ciara pop into my head, and I realize how badly I just want to be with her right now. Will she be okay if I tell her what happened today? Memories of Erica begging me to quit my job threaten to drown me, but Ciara's words pull me back. *"It takes a special person to accept that."* Could she be that special person for me? She said that being loved and cherished by someone like me would be an honor. She also said it'd be cruel to ask me to step away from what I've dedicated my life to. She said all the right things. My head wants to dismiss what she said as impossible to believe, but my heart is telling me to trust her. To lean into her. To stop letting the past hold me back.

"Make a choice, Lincoln. Between your past and your future." I choose my future as I make my way to Ciara's apartment.

She answers the door wearing shorts and a tank top that I want to rip off of her. "Hey, you. You're early," she says. I lean in to kiss her. It starts soft, but when she wraps her arms around my neck, I deepen the kiss. I kick the door closed behind me and flip both locks without ever taking my lips off hers. She moans into my mouth but then pulls away.

"Hey. What's wrong?"

"Nothing's wrong." I rest my forehead against hers.

"Then why are you early? I wasn't expecting you until tomorrow. Did something happen?"

I sigh. "They sent me home."

"Why?"

I start to fill her in on what happened on the scene, but for some reason when I go to tell her about the man, my brain freezes. I don't feel right telling her about it. I want more answers about that before I loop her in. I can barely wrap my head around it, so how could she?

Her eyes are wide with concern. "Jesus. Are you okay?"

"Yeah, I'm all good. My chief just decided to send me home, but I'll go back on my next shift as normal."

She eyes me skeptically. I know she doesn't believe me. She knows me better than that by now, and I don't fully understand why I'm not giving her the full story, but in my heart of hearts I know I'm making the right choice.

She seems to decide to let me be shady for now, and I'm grateful. "Okay, well, what do you need? How can I help you unwind?"

"I just need you." She gives me a sexy smile and wraps her arms around my neck again. What's crazy is that when I said I just need her, I didn't even mean sex. I mean, of course I'm going to take what she's offering me because I'd be dumb as hell not to, and I do want to, but being here, in her arms, with her checking to make sure I'm okay and rubbing circles on the back of my neck is more than enough.

She kisses my neck, and it snaps me back to the here and now. I squeeze her ass, and when she giggles I'm immediately rock hard for her. She pushes me down on her couch and straddles me. I cup her through her shorts, and she starts grinding against my hand.

"Stop trying to distract me," she rasps.

I smile. "Distract you from what?"

"You're the one who had a long day, so this is for you." She slides down on her knees between my legs and pulls my cock out of my pants. Before I can even register what she said, she strokes me from base to tip twice, and I rock forward on instinct, my dick glistening with pre-cum.

"Baby, you don't have to."

She cuts me off. "You had me for breakfast. I'm having you for dinner. Now hush." Ma'am yes ma'am. In the next moment her mouth is on me, and all coherent thought leaves me.

"Oh, shit," I moan. Her tongue traces the vein in my dick, and I am powerless to this woman. When she relaxes her throat and takes me in deep, I'm lost looking at her. Before long, my hands are in her hair, and my hips are driving forward so she can take me deeper. Her mouth is so wet and warm, I could stay here forever. She snakes her hand up her thigh and starts rubbing lazy circles around her clit and moaning. The hum of her throat against my dick and the sight of her being turned on by pleasuring me brings me so close to finish, but I'm not ready for this to be over so I force myself to tame it down. Her mouth is like ecstasy, though, and soon I can't hold back anymore.

"Oh fuck. I'm gonna come," I warn her, but my words only spur her on more until I spill my release and she drinks me down. She looks up at me with mischief in her eyes, and I swear the Big Guy, or excuse me, Khal Drogo or Jay Z, is ready to go again.

She stands up between my legs and wipes her mouth with the back of her hand, looking completely satisfied with herself. "Feel better?" she asks as she kisses me.

"I'm not sure I could possibly feel any better." Yes, I could. If I was sinking inside her right now I would feel ten times better.

"Perfect. How do you feel about leftover chili for dinner? I just made it yesterday." She whispers, "it'll be my second dinner" to herself and quietly laughs to herself. What a fucking nerd. I love it so much.

But umm...if she thinks we're going anywhere but her bedroom right now she's lost her mind.

"Do not look at me like that, Linc. I know your ass hasn't eaten yet, so let's eat. You're gonna need your strength for the plans I have for you later anyway."

The thought has me laughing and getting hard at the same damn time. "And what plans would those be?"

She tosses me a playful shrug before walking over to her fridge and pulling out her chili.

"Okay, wait a minute. Please tell me you're lying." She throws her head back in laughter. We've been sitting here eating and sharing old stories.

"No, I swear on my mama that happened."

"So three of Shane's exes end up at the same party, and his solution to dealing with all of them confronting him was to pull the fire alarm? At a work function? In a fancy hotel, surrounded by his bosses and important clients?"

"Oh, yeah. In his mind that made perfect sense," I say with a chuckle. "Shane is great at what he does, but he hates personal confrontation and especially with women. His brain usually short-circuits so he ends up doing dumb shit like dramatically pulling the fire alarm to get away from them."

"But isn't falsely pulling a fire alarm illegal?"

"That's the best fucking part. He knew that so he went into the bathroom, started a literal trash can fire, and then ran out and pulled the fire alarm so when the cameras showed he was the one to do it he had a legitimate reason for doing so. The hotel actually fucking thanked him for being so quick to pull the alarm and call attention to it. Believe me, Dom and I reamed him the fuck out when our crew got there and he told us the whole story, but when we think back on it, it's damn funny."

She has tears in her eyes from laughing so hard, and I'm right there with her.

"Your friends are something else. How did you all meet again?"

"I can't tell you that."

She laughs again but blinks when she realizes I didn't actually follow that up with the story.

"Are you guys secret agents or something?"

"Ha! No. We met nine years ago, but the story is so wildly stupid and unbelievable. We swore that night we would never tell anyone the real story. Not until each and every one of us were married and settled down."

"Why the hell was that your criteria for telling the story?"

"Because at the time we were all convinced we'd never actually settle down and get married. At least not all of us, so we'd never have to tell the story." It was Isaiah who suggested that be the criteria. He was nineteen at the time and was solely concerned with getting his dick wet at any given moment, so he never imagined himself settling down. Kai immediately agreed with the plan, and to this day I don't know why he was so quick to accept it. The rest of us took some convincing but then we just sort of thought Isaiah and Kai would be our holdouts so we'd never have to deal with it regardless. It's been working so far.

"Men are so fucking dumb," she says as she doubles over with laughter. "I wish Simone was here. She'd be frothing at the mouth to meet your friends." Ciara has told me all about her childhood friends Simone, Sarah, and Brittany. They're her extended family like the guys are for me. Every time she speaks about them, she has a layer of sadness in her voice which makes me want to know even more why she left home, but I won't push her on that. I have faith that she'll tell me when she's ready, and I'll be here for her whenever that is.

"Which one do you think Simone would latch on to?"

"Oh, I mean all of them. So I guess the real question is which one would she latch on to first." She takes a minute to think. "Definitely Shane." She brings her finger up to her chin in thought. "Yep, Shane. He's got this arrogance about him, but he's also kind of shy, and she would eat that shit up. She lives for making guys blush."

"I would love to see that."

She chuckles at that. "Do you ever feel like your entire life is an out-of-body experience? Like you put this husk version of yourself on display for everyone to see, but inside you're slowly dying but you don't know how to stop it?" I tentatively reach for her hand. When she doesn't pull away, I grasp her hand in mine and squeeze. She turns to me with a fragile smile and squeezes back.

"Yeah, I have. When Erica left me, I was hurt, and I didn't think I'd ever be myself again, but when she died, I really lost it. I kept up appearances like everything was fine, but inside I was questioning every single choice I ever made and regretting everything and just losing more and more of myself."

"How'd you fix it?"

"Honestly? I didn't realize I hadn't truly dealt with it until I met you."

"Me?" Her mouth is agape in shock, and I curse myself.

Shit. I did not mean to say that. I don't think Ciara is ready to hear how deep my feelings run for her. Hell, I don't think I'm ready to say it. But the more I think about it, the more I realize it's true. I have not felt this way about a woman since Erica, and the really scary part is that these feelings might even surpass that. I didn't think I was capable of these types of feelings anymore, so this is just making me realize how much I haven't dealt with my shit.

"Yeah. I just…I care about you. I care about you more than I thought possible."

She blinks. "I care about you too." She looks away and curses under her breath.

"Is that not a good thing?"

"I don't know. You are so unexpected. You were never part of my plan, and I'm just worried that—" She cuts herself off.

"Worried that what?" *Come on, Angel. Give it to me.*

She tries to blink away a tear, and I reach out to wipe it off her cheek. "Ugh, nothing. This is too much. Please." She cuts herself off again, but I know what she's asking. She's not ready. That's okay.

I lean in and kiss her, and she deepens the kiss. She stands up and grabs my hand. I let her lead me to her bedroom, and I show her with my body everything I'm not saying with my words. I just hope it's enough to get her to trust me with her pain.

CHAPTER
Seventeen

Eddie

I HATE YOU.

Do you know what I had to do today?

I set a fire. I've never set a fire in my entire fucking life. And yet I had to in order to teach you a lesson. You're so sure this man can protect you because what? He willingly runs into burning buildings? He's just as flammable as you, and I'll gladly burn him alive to make you see that. I didn't think that you could ruin me any more than you already have, but you're so determined to prove me wrong.

I hate you.

Do you know what burning skin smells like? I do. I've known since I was twelve years old and that sadistic bitch who popped me out of her cunt held my hands on top of the stove. You never forget that feeling. That smell.

You know, when I disposed of her I had to make it quick. Pity. She deserved a much slower, much more brutal death. Suicide, they ruled it. In a way it was. Every slap, every kick, every cut, all the pain she inflicted on me only led to her own demise. Slitting her wrists was easy. Watching her bleed out until the dim light in her eyes went out for good was a treat. But it wasn't enough. I wanted more. If I had my way it would have taken them days just to be able to identify her.

I'll take my time with you though. By the time I'm finished with you, you'll be begging me for the sweet release of death. Maybe I'll grant your wish. Maybe I won't. I decide. I hold your life in my hands and I'll crush it beneath my fingertips.

I hate you.

CHAPTER
Eighteen

Lincoln

THE NEXT TWO WEEKS FLY BY. CIARA AND I ARE TOGETHER DAMN NEAR every day at this point. There's not a lot of sleeping apart. Nevaeh has officially replaced me with Ciara as her favorite human being, not that I blame her. I've officially met her mom and friends through FaceTime. Ciara insisted on meeting Mrs. Townsend after she sent more cookies for her, and Mrs. Townsend has taken to planning our damn wedding every time I see her in the neighborhood now.

I'm supposed to head to her place tonight, but I just got home from my shift and it was a particularly tough one. We responded to a car accident where one of the passengers didn't make it. Failing to save someone is hard no matter what, but car accidents are especially hard for me.

I don't think I'll be good company for anyone tonight, so I send a text to Ciara.

Me: Hey, I think I'm gonna stay home tonight. Rough day.

Ciara: Are you okay?

Me: Yeah I'm just not gonna be good company so I'm saving you

Ciara: Always the hero. Anything I can do?

Me: I've heard that nudes that can solve all problems

Ciara: Haven't heard that one

Ciara: *image of a cat*

Me: What's the cat for?

Ciara: It's a picture of a pussy. Enjoy *smiley face*

Ha! It was worth a try.

Twenty minutes later I get a knock on my door. When I open it, Ciara is standing there wearing a trench coat, holding a box of pizza and a six pack of beer.

"I don't send nudes, but I can deliver them in person." She saunters in, sets the beer and pizza down on my kitchen counter, and unties her trench coat. My jaw hits the floor when I see the lingerie she's wearing. "So? Did this solve all your problems?"

"Oh, it more than solved them." And created another in its place. *How do I hold on to your heart forever? Because I think I've handed mine over to you.* She hops up on my counter, grabs a slice of pizza, and beckons me with her finger. I'm on her in seconds. "You know? I think I'm hungry for something else right now." She smirks and spreads her legs wide.

"Feast away then." I grab the band of her panties, and she lifts her hips so I can pull them down her legs. I start at her ankles and leave biting kisses up both her legs, watching as her breaths become labored and her eyes darken with desire. I reach the heaven between her thighs, gently massaging her folds. She's so wet for me already. I waste no time diving in.

As soon as my mouth is on her, she throws her head back and moans. She runs her hands through my hair and lifts her hips more. I know her body so well at this point, I know exactly what she needs. I trace my hands up her thighs and curl two fingers inside her and use the other hand to squeeze her ass.

She is absolutely gorgeous. She still has a white lace corset on, and it really feeds into the whole Angel moniker I've given her. She's pure perfection. Watching her writhe beneath my hold is addicting. Her soft whimpers spur me on. She grabs my hand from her thigh and places it on top of her corset. I love that she has no problem showing me what she needs. I massage her breast and pinch her nipple, eliciting a groan from her.

"Fuck! I can't take anymore. I need you inside me," she cries out.

Nope. I'm not done with my meal. I look up, and her eyes are shut so tight. I slap her ass, and her eyes fly open as she whimpers and looks down at me. I wink at her. "Give it to me first." I want her first orgasm from my mouth and her second, third, and fourth from my cock. I push deeper until she shatters, and her taste coats my tongue.

"Fuck, you are beautiful. I could watch you come all day every day." I can't get enough of her. She owns me.

She laughs while trying to catch her breath. "Yeah, you are definitely giving me Khal Drogo vibes today."

I throw my head back in laughter. "I'm okay with that. As long as you don't get witches involved."

"I would continue the joke but if your dick is not inside me in two minutes, I may die, soooo…"

Say no more. I toss her over my shoulder and carry her to the bedroom.

"See, that's some Khal Drogo shit. Oh look, I still had one in me."

We're lying in my bed, her legs draped over mine, her arm wrapped around my waist, and her face pressed against my chest. Her natural orange and vanilla scent surrounds me, putting me under her spell. I move a piece of her hair off her face. She stirs but just barely. I'm in fucking trouble.

I'm falling for this girl. Hard.

It terrifies the ever-loving shit out of me. I don't know if I'm ready for this. I put my heart on the line once, and it ended in tragedy. But I know I'll regret it ten times more if I let her go now.

CHAPTER
Nineteen

Ciara

I WIPE MY SWEATY PALMS AGAINST MY SLACKS AS I STEP OUT OF MY CAR. *After the day I had yesterday, I'm not looking forward to being back at the office today. I'm so tired of the police in this city. I don't know how else to prove to them that it's him doing this to me. Who else would it be? I spent hours at the police station yesterday trying to file a complaint after I received yet another dead rat delivery to my mom's house. They assured me that they're "looking into it," but as a black woman in Baltimore city, I'm not confident in their assurances at all.*

The street is eerily quiet, but that's not unusual for me since I normally come in earlier than most people. As I turn the corner to the last stretch of street before my office building comes into view, I feel uneasy. The hair on the back of my neck stands up. I dart my eyes around the empty street, but I don't see or hear anyone. I pick up my pace, and all I hear is the click of my heels against the pavement. I probably look crazy hustling down the street, but I don't care. I'll breathe easier once I step inside the confines of the building.

Oof.

A large, scarred hand wraps its way around my waist and yanks hard. I yelp, but his other hand slaps across my mouth so hard it stings. I scream into his hand, but the wind absorbs it until it's nothing more than a whisper.

He leans down to whisper in my ear, the stench of cigarettes potent. "You'll never get away from me. Don't you know that by now?" His voice triggers my fight or flight response. My brain races into overdrive, and I do everything in my power to release myself from his hold. I thrash around, but his grip only tightens. I drive my heel deep into his foot, and he cries out in pain, giving me a window. I rip free from his hold and take off running and screaming, but he's on me in seconds.

"Stop fighting the inevitable," he growls. I'm searching frantically for any sort of weapon I can grab. Anyone I can call for help, but there's nothing. No one. He squeezes my shoulder so hard I can feel the bruise forming already. I manage to elbow him in the gut, but he only stumbles for a split second before I feel the pain against my skull. What did he hit me with? Whatever he used was hard and heavy. My vision is already doubling, and I feel myself going under. I try to fight it, but it's no use.

I come to and I'm in a tight, dark space. My hands are tied in front of me. My legs are bound too. Fuck. I have no idea where he's taken me, but I can tell I'm in the trunk of a car and we're not moving. I do a quick search around the trunk looking for anything I can use to cut myself free. I need to be ready to fight when he opens this trunk. If I don't, I'm as good as dead. There's nothing here but me. Fuck. Fuck. Fuck.

Don't panic. I will survive this. I scream and rock my body back and forth, but I don't hear any noise outside. No footsteps, no voices, nothing. Minutes, or maybe hours—I'm honestly not sure—go by. He hasn't come back for me. Is this his grand plan? Leaving me here to run out of air God knows where? Right as the thought enters my brain, my chest starts heaving in panic. My throat feels tight. The air around me is thick.

"Help me!" I scream, using every bit of my strength to bang my constricted hands and feet against the top of the trunk. Time is running out. I don't have the strength to lift my limbs anymore. My throat is too dry to scream. A single tear falls down my face.

I'm so sorry, Mom. I'm so sorry, girls. This isn't how I wanted this to end, but maybe it's better that it's over. I love you.

When I wake up, tears are streaming down my face. Lincoln's arms are wrapped around me tightly. I try to pull away, but he pulls me in tighter. I can't help but laugh at the fact that his tight embrace feels comforting to me. Safe. He looks so peaceful in his sleep. I lean over and kiss the bottom of his chin. His mouth tips up in a smile but he remains asleep.

Usually after one of these nightmares, I'm inconsolable. But in Lincoln's arms, I feel like I might make it out of this.

I might be okay.

CHAPTER
Twenty

Eddie

Y OU SEEM TO HAVE FORGOTTEN ABOUT ME, DOLL. YOU AND THAT
Lincoln have just been walking around town like the perfect couple.
You seem so happy.

You have some nerve.

Every day you're at that damn coffee shop with your laptop, and every night you're working at that bar. Every free moment you have, you're with him. You've become so predictable. It's sad. I expected better from you, but you've proven to be nothing more than a disappointment.

I've given you too much power over me lately. I don't deal with fire. And yet, I've set countless fires since being here to keep your little boyfriend busy. That's not how our arrangement is supposed to work, doll. You've forgotten your place.

I think it's time I reminded you who's really in charge here. I was going to wait a little longer to announce my presence, but you've become far too comfortable.

Watching your pupils dilate at the sight of me will be my reward.

Watching the color drain from your face will charge me for days to come. Your pain fuels me.

I know exactly where you'll be in one hour. It's time for our long-awaited reunion. Get ready.

CHAPTER
Twenty-One

Ciara

THE LAST MONTH WITH LINCOLN HAS BEEN A DREAM. HE'S TRULY MY best friend. I think I've told him more than I've told Sasha and Nina, and I've told them almost everything. Everything but the most important detail—the real reason I moved here in the first place.

I haven't felt like I'm being watched in weeks. I'm really finding my groove here. If only I could stop the recurring nightmares, I'd be golden.

And the sex.

Good Lord, the sex. I think the man has broken me. I'm pretty sure I'm ruined for all other men. I used to hate when women said that, but holy shit, I get it now.

The problem? Lincoln has opened up to me about everything that scarred him in the past, and I'm still being a fucking coward and not telling him about Eddie.

This is stupid. I want to tell him. I want to share my burdens with him, and I know if we're going to have a real chance, I need to trust him with all of me but…fuck.

The smile on my face falls when Dr. Goodwin asks her next question. "So things are going well with Lincoln?"

"Things are going amazing with Lincoln." Amazing is an understatement, but I don't really want to get into the details of my sex life with my therapist.

"But I sense some hesitancy there."

"I'm lying to him. I'm lying to everyone. Lincoln, Sasha, Nina, his parents, his brother, his other sister, his friends. They've all taken me in, no questions asked, and accepted me into their circle, and I'm not being honest with them about what I'm running from and the danger they could be in just being around me."

Dr. Goodwin takes in my silence and keeps pushing on. "Are you afraid that if you tell them they'll no longer accept you?"

Am I? "Umm…I…I don't know. I don't think that's the reason."

She clearly doesn't believe me, but like the good doctor she is she just probes further. "Okay. What do you think the reason is?"

I don't answer right away, and Dr. Goodwin just sits there patiently. "Shit. Maybe that is the reason. I don't know. They would be well within their rights to tell me to fuck off. That they don't want to be brought into my drama. Part of me wants them to do that, because if Eddie found me and hurt them to get to me, I would never forgive myself. But part of me…" I bury my face in my hands and Dr. Goodwin just does her patiently waiting thing again. How does she do that?

I continue. "Part of me doesn't want them to let me go. But how selfish is that?"

"You think it's selfish to want love and acceptance?"

Yes. I'm not worth the trouble. "No."

"Do you trust these people?"

"Yes," I answer with no hesitation. I do trust all of them. I know they care about me. I just don't know if they should.

"But you don't trust them not to hurt you or toss you aside?"

Hmm. "I think that if I tell them what happened to me, that'll make it real."

"You think telling them about this part of your history will invite your past to join your present?"

That's it! "Yes! Is that crazy? It's like Eddie is this ghost. Like Beetlejuice. If I say his name three times, he'll show up and fuck up my life again."

There she goes writing in that fucking notebook again. "I don't think you're crazy at all. But I do think you need to make a choice. Are you willing to take that risk to have Lincoln and everyone else close to you?"

The question of the year right there.

Lincoln and I are sitting outside at a restaurant for lunch. It's a gorgeous day outside, but Lincoln has on a jacket and a hat.

"Are you cold?"

"Yeah, why?" He looks at me like he can't fathom why I'm confused at his response. And I'm looking at him like I can't fathom how he's confused that I'm confused.

"It's seventy degrees out," I deadpan.

"Yeah, that's kinda cold!"

I shake my head in mock disappointment. "Such a Texas boy."

"And don't you forget it." He's so damn cute I can't stand it.

We're walking arm in arm after lunch, but I'm stopped short when I look across the street and see a face I hoped never to see again. There's no mistaking the coldness in those eyes. I jump away from Lincoln and stumble backward but barely catch myself before I hit the ground. Lincoln grabs my elbow to steady me, but I snatch my arm away from him. I can't have him touching me right now. My skin feels like a thousand needles, I'm so on edge. The man I saw is nowhere to be found.

Did I imagine that? No. I know what I saw.

Do you? Fuck. I…I have to go. I need to get out of here.

"Ciara, what's going on? Are you okay?" Lincoln's eyes are wide with concern.

"I'm fine. I have to go." I don't even recognize my own voice. I sound so meek. So soft. I hate myself for it. My throat feels like it's closing. My chest feels heavy, like an elephant's sitting on it.

"Wait, talk to me." He reaches for me again, but I back away. To the outside world, I look like I'm having a full-on panic attack, and I am. I am not okay. I can't even bring myself to look at Lincoln right now. I don't want to see the pity there.

"I have to go. I'm sorry." I turn and run as fast as I can. I run inside a clothing store, and the cashier looks uncomfortable with my presence. I can't blame him; I look shady as fuck standing by the door looking outside. He doesn't approach me though, and that's a good thing because I don't think I even have the ability to speak right now. I stand in the store's window until the Uber I called pulls up.

When I get to my building, I run up all six flights of steps and don't stop until I'm inside my apartment. I rush through my security checks and sit on my couch, knife in hand. I sit on my other hand in an attempt to stop the trembling, but it doesn't work.

I've missed four calls and three texts from Lincoln.

Lincoln: What happened back there? Are you okay?

Lincoln: You're scaring me.

Lincoln: Please just tell me you're somewhere safe.

I let out a deep sigh. I have to deal with this.

Me: Yeah I'm okay. I'm home.

Lincoln: Can I come to you?

I'm torn between ignoring him and telling him I need him and to come over.

You need to make a choice. Are you willing to take the risk to have Lincoln close to you?

He has to know. If I really saw Eddie, then he needs to know what I've done. The danger I've put him and his family in. Even if I decide to leave town, they still need to be vigilant. I send the text before I can chicken out.

Me: Please do.

Moments later, he's knocking on my door. I wonder if he had been outside waiting for me to respond to his text or if he just broke a million traffic laws to get to me. When I let Lincoln inside, his eyes track to the knife sitting on the coffee table and back to my eyes. He caresses my face with his hand.

This may be selfish. But I don't know how this conversation is going to go, and if this is the last time we'll be together like this, I want to have him completely.

I lean into his touch and kiss the palm of his hand. "Please. No talking yet. I just...I need you." He searches my eyes, and I don't know if he finds the answers he's looking for, but he nods and grabs my hand, leading me to my bedroom.

He kisses me deeply and then trails his kisses down my throat while pushing my shirt off my shoulders. He trails his fingers down my tattoos, letting me know with his gentle touch that he accepts me completely, and my heart bursts for him.

He sucks on my puckered nipple through my bra, and the thrill of the feeling has me ripping the cups down to give him more access. He helps me shove his pants down his legs, all while releasing my nipple with a pop before switching to the other one. He sits on the edge of the bed and in one swift motion, he shifts us so I'm straddling him and hands me the condom. He knows I need control right now without me saying anything. I stroke him a few times, letting his soft grunts guide me. I look directly in his eyes as I sheath him with the condom, and the look there makes me fall a little deeper for him. He lifts my hips and lines his cock up against my entrance. I take him in inch by inch until I'm fully seated, never taking my eyes off his. My hips start to move, and I bury my face in his neck.

I don't even realize I've started silently crying until Lincoln lifts my face and kisses my tears away. He looks at me, a question in his eyes. I give him a nod, and he takes control of our pace. He flips me onto my back and kisses me passionately.

"I'm here, Angel."

Angel. He doesn't know how much I needed to hear that. I have no idea why he chose the nickname Angel for me. I'm not an angel. The things I've seen. The things I've been through. I'm too damaged to be an angel. I'm so close to the side of the devil I can feel the flames of hell nipping at my feet, but God, with him I feel like I could be one. This is different than any other time we've had sex. We've always been this passionate, and we've always had fun in the bedroom, but this is more than lust and this is anything but funny. This is healing.

"Lincoln!" I scream his name as I come undone, and he joins me a moment later.

He gets up and runs to the bathroom to dispose of the condom and runs back to bed as fast as possible. As if he doesn't want me out of his sight for a moment. He crawls under the covers and pulls me against his chest, rubbing his hand up and down my tattooed arm. I know he has felt the scars under my tattoo, but he's never asked about them—a fact I'm grateful for, but I need to address everything now. I take a deep breath. "Okay, go ahead."

"Go ahead what?"

"Ask me. Whatever you want to ask me."

He turns me so I'm looking him right in the eye. "Ciara, I don't want to ask if you're uncomfortable. I will never force you to tell me anything. But please don't mistake my not asking for my not caring. I want to know everything about you, and I want to help you carry whatever burdens you have. I'm here. Whenever you're really ready."

And that right there is what changes this conversation from my telling him out of obligation for his well-being to my telling him because I trust him more than anyone else in this world and I know he'll catch me when I fall.

"Two years ago, I was in a really bad car accident." He winces, and I know part of his mind went to Erica, but he stays present with me and rubs my arm in support.

"A man driving an eighteen-wheeler crashed into me, and my car rolled four times before stopping. A few witnesses pulled me out before the car caught fire, but I still had a broken leg, a broken collar bone, a ruptured spleen, a collapsed lung, and I had to have surgery on my arm. It left extensive scarring. I hated the scars at first. It's why I covered them up with these." I gesture to the tattoos. He lays a kiss against my tattoo, and I already feel my composure falling, but I suck my tears back in. I need to get through this. "But now I see the scars and the tattoos as a reminder that I survived. The accident is what started the path my life took, and it was very traumatic, but it seems like nothing now in the grand scheme of things." Lincoln still doesn't say anything. He just continues to be a supporting presence. "The man who drove the truck is named Eddie Brighton. Apparently, he was drunk and high when he crashed into me. So naturally, he was fired. And he had his CDL revoked. He faced criminal charges, but he ended up just getting probation. He came to visit me in the hospital. I didn't know who he was at the time. He was just some random white guy who stood over my bed, but the look in his eyes made me uncomfortable. He had these severely scarred hands, and he kept rubbing them together while looking at me. I remember looking at the call button on my bed, but it was actually a little out of my reach, closer to where he was standing, and he just looked me in my eyes like he dared me to try to reach for it. I asked him who he was, and he just said he worked in the hospital, but I knew that was a lie. I called out for a nurse and he left, but he said he'd see me soon. I found out it was Eddie later when a nurse said she saw him on TV regarding the accident." I've researched Eddie, but I've never found anything besides the articles about my accident. I have no idea why he set his sights on me. It could be the influence of the drugs, but I doubt it. There's more to it. There has to be. I take a minute to wipe the memory away before continuing. At least I try to. I start and stop my sentence three times before Lincoln steps in.

"We can stop if it's too much," he says.

I shake my head with so much force the tears fly off my face in all different directions. "No, I want to share this with you. Just…stay with me, okay?" He nods and squeezes my hand. I take a deep breath and continue. "I went through physical therapy after the accident, and the company Eddie worked for approached me and offered me a huge settlement so that I wouldn't sue. I took it, of course, because I know better than to go up against a large corporation like that, and it was more money than I knew what to do with. I thought that was the end of it, but it was just the beginning."

"What happened?" he asks. I chuckle because he knows me well enough to know I needed him to ask a question so I'd keep talking and not shut down.

"It started with phone calls from restricted numbers. The caller would breathe if I answered or on the voicemail if I didn't but not actually say anything. Then I started getting deliveries to my house. Flowers, stuffed animals, chocolates. Then it escalated to dead flowers, stuffed animals with the heads cut off, rat poison covered in chocolate. The police told me that though it was weird Eddie visited me in the hospital, they couldn't prove he was the one sending me the deliveries. The death threats started after I went to the police. He told me he'd kill me before he ever let the police catch him. I kept going to the police, and they kept doing nothing. It's like they couldn't be bothered. He would stalk me everywhere I went. He'd make himself seen only to me but would never put his name on any of the threats he sent me, so I had no proof it was him. Then he started sending me pictures of myself. Me walking into work, me out with my friends, me at the grocery store. I stopped going out. I basically became a recluse. Then he started sending me pictures of me in my house. In my bedroom and in my living room. I always kept the curtains closed so he couldn't see inside, but the pictures looked like they were coming from inside my house. He had to have cameras set up inside my fucking house." Lincoln clenches his fists, and he clenches his jaw so tight I think he may break it. I tap his hand and ask him with just a look if he's still with me. I can't handle him flying into a blind rage right now.

"I'm with you," he says.

I smile and clear my throat. Thinking about the next part of the story makes me sick. I need to stand up. I jump up from the bed, and without a word, Lincoln follows me out to the kitchen and sits me down on a stool. He grabs me a glass of water, and I'm so grateful for this man. *Deep breaths.* Here we go. "I moved back in with my mom and called a company to come check for bugs in my house. They found five cameras and a wired bug. I had no idea when he had been in my house, but I felt so violated. I was losing my mind. One day, I was walking into work when he grabbed me and slapped his hand around my mouth so I couldn't scream. I fought him with everything I had, but he hit me in the back of the head with something and everything went black. When I woke up, I knew I was in the trunk of a car. We weren't moving. I looked around for a weapon or anything to cut myself loose and hit him with when he opened the trunk. But then, he didn't open the trunk. Everything was just silent. I screamed and kicked the trunk as hard as I could. I knew I was running out of air. Up until then, drowning had always been my worst fear, but being trapped in a closed space and running out of oxygen blew that out of the park. I think that was the moment I accepted that I was going to die. I tried to scream again, but my throat was so dry I couldn't. I kicked some more, but I was weak. Finally, someone noticed the car shaking and called the police. They got to me right as I passed out. Do you know where he left me?"

He lifts his brows in question.

"The fucking parking garage at my job. He never left the premises. He just left me there as some sort of sick fucking joke. The police found a note in the trunk with me that I didn't see. It said 'I can get to you anywhere.' Still I couldn't get a goddamn protection order against him because they still couldn't prove he was the one doing it. The car he shoved me in? Stolen. From someone who worked in my building. I told them it was Eddie. That I saw his face when he grabbed me and that I had seen his face stalking me all over the city, but my word meant nothing." I feel the anger from being so helpless rising, and I try to force it back down, but then I let it take over. I want to let the anger burn when I tell this story. I'm tired of wasting my tears on this monster of a man. "I pulled back from everyone. I stopped talking to people at work. I didn't speak to strangers. Finally, my boss told me I could work from home for awhile because I was having panic attacks just walking to the building. Brittany, Simone, and Sarah wouldn't let me get away with pulling away though. They were there at my mom's house every day forcing me to let them in. Being my personal bodyguards. Not allowing me to drown myself in sorrow, but I think I had already lost myself by then. Fuck." I stop when the tears come back, and I'm so mad at myself for letting them fall. Lincoln tugs my hand.

"Angel, we can stop. You don't have to keep going tonight if you don't want to. We can take it in stages."

"No, no. I need to finish." He nods and gives me a moment to collect myself. "My mom didn't want me to be a recluse, but she understood, so she never tried to force me to go anywhere. But I wanted to be the woman she raised me to be, so I thought my big accomplishment would be stepping outside to get the mail. The fucking mail. I don't know what I was thinking. I would always look outside before opening the door, but I didn't that day. And when I opened the door, he was there. He stabbed me in my stomach and gave me this cruel grin as he twisted the knife. He left me there, bleeding out in front of my mom's house." Lincoln lays a gentle caress on the raised scar on my stomach, and it warms me. "Here's the part no one knows. I never told my mom or the girls. He came to visit me in the hospital again. It was after hours. I have no idea how he got in there without anyone seeing him, but how was he doing any of this shit without anyone seeing him, right? I went to scream, but he pulled out a knife again. Honestly, at that point I was hoping he'd just kill me and put me out of my misery. But then he told me that he would never be done with me. And that if my friends and my mom tried to get in his way, he would tear them limb from limb just to get to me. He told me if I didn't tell them to stand down from guarding me, he'd kill them all and make me watch. I knew they'd never stop. They would never stand down. If it were any of them in my situation, I wouldn't stand down either. I'd sacrifice myself for them in a heartbeat, but I couldn't let them do that for me. So I decided to leave. I told them I needed to get out, and I left. And now here I am. I wanted to self-isolate here so that if he ever did find me again I'd be alone and he couldn't threaten anyone else on my behalf. But then Sasha and Nevaeh happened. And you happened. And Nina happened. And I'm so sorry, Lincoln. I'm so sorry. I've put you and your family in so much danger. I'm so sorry." He hauls me into his lap and kisses my head repeatedly.

"Ciara, stop. You have nothing to be sorry for. Nothing."

"No, Linc. I do. I think I saw him today. That's why I freaked out. I swear I saw him watching me across the street. I think he found me. I have to leave."

"No, you don't." That's it. That's all he says. Did he not hear what I said?

The source of my terror is probably here, in our city. And he doesn't think I have to leave? Is he just as nuts as I am?

"Yes, I do. I have to move again and become a true recluse. I can't risk you or your family. I can't...I am not strong enough to handle this."

"That's where you're wrong. You are the strongest woman I know." I roll my eyes, but he kisses me again before continuing. "You are. For the past two years you've been through hell. There are so many people who would've given up a long time ago. But you have stayed strong. You say you've become a shell of yourself, but the real you continues to shine. It's what drew my sister and niece in. It's what drew me in. Your beauty, your confidence, your strength—they can't be contained. You moved to a new city where you knew absolutely no one just to attempt to keep your family safe. That's brave. You are so strong for everyone else. Let me be strong for you. Please don't run. Please let me be here for you."

How the hell is this man real? I shake my head in disbelief. "I can't ask that of you."

"You're not. I'm asking you. I am honored you've shared this with me, Ciara. I'm honored you trusted me with this. So now I'm asking you to trust me to make my own choice with the information you've given me. I choose you. I choose to be the person you lean on, the person to keep you safe, the person to be your strength when you feel like you don't have any."

Fuck.

Deep down, I knew this is what he'd say. But actually hearing it, I have no words.

"Please," he begs again.

I look in his eyes, and I see a chance at a future. For so long, I've felt like I was on borrowed time. That I was just existing until Eddie got tired of toying with me and finally decided to kill me. But with Lincoln, I see a real future, and fuck, do I want it. Dr. Goodwin's words play in my mind again, and for the first time I feel my head and heart align.

"Okay. I'll stay."

CHAPTER
Twenty-Two

Ciara

L INCOLN AND I SPENT THE REST OF THE NIGHT TALKING IN MORE DETAIL about everything. It feels so good to have someone know the entire story. Not even my mom or the girls know the full reason I left home, and that's been tearing me apart.

I still have no idea why I became the target of Eddie's obsession, but I find myself not caring. I know Dr. Goodwin said that I can't dive into the psyche of someone else, I can only focus on myself, but I've been racking my brain looking for a reason this all started. But with Lincoln, I find myself letting go of the things I can't control. I can only control my reactions, and I will not let Eddie win by not living. If he wants me to not live my life, then he'll have to put his money where his mouth is and actually fucking kill me.

I'm on a FaceTime call with my little cinnamon roll, Brittany, and I'm really glad to be having this talk one-on-one because I am too tired for Sarah and Simone's energy right now. I'm exhausted from all the crying, plus Lincoln kept me up for more delicious reasons after we were all talked out. "You sound happy," Brittany says with a smile.

"I am happy. Guess what I did?"

"Umm, anal?" Her huge eyes double in size. She can't believe what just came out of her own mouth.

My eyes bulge out of my damn head. Anal? I am scandalized. Did my little cinnamon roll actually say that? "What the fuck?" I double over in laughter. "Okay, I really have left you alone with Simone for too long. Anal, bitch?"

Her eyelashes flutter so fast it's like she's trying to shake the thought from her head. "Girl, I don't know. You sound so giddy. It just came out."

It just came out? I'm still baffled by the idea that I would say "guess what I did" and her immediate thought would be anal. My little Britt might not be so innocent after all. The thought of that cracks me the hell up. "Umm, no ma'am, we did not do anal." I shiver at the memory of Lincoln's finger against my hole. It's not something we've tried, and it's not something I was ever interested in before. That's always been a do not enter zone for me, but he makes me feel all the things and want to try all the things. "But I'm not saying it won't happen." I overexaggerate my wink.

She cracks up at that. "Okay, so what did you do?"

"I told him about…everything."

She gasps. "You did?!" I nod.

"And? How did it go? Good, I assume based on the smile on your face."

"So good. I've never felt so…free." Free is the best word for what I'm feeling. I know I still have to deal with Eddie and whatever his plans are for me, but my soul is free. I don't feel bogged down by all the lies I've told. One day I'll have to come clean to my mom and the girls about Eddie's threats, and I'm in no way prepared for the guilt I'll feel over that betrayal, but I'm not shouldering the burden alone anymore. And that is a powerful feeling.

"Oh my God, you love him."

"Slow your roll," I tease, but shit, I think I do. I know I do. I'm nowhere near being ready to address that though, so I'll just let it sit there.

Brittany narrows her eyes at me, and I avert my gaze. I can't let her get too deep in my head. "Okay, okay. It's just so good to hear you so happy. I know you thought you had us all fooled, but you didn't. We could see the misery dripping off of you. We just wanted to be there for you—it's why we were so worried when you said you were moving."

And here comes the guilt train again. "I know. I'm sorry."

"You don't have to be sorry. I'm sorry." She chokes on her last word and my brows rise.

"Hey, what's going on?"

"I just…I'm sorry. I should've known. I should've realized you weren't there that day, and I didn't. You could've died, and what kind of best friend am I that I didn't even know you were gone?"

Oh shit. I had no idea she was holding on to this. Brittany and I used to work together for the same management corporation. Brittany still works there. She's the Executive Assistant for the CEO, and I worked in Human Resources. We didn't even sit on the same floor, but we used to grab a quick breakfast together in the building's cafe every morning. The day Eddie grabbed me, Brittany had a last-minute morning meeting, so she didn't come to our breakfast, therefore she didn't notice I wasn't there. I have never blamed her for what went down that day. There is no one to blame but Eddie himself.

"Brittany. Do not do this to yourself. It is not your fault. You had a busy morning and forgot our breakfast meeting. It happens. We didn't even sit on the same floor, Brit. How would you have known I didn't show up?"

She scoffs, her disgust aimed completely at herself, and I just want to hug her. "I should've noticed you didn't text me wondering where I was, but I was so stuck up my own ass."

And I was so stuck up my own ass I didn't know Brittany had been beating herself up over this for the past year.

"You were not and are not my babysitter. You're not responsible for knowing where I am all the time. And even if you had noticed I wasn't there, what would've changed? No one would've thought the sick bastard would've left me in the parking garage."

She blows out a big breath. I hate seeing her like this. I know that pain. That guilt weighing you down until you can't breathe anymore. "I just wish so many things were different."

"I do too. But I am learning that I need to focus on the things I can change and not stress about the things I can't. I love you, Britt."

"I love you too." She gives me a weak smile.

"Are we okay?"

"We're always gonna be okay."

"Are you okay?" I ask.

She pauses at that. "I'll get there. I promise." She takes a brief pause, and her cheery smile is back on display. "So, I was talking to the girls, and we were trying to figure out why you've been so cagey with us about us flying out to visit you."

Fuck. "Wait, do you think I'm pushing you away because I blame you?"

"No, no. I never felt like you blamed me. I just blamed myself. But no, we're just wondering if there's more you're not telling us."

I debate ripping the Band-Aid off and just telling her the rest of the story, but I know if I do they'll be on the first flight out here, and I'm not sure if I want that just yet. I want to figure out if Eddie is truly here first and figure out a plan of action if he is. I don't want to shut anyone out anymore, but I don't want to go into this blind.

"No, it's not that. I just hadn't made up my mind about this place yet. I didn't know if I was going to come back home or pick up and move somewhere else, so I didn't want to waste your time."

"Okay." She drags out the word. "But, now that you and Lincoln are happily dating and you've made friends, you're pretty sure you're staying, right?"

"Yeah, I'm staying."

"Okay, so we can plan a visit then?"

"Yeah, we can," I say, using Nevaeh's methods of word play.

"Okay, good. We miss you so much."

"I miss you guys too. You have no idea." As close as I've become to Lincoln, Sasha, and Nina, a part of me is dying without my girls. I need a hug from Brittany. A binge session of *90 Day Fiancé* with Sarah. A twerk session with Simone. A nugget of wisdom from my mom.

"Guess what?" Brittany asks.

"You did anal?" We both laugh hysterically at that.

"Shut the hell up. Thank God Simone and Sarah weren't witness to that moment. That does not leave the vault."

"My lips are sealed." I make the zipped lips motion with my fingers.

"Those fingers and crusty toes better not be crossed."

"Crusty?!" How fucking dare she?

She shrugs with a laugh. "Anyway. I had a date. It was a disaster. I mean worst date of all time."

"That bad?" Brittany has had some epically bad dates, so for her to say worst of all time tells me I need to be prepared for something monstrous.

"He brought his mom and sister with him."

"Oh, shit."

She dives into the story of the creepiest date of all time, and I feel like myself again.

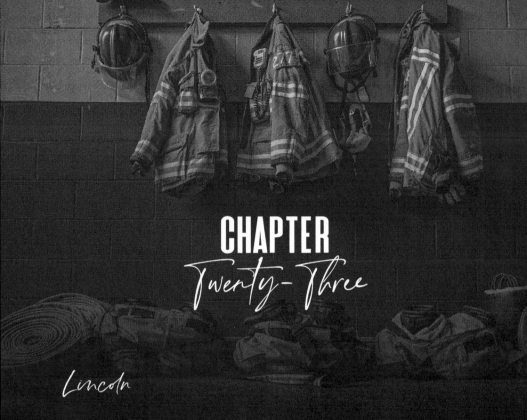

CHAPTER
Twenty-Three

Lincoln

K NOWING THE LAST PIECE OF CIARA'S STORY HAS ONLY INCREASED MY feelings for her. I just want to hold her close and keep her safe.

I love her. I am completely and desperately in love with Ciara Jeffries.

Ciara asked me to tell my family about Eddie, so that's what I'm here to do today. She felt it was time they knew just in case the fucker is here so they can be aware of their surroundings, but she didn't have it in her to tell the story again. She's going to tell Sasha and Nina today, but I told her I'd handle everyone else.

Eddie. I growl at the thought of his name.

If I see that motherfucker, I'll kill him myself. I think back to the day I was trapped in the fire, and I know now that was my real first introduction to Eddie. Those scarred hands. As soon as she mentioned them, I knew. He's been here much longer than Ciara thought. *Fuck.* I should've told her. If we're going to deal with this together, we need to be on the same page.

"What the fuck?" This from Isaiah. I just finished telling the guys Ciara's story, and they're just as pissed as I am.

"So is that fucker in town or not? Let's find him." Dom stands up but Kai pushes him back down.

"Believe me, I'd be all too happy to kill this guy with my bare hands, but my main priority is Ciara. I need to make sure she's safe."

"We got your back, Linc."

"Just tell us what you need."

"How's she doing?"

"She's doing okay. She's happy the truth is finally out there, but she's worried that he's really here and that we're all in danger because of her." I want to take that feeling away from her. I would happily lay down my life for her. Life wouldn't be worth living without her anyway. She's so insistent upon taking on everything by herself but those days are over. She'll never be alone again.

"Fuck that. She's family and we look out for family." It means a lot to hear my brother say that. The guys nod their heads in agreement and that's why these assholes are my family.

I want to do something for her to show her how much she means to me. For that, I'm going to need my sister. I pull out my phone and call her.

"What's up, Linc?" she asks.

"I need a favor." I tell her my plans for Ciara and she hums in approval.

"I knew I raised you well."

I roll my eyes, and I hope she can hear that motion through the phone. "For the last time, Sasha. You did not raise me. That was Mom and Dad."

"Close enough."

We get to work on setting everything in motion.

"Where are you taking me?" Ciara asks as she climbs into my passenger seat.

"It's a surprise."

"Okay, but you made me wear workout clothes. What are you up to?"

"Maybe I just wanted to see your ass in those tight-ass leggings."

She shakes her head and turns back toward the road. "Impossible man."

Twenty minutes later, we pull up to the gym, and the smile on her face hits me right in the chest.

"You're taking me rock climbing?"

I nod. I take a stray braid and push it behind her ear. "Figured after unloading everything you could probably use a day of stress relief."

"You gonna be my belayer?" She smirks.

"Always, Angel." I give her a look that says I'm not just talking about rock climbing. She squeals and jumps over the middle console to plant a kiss on my lips. The entire gym is about to get a show if she doesn't get off my lap, and I never took myself as an exhibitionist but I'm about two seconds from saying "fuck it." I give her one last kiss before jumping out of the car and helping her down.

When we head inside the gym, it's bustling with people. Ciara looks right at home. She immediately starts chatting with the instructor who has been watching her ass since she walked in. I can't blame him—it's a fantastic ass. But I will lay this man out if he tries to touch her. She looks at me over her shoulder and winks. I love being the person to put that smile on her face.

We gear up and get to work. I am in complete awe watching Ciara handle this wall. She doesn't rush. She takes her time finding the exact footholds and handholds she needs so that she never has to come back down, but at the same time, she's so good at finding exactly the right place to go that she's still flying up the wall. She rings the bell in no time at all and catches me staring at her ass, but I'm not even sorry. Her ass really does look fantastic in those pants.

"Bring me down, perv."

We spend another two hours at the gym, and I can see the weight flying off of her shoulders.

"Thank you for today. I really needed that." She kisses me when we walk in her apartment. I lock her door and go through her security checks for her. When I come back to the living room she's giving me those fuck-me eyes. We have somewhere else to go, so I need to get her back on track.

"That's just the beginning, Ci."

"What else do you have planned?" She eyes me curiously.

I whistle while walking over to the fridge to grab a water. "Go shower and get dressed for a date. I'm taking you out."

"Hmm okay. Well let's go then."

"Let's go what?"

"Shower."

My dick is immediately at attention. "Angel, you're gonna make us late."

She gives me her most innocent shrug, and let me tell you, it's not innocent at all. "Nonsense. I'm just trying to save water. Besides, shower sex is highly overrated. I don't want to fall on my ass. No funny business. I promise we won't be late."

We are most definitely late. Fun fact, shower sex is not at all overrated.

"Okay, so I lied. But say that wasn't fun." I can feel her smile burning the side of my face. "Plus, it's your fault I had to get dressed twice, I'll remind you." Ciara walked out to the living room wearing an off the shoulder yellow dress that hugged to all of her curves perfectly and then flared out at the bottom with a slit on the side to showcase her toned thigh. I yanked the dress right back off of her for another round, and now we are really, really late. I'm trying to find a fuck to give about that, but I can't find it anywhere.

Ciara doesn't ask questions as we drive to our destination. She just sits back and enjoys, intertwining her fingers with mine. We pull up to Sasha's shop and I wait for her reaction. "We're going to Sasha's for our date?" She doesn't seem disappointed by that fact at all. In fact she seems sort of excited and that just makes me love her more.

"No, we just need to make a quick stop here first." I bring her knuckles to my lips for a kiss and escort her out.

We walk in and I watch Ciara's jaw drop to the floor. Before she can even register what's happening, she's being wrapped in a hug by her favorite people in the world—her mom, Brittany, Sarah, and Simone. She turns to me but she's still speechless.

"You...you did this?" She seems to be warring with her emotions. She looks like she wants to kiss me and kill me at the same time.

"Yeah, lover boy and your new bestie, who we've now claimed as our new bestie, called us and arranged everything," Simone answers, giving credit to Sasha and me. I'm too caught up in Ciara's eyes to answer further. She steps into my space, grabs my face, and kisses me hard and deep. I guess kissing won out.

"Thank you," she mouths. I nod and spin her back toward her friends. She hugs her mom extra tight then picks up Nevaeh and gives her a huge squeeze before hugging Sasha and Nina.

Isaiah walks in at that moment. "Hello ladies, your second chariot has arrived." He and I are driving everyone to dinner tonight. Isaiah makes eye contact with Nina, but she looks away and walks out with Simone.

Ciara, Ms. Angela, Brittany, and Nina ride with me. Sarah, Simone, Nevaeh, and Sasha ride with Isaiah. Ciara holds my hand the whole way to the restaurant, and she and Nina tell her mom and Brittany all about Texas life. I make eye contact with Ms. Angela in the backseat and she winks at me.

Our party commandeers a corner of the Tex-Mex restaurant we're in. There are fajitas, nachos, and chili con carne everywhere. Nevaeh has made a complete mess on herself but she doesn't care. She's too busy focusing on the conversation to worry about the food actually getting into her mouth. "So you've been friends since you were ten?" Nevaeh asks. She is obsessed with Simone. She thinks she is the funniest person she's ever met, and she's trying to soak up every gem Simone unleashes.

"Yep! I kind of bullied Brittany into being my friend first, and then Sarah and Ciara wormed their way in there."

"Ooooh, bullying is bad." Nevaeh's jaw drops. She looks like she's been let in on a huge adult secret and she can't get enough.

"Yeah, Simone. Bullying is bad," Brittany admonishes.

Simone chuckles. "Bullying is very bad, but I had good intentions. Brittany was so quiet and shy. She was sitting all by herself and I didn't want her to be lonely, so I made her sit with me. It was the best thing to ever happen to her." She reaches over and pulls Brittany in for a side hug, laying a big kiss on her cheek, and Brittany smiles.

"No, actually I think that was the kiss Grant Kimball planted on me in the sixth grade."

"Not Grant Kimball!" Sarah shrieks. Ciara smiles but doesn't add to the conversation. She's been watching her family with love in her eyes all night. I'm so glad they're here. I know she has me and my family, but she needs them.

The waitress delivers a drink to Ciara that she didn't order. Her eyes fly around the restaurant only to go back to the waitress in confusion. The hairs on the back of my neck stand at attention. The waitress explains that she thought it was Ciara's birthday. Ciara thanks her and winks at me, but something doesn't sit right with me. I ask her if I can try it. It's tequila and pineapple juice which doesn't interest me at all, but I want to see if it tastes and smells right. It seems fine, but I'm still on edge as Ciara's mom stands up.

"I'd like to make a toast." Ms. Angela raises her glass and everyone follows suit.

"To you, Lincoln. To Sasha, Nina, and Isaiah. And to you, little Ms. Nevaeh. Even though my daughter is over a thousand miles away, I feel like she's finally come back to me. And I think I owe that to you all." Ciara's eyes water, and she squeezes my leg under the table.

"I second that, and I'd like to propose another toast. To Ciara. I knew the moment you walked into my coffee shop that we would be friends, and I could not be happier that you're now not only my friend but my family too. I thank you for being a badass my daughter can look up to." Nevaeh raises her finger, but Sasha cuts her off. "I'm not starting a swear jar, little girl."

"Ciara," Isaiah stands. I really didn't think this was going to turn into a night of toasts, but I'm interested to hear what my brother has to say. "My brother was lost for a long time. You know why. You're bringing the old Lincoln back to us, and for that I will forever be loyal to you. It's an honor to know you." Well, shit.

Everyone takes turns showing love to Ciara. Even Nevaeh jumps up to thank Ciara for being so cool and showing her how to play TV tag because it's the one game she's better at than Malcolm and Niecy.

Ciara is the last to speak. "This night was completely unexpected, but it's exactly what my soul needed, and I'm so glad to be here with all of you. I don't know what I did to deserve this or any of you, but I'm grateful." She turns toward her mom, and Ms. Angela's eyes immediately start watering.

"Mom, you raised me to be this confident, fearless queen, and I allowed a monster to steal that away from me. Thank you for believing that the woman you raised was still in there somewhere." Ms. Angela doesn't speak, but she nods and taps her heart in gratitude. Ciara turns to look at Simone, Brittany, and Sarah. "Petty squad, we've been riding together for eighteen years now, and we'll keep riding until the wheels fall off. I could not have asked for a better crew." Simone lets out a loud "we love you, girl" while Brittany gasps out a sob and Sarah blows her a kiss. Ciara winks at them before turning to Sasha and Nevaeh. Nevaeh sits up taller in her chair, waiting for her praise. "Sasha and Nevaeh, thank you for seeing in me what I couldn't see in myself. Without you, I would've faded away to nothing in this city." Nevaeh beams at her compliment, the pride evident in her eyes. Sasha gently squeezes her shoulder, and Nevaeh flashes those bright teeth at her. Ciara chuckles and turns to Nina. "Nina, thank you for taking a chance on me. You inspire me to find that badass Sasha thinks I am again." Nina waves her off, but you can see her eyes are glistening. Ciara turns to Isaiah, and he looks nervous. "Isaiah, thank you for being the brother I always wanted. Your loyalty means everything to me." He nods at her with respect. She stops and turns to me, and the look she hits me with would knock me on my ass if I weren't already sitting. "Lincoln, you are a dream I long thought impossible. Thank you for dragging me out of my darkness and into your light, and thank you for allowing me to carry your darkness too. I'll treasure it the way you treasure me." Knocked. On. My. Ass.

"Cheers!" Everyone raises their glasses. I join in, but my eyes never leave Ciara's and hers never leave mine.

"Wait, Mom. You're leaving?" We all came back to Ciara's so that her family could see her place. Isaiah and Nina have been ribbing each other all night, but I'm not sure if they want to rip each other's clothes off or punch each other in the face.

"Yeah, girl. Your friends can camp in here on your couch all they want, but I'm too old for that. Lincoln booked a hotel for me."

Ciara steps into my arms. "So I guess that means you're leaving too?"

"Yep. I'm gonna drop your mom off at her hotel, and Isaiah and I are gonna have an uncle sleepover with Nevaeh at my place. You and the ladies are on your own for the rest of the night."

She looks at me in awe. "I seriously can't thank you enough for tonight."

"I would do anything for you, Angel."

Her eyes slam shut, and when she opens them they are red-rimmed with tears. I know they're tears of joy but I want to kiss each one away. "I'm getting that."

"Alright, alright, lovebirds. Say goodnight to your boo so we can drink more wine and talk about him," Sarah teases.

Isaiah chimes in. "Enjoy your night, ladies. If you decide to have a pillow fight, feel free to video chat me. Actually, wait. Sasha, I forgot you were here. Never mind, please don't." Sasha slaps Isaiah on the shoulder.

Ciara hugs her mom, Nevaeh, and Isaiah goodnight and kisses me one more time. Simone waits until the door is almost closed behind us to yell, "Okay, so real talk, how big is the dick?" I laugh the whole elevator ride down.

CHAPTER
Twenty-Four

Eddie

THE FAMILY'S ALL HERE, HUH? YOUR OLD BODYGUARDS AND YOUR new ones all in one place.

I'd love nothing more than to slice the happy smiles off all of their faces. You all think you're above me. Your friend, what's her name? The black, loud-mouthed one? Simone. That's it. She hasn't stopped running her mouth all night, thinking she's so funny and entertaining. Your obnoxious mother has been showering you with hugs all night. You're all dying to be the center of attention. It makes me sick.

Did you enjoy the drink I sent you, doll? I know tequila and pineapple juice is your favorite. I know everything about you. I instructed the waitress to tell you it was from the restaurant and not from a person. Don't worry, doll. I didn't do anything to the drink. It just gave me great satisfaction to see how easily I could get to you if I want. It would be so easy to slip something in your drink, wait for you to excuse yourself to the bathroom, and cart you away. Too easy. You've got to make it a little challenging for me, doll. It's no fun to play with my toy when you just lie there.

That asshole Lincoln was onto me though. I saw the way he sniffed and tasted the drink before you. He's becoming more and more of a pain. I may have to dispose of him earlier than I planned. Maybe he needs another warning. He needs to stay in line. I have a plan for you, and I'm not going to let him get in my way.

CHAPTER
Twenty-Five

Ciara

"**C**IARA! WAKE UP!" MY EYES FLY OPEN TO FIND I'M SURROUNDED by Brittany, Sasha, Simone, Nina, and Sarah. Their eyes are full of concern and fear.

"What happened?" I ask. I wipe the sweat from my brow. I know what they're about to tell me. The looks on their faces tell me everything I need to know. He got the best of me yet again.

"You were having a nightmare. You were screaming and thrashing around in your sleep." *Fuck.* I haven't had one that bad in awhile. I've been seeing Dr. Goodwin for long enough that I can imagine what she'd tell me this means. I've finally decided to open my heart completely to these people, and my subconscious is trying to convince me that it's a mistake.

"Are you okay?" Sasha asks as she hands me a glass of water.

"Yeah, I'm fine." I sit up straighter in bed and wipe the sleep from my eyes.

"Enough. Okay?" All the heads turn toward Brittany. "You're clearly not fine. Please stop holding everything in. Just let us be here for you." Simone looks at Brittany with pride, and Sarah looks at her with shock. Nina and

Sasha just watch me to see what I'll do. She's absolutely right. I can't half-ass this. If I'm going to let them in completely, I need to actually do that. The fact that it's my little cinnamon roll yelling at me that enough is enough tells me I've pushed this too far.

Deep breaths. "You're right, you're right. I've been having nightmares since the car accident, and they were getting worse as everything was escalating with Eddie, but they haven't been that bad in awhile."

"What happens in the nightmares?" Nina asks.

"He kills you. All of you." Sarah gasps. Everyone else watches me with rapt attention.

"It started with somebody taking my place the day of the stabbing. Him stabbing me but when I turn the body over I morph into one of you. But last night, he took every single person I care about and made me watch as he killed you in the most brutal ways. I was standing there, not even tied up, but I couldn't move. I had no control. I was helpless. And you were each looking at me, begging with your eyes to save you and I couldn't do shit." Sarah jumps when I slam my fist into my coffee table and storm into the kitchen.

"This is why you left, isn't it?" Simone pins me with her eyes and demands the truth.

"Yes," I sigh. "He snuck into the hospital that last time after hours." Simone curses while Sarah's eyes widen and Brittany's fists clench. I honestly didn't even know she was capable of forming a fist. "He told me that if you guys or my mom ever tried to get in his way again, he'd kill you all. I love you all. You know how much I love you, and you know how well I know you. If I had told you what he said, you'd just double down."

"So you made the decision for us and left town," Sarah says, her voice full of venom.

"Yes. And I'm not sorry. I needed to get out of there. I was having panic attacks daily. I needed to keep you all safe."

"So what was your plan exactly? You get farther away from us and then what? What would you have done if he found you here?"

"My plan was to fly under the radar here, alone. That way either he wouldn't find me or he would and he would just kill me and you'd be safe because you were far enough away that you couldn't stop him. He didn't really care about hurting any of you, so long as you stayed out of his way. You're plenty out of the way with me here and you there. Then everyone could move on with their lives."

"Just that easy, huh?" I can feel the anger and hurt in Simone's voice. "You think you'd die and we'd just move on with our lives? Like we don't love you with our entire souls? Like a part of us wouldn't die when you did? Who the fuck do you think you are?"

"Calm down, Simone," Brittany pleads.

She brushes her off and whirls on me. I've earned her resentment, so I welcome it like an old friend. "No, fuck that. No one asked you to be a goddam martyr, Ci. We are a team. We have always been a team. You are not the only one in this weird-ass sisterhood willing to risk her life to protect the ones she cares about, and I don't appreciate you taking away our choice to make whatever sacrifices we want."

Well, shit. I feel like a child who was just reprimanded by a parent, but I deserve it. I've been so obsessed with having some semblance of control over something in my life—because I didn't have it anywhere else—that I took away theirs in the process. I've been plagued by the guilt I would feel if something happened to them. I didn't even consider the guilt they would have to live with if I died and they found out what I had kept from them.

I thought it would be selfish of me to ask for love and acceptance when what I was going through could threaten to bring them all down with me. But the real selfishness is cutting off the ones who have always loved me unconditionally and leaving them to figure out why.

"Okay. I'd like to amend my statement."

"Well, get to amending, bitch," Simone demands with a weak laugh, trying to mask her hurt.

"I'm not sorry for moving here, because I've found people who I cannot imagine my life without. I can't bring myself to be sorry for that. But you guys were my family first, and I will always love you. I'm sorry for the way I've handled things, and I promise to do better."

"That's all I ask."

"Aww, yay. I was worried Simone was going to kill you herself for a minute there." Sarah claps as she brings us in for a group hug.

"Yeah, it was getting dicey there for a minute. I know we always said we'd be there for each other if we ever had to bury a body, but I was not prepared to actually follow through on that." Brittany chuckles as she joins the hug.

"Yeah, and I was gonna feel guilty for cutting your life short when you were finally getting consistent dick," Simone says as she wipes away a tear and lets out a genuine laugh.

"I'm so glad we can joke about my impending death now." Sarah slaps my arm. I motion for Sasha and Nina to join the group hug, and the ladies welcome them with open arms.

"Okay, but for real, what's our plan if his bitch ass really is here in town?" Nina asks. With that question, reality comes crashing back down on us. Because what is the fucking plan? I sure as hell don't have one.

The ladies have all decided to spend the day shopping while I've decided to spend some quality time with my mom. Being raised by a single mom wasn't always easy, but I never wanted for anything because of that woman. She's my rock, and I didn't realize how much I missed having her nearby to draw strength from until she was here visiting.

"You're too much like me," she says after our lunch entrees are set in front of us.

I take a huge bite of my burger and chew before I even bother to respond. "Is that a bad thing?"

"In this case it is. Because you always feel like you have to take care of everything by yourself," she says, taking a more ladylike bite of her chicken sandwich than I would have.

I don't even know what to do with that statement. Growing up, my mom did everything for us. She didn't have anyone she could call on. She worked relentlessly every night to put food on our table but still managed to be at every dance recital, every parents' day at school, every game. I was never one to ask for overly expensive Christmas gifts, but what I did ask for, I always got. She made that happen. Her. By herself. When I needed a shoulder to cry on over the first boy to break my heart and every idiot after that, she was the one to put me back together. When I needed help with homework or life advice, she was always there for me. She single-handedly shaped me into the woman I am today, and I'm just trying to be a quarter of the woman she is. "I mean, Mom, you literally had to take care of every-thing by yourself."

"But you don't. You have a support system. Use them."

"I'm trying."

"I was a one-woman show because I didn't have any other options. If I'd had a support system I would've used it. Don't put me on some unat-tainable pedestal. The same strength I have inside of me, you have inside of you. Never forget that." She takes a brief pause, and it's a good thing she keeps going because I'm about to start sobbing uncontrollably at this table. "I like Lincoln. He's a nice boy."

That brings a smile to my face. "I like him too."

"Do you love him?" I almost spit out my drink. I was not expecting that question.

"Umm. It's just too early to think that way."

She tilts her head and wrinkles her brows. "I didn't ask that. I asked if you love him."

I cannot even go there with her right now. Leave it to my mom to force me to have a conversation with her that I haven't even had with myself or Lincoln yet. "Umm, well. I, umm. I just don't think we're ready to say—"

"Ciara," she cuts me off. "Don't talk in circles. I know your deflection game. Spit it out."

Sheesh. "Yes. Yes, I do."

"Okay."

"Okay? That's all you have to say? You just bulldozed me into confess-ing that, and all you have to say is okay?"

"I asked a question. You answered it. Thank you." My mother, ladies and gentleman.

This has been a whirlwind of a day. My nightmares have reached unbearable levels. I've unloaded my truths to the girls. I've confessed to my mom that I am in fact in love with Lincoln. I'm emotionally spent. What I need is to sleep for a full twenty-four hours, but no such luck. Nina and I are working tonight. The ladies—except Sasha who decided her carriage has turned back into a pumpkin and she goes back to wife and mom duties tonight—have decided that they'll be spending the night at Neon scoping out what Austin has to offer in the man department. This is the perfect excuse to have Lincoln pay me a visit.

Me: What are you doing tonight?

Lincoln: Hmm well you still have a whole coven sleeping in your living room so I'm gonna say not you

Ugh, I need the release only that man can give me like yesterday.

Me: Don't remind me

Lincoln: Khaleesi misses her Khal Drogo?

Me: Oh I'm definitely Beyoncé today

Lincoln: Oh well then in that case

Lincoln: *inserts gif of Jay Z fixing his cap in Change Clothes music video*

I literally laugh out loud at that, and Nina laughs at me so I give her the middle finger. Let me sext my man in peace.

Me: That's the stuff right there *inserts gif of Beyoncé removing her glasses sexily*

Lincoln: LOL so what'd you have in mind for tonight?

Me: Come visit me at work!

Me: And bring the guys

Lincoln: Oh boy, Simone trying to sink her claws into Shane?

Me: I think you spelled 'all of your friends' wrong

Lincoln: *crying laughing emoji* We'll be there

Lincoln: Btw, what's Nina's policy on quickies in the back room? Asking for a friend

Me: Wait…we were just talking about Simone so now I'm confused if you are really asking for a friend or for us

Lincoln: *three crying laughing emojis* See you tonight, Angel *wink emoji*

Me: *kissy emoji*

Later that night, Nina and I are busy behind the bar. I've just served yet another round of buttery nipple shots to a bachelorette party. The bride has on a white T-shirt that reads "Savage" while her bridesmaids have on black T-shirts that each state a different word—Sassy, Moody, Nasty, Classy, Boujee, and Ratchet. Meg Thee Stallion would be proud. It's fitting that their personalities all seem to match up with the shirts they're wearing. They've been the main source of entertainment tonight. The maid of honor aka "Ratchet" has been downing shots like a champ, celebrating each one with a clap of the booty cheeks. The "Boujee" bridesmaid has been demanding they switch to top-shelf liquor while the "Classy" bridesmaid has been downing her shots in between sips of her martini. The bride has been pitching her idea to her girls about creating a brand of lollipops in the flavor of her man's dick. Needless to say her girls are not fans of that idea. Her man might just love it, who knows? I wish the happy couple the best. Looking at the bride's flushed face though, I know someone will be cleaning up vomit tonight, and I hope it's not me.

Right as Ms. "Sassy" starts dancing to Drake's "Toosie Slide," my girls walk in. I crack up because it never fails that we always look like a band of misfits when we go out together. Simone has on a short leather skirt with a V-neck, sleeveless bodysuit on and black strappy heels. Sarah has on a denim dress with brown thigh-high boots. Brittany has on light distressed jeans, a white off the shoulder crop top, and white Chucks. All they need is me in one of my bodysuit and jeans outfits to round out the weird crew. And if

Sasha were here in one of her bright-ass dresses and Nina were decked out in one of her graphic tee outfits, we would really stand out. We'd be the re-imagined Spice Girls.

The girls make their way to the bar, and I hug each one of them before getting their drinks. A tequila sunrise for Simone, a lager for Brittany, and a vodka cranberry for Sarah. Of course, the bachelorette party is drawn to my girls, and they become fast friends. Simone and "Ratchet" are engaging in a twerk contest, as much as Simone's leather skirt will allow.

The air in the room changes and Simone's jaw hits the floor letting me know the guys are here. I look up and these fools seriously look like the sexy cast of an action movie. They're walking side by side, and every man and woman is clearing out of their way. I'm waiting for something to blow up behind them for special effect. Fucking fools.

"Holy. Shit. Those are Lincoln's friends? How the fuck do you move to a new city and find a group of guy friends who look like the United Nations of gorgeousness?" I think it's safe to say that Simone is pleased with me for having Lincoln bring his friends tonight.

Finally the two crews come together, and Simone wastes no time. The guys are great sports while she objectifies and lightly gropes them all night long. After the whole production, Simone ends up latching onto some random guy who's not part of Lincoln's crew.

I look out at my old family and my new family and my heart is full.

Oh and on a side note, I'm pretty sure Nina knows what Lincoln and I did when we disappeared for a little while, and I still have my job so I'm counting that as a win.

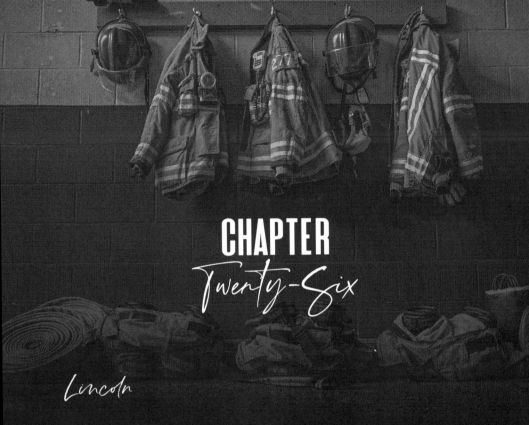

CHAPTER
Twenty-Six

Lincoln

I MISS HER.

I know that's weird considering she didn't go anywhere, but that's just the bottom line—I miss her. Bringing her family here to visit was the best decision I ever made. I'd do anything to keep that smile on her face, but I did not think the ladies would insist on sleeping on her living room floor while here, preventing me from making my woman scream my name every night.

I'm so proud of how far Ciara has come. It motivates me to do better for her and to do that I need to address the shit that's been clouding my judgment for years.

While Ciara is driving her family to the airport to say her goodbyes, I'm making the one and a half hour trek to San Antonio to see the people I haven't seen in three years.

The door opens, and shame fills me at the sight of eyes that have haunted me for so long. Erica looked so much like her mother. After she died, it was too hard to look at her mom and see those same eyes, knowing Erica would never grow old with me like we planned.

"Lincoln! It's so good to see you. Please, come in." She steps aside so

I can walk in, and I'm immediately hit with the ghost herself. Right in the entry hallway, there are two side-by-side portraits. One of Erica's younger sister, Christina, and one of Erica. I look at Erica's mother and she gives me a sad smile, silently taps my hand, and leads me into the kitchen. Erica's dad is making grilled cheese sandwiches and turns to me with a smile.

"Lincoln. How are you, son?" He sticks his hand out for a handshake, and I'm suddenly at a loss for words. I have no idea what I'm supposed to call these people. Do I call them Michelle and Henry like they insisted I do when Erica and I were together? Do I call them Mr. and Mrs. Sanders? These people were once going to be my family. That was taken away from us, and I put the final nail in the coffin when I distanced myself from them.

"I'm good, Mr. Sanders. How are you?"

"You can still call me Henry, son. We still consider you family." Well, that answers that.

"Thank you. That means a lot."

"We told Christina you called to say you'd be visiting. She's so sad to be missing you. She's on vacation in Puerto Vallarta with her husband, but she said to tell you hi." I still can't believe little Christina is married. Three years ago she was a twenty-two-year-old college grad set on taking the world by storm. Now she's doing that with a husband in tow. The family invited me to the wedding, but I couldn't do it.

"Tell her I said hi and I hope she's doing well."

"So, how are you doing, really?" Michelle always reminded me so much of my mom. Strong, supportive, intuitive.

"I just want to say I'm sorry." Michelle and Henry both look baffled at my admission. I know I'm three years overdue with this apology. "I'm sorry for everything. I'm sorry for pushing you away and not returning your calls when Erica died. I'm sorry I couldn't save her. I'm sorry she wasted her time with me. I'm so sorry."

Henry's eyes crinkle in understanding. "Sit down, Lincoln." Henry leads me to the couch, and Michelle passes me a glass of iced tea. She always has some on hand. "I want to make this very clear. You have nothing to be sorry for. You never have. We missed you after Erica died. You were the son we always wanted, but we understood why you distanced yourself. You had to do what was right for you. And you are under no circumstances responsible for what happened. There was nothing you could have done to save her. It was her time to go, and we have come to accept that. It will never be easy to cope with, but we've taken steps to move forward. Why do you say she wasted her time with you?"

I clear my throat before continuing. "Well, you know we were broken up when she got into the accident. She said I didn't love her enough and that I put my job before her, and she's right. She asked me to step down as a firefighter and I refused. I was selfish. I'm still selfish, and she deserved better. She left this world heartbroken, feeling like the man she spent three years with didn't love her enough to put her first."

Michelle and Henry exchange a concerned look, and Michelle taps Henry's hand before speaking. "Lincoln. I loved my daughter with all my heart. I still love my daughter with everything I am, but she wasn't perfect. No one is. Can I be honest with you? I didn't have high hopes for your relationship."

I'm sorry, what? They just told me I was the son they always wanted. Erica and I were engaged. I was literally going to marry their daughter, and they're telling me now that they didn't see us lasting?

She continues, "I wanted so badly for you two to work because you are a good man. You were so good to her, and you were good together. But Erica was never going to accept you."

I shake my head. It's all I can do. "I'm sorry, I don't understand."

"What she means is Erica had it in her head that she could change you. She loved you, but from day one she was convinced that she'd eventually get you to quit being a firefighter and find a 'mainstream' career elsewhere. We knew that would never work. Public service is in your blood. I saw that in your eyes the same way I saw it in my father's eyes. He was a police officer. He bled black and blue and there was not a damn thing that would stop him from putting that badge on every day. If my mother had asked him to quit, he would've refused her too, but he loved her and us something fierce and we never doubted that."

174

Michelle adds, "She knew you loved her, Lincoln. Anyone who looked at you two knew that you loved her completely. I just think she finally accepted that she wasn't going to get her way, and she couldn't deal with that. That is nothing against you." She takes a pause. "Being the spouse of someone in public service is not for everyone." Ciara's words jump out at me again.

"My daughter had a lot of insecurities, Lincoln. And I pray that she found peace when she left this world. But you're still here. Do not let her insecurities become your own and drag you under."

I leave Erica's parents' house with a lot of unresolved emotions. I think I've known all along that I'm not to blame for what happened to Erica, but that guilt has been eating me alive for so long that I don't know how to function without it. I'm not fully prepared to let go of everything that I've felt these past three years, but I'm ready to start clearing the fog.

I'm lost in my own thoughts on the drive home until a bright pair of high-beams blinds me from behind. I look up to find a truck speeding toward me. The truck taps my bumper, and I speed up to get away from the asshole. The truck catches up and I reduce my speed because I know if he hits me at this speed the outcome will be ten times worse.

I try to get a good look at his face, but he's wearing sunglasses, a hat, and a hoodie so I can't see. I'm willing to bet my paycheck that this is the infamous Eddie though. I look at his hands on the steering wheel, and I think I make out a few scars from here but I'm not sure. Fucker. I'm ready for your ass. Next thing I know, Eddie's window winds down and he pulls out a gun. I swerve to avoid his shot but he shoots my front left tire. My car immediately swerves to the side of the road to slide into a nearby ditch. Eddie speeds off, and I punch my steering wheel in frustration.

I know there won't be much the cops can do in terms of evidence, but I call a friend of mine in the Austin Police Department to come to the scene and look around. We've told the police everything about Ciara's past and Eddie, but they've given us the same bullshit the Baltimore cops did. There's nothing proving Eddie is here in town. No credit card usage in Austin. No residence, no car registered here. No sight of him on any security cameras. The man really is a fucking ghost.

I call a tow truck and I call Shane for a ride. I text Ciara to make sure she's home safe and remind her to keep the door locked, but I don't tell her what happened. Not yet. I want to see her face to face for this.

Shane pulls up to Ciara's building, and I take a deep breath about to step out of the car when he snags my attention. "By the way, man. I told Ciara what happened, and she sounded pissed that you didn't tell her when you texted her, so watch your back,"

Shit. "What the fuck did you tell her for?"

"She low-key scares me, bro." Fair. I thank Shane for the ride and head up to Ciara's floor. She rips the door open before I even knock, so she must have been checking the peephole for me. She grabs me and yanks me inside before pulling me in for a hug.

"Are you okay?" she asks with her hands on my shoulders, looking me over from head to toe.

"I'm fine, Angel. I promise."

"It was Eddie. I'm sure of it."

There's no point in trying to deny it. Denial gets you killed. "I think you're right."

"Fuck. This is exactly what I didn't want. I hate this."

"I know but I'm fine." I try to reassure her but I know I've said the wrong thing.

"He had a fucking gun, Linc! What if he had decided to shoot you instead of your tire?"

"We will deal with this. Together." I take a deep breath and tell her about the day of the fire where I was trapped. I might as well rip that Band-Aid off while she's still riled up.

She gasps, pushing me away. "Are you fucking kidding me? Why didn't you tell me about that? He's been here for so long! Fuck, every time I felt like I was being watched, he probably was lurking around somewhere. He just didn't make himself seen. Fuck!" I grab Ciara by the shoulders and push her head into my chest. She immediately releases a sob but then lightly punches my chest and pulls away.

"This is fucked, Linc! He's coming after you! Just like I thought. I can't…"

"Ciara, do not finish that sentence. You promised you'd stay. You promised to give me the chance to protect you, and I will."

"And who's going to protect you?"

"You." She freezes. "You have me and I have you. That's how this works. Don't freak out on me now. Okay?"

She nods. It starts off slow but as my words sink in it gets quicker, more certain. "What do we do?"

I have no idea what we do next. But I do know, there's no way in hell I'll ever let him get near her.

"We call in reinforcements."

CHAPTER
Twenty-Seven

Ciara

I'VE BECOME THE DAMN PRINCESS IN THE CASTLE WITH EVERYONE acting as my bodyguard by order of the king. I hate it.

I spend each day at Sasha's writing and editing but now, conveniently, everyone in our circle has decided they want to spend all their time at Sasha's as well. Isaiah comes to visit his sister, but his eyes are always on me. Shane stops by on his lunch break and pretends to be shocked I'm there. Kai comes in claiming to crave some of Sasha's pastries even though I've never once seen him eat one. Dom stops by to "check on Sasha's alarm system" an awful lot. Nina already spent a lot of time with me at Sasha's, but she's taken to spending every free moment with me now and bringing Jada and Logan along when her parents take off on yet another trip.

Nevaeh is the only one who is honest with me about her new duties. She runs into the shop behind Carter and gives me one of her infamous hugs. "Ciara! I asked Mommy if I could help babysit you today."

Sasha sucks her teeth. "Little girl! No one is babysitting Ciara."

"Oh, well you said everyone is coming by to keep an eye on her so I thoughted you meant babysitting."

My grin grows even wider. At least she's honest. "I gotta say that you are, by far, my favorite babysitter." She takes pride in my compliment and stands as tall as possible.

"Thank you! I like being the babysitter. It's usually me getting babysitted."

"I bet. You should get your mom and dad to give you a brother or sister so you can practice babysitting with them." I stick my tongue out at Sasha over Nevaeh's head. She flips me off and then calls Nevaeh over to pick out a muffin for her snack.

I pull out my phone to find Lincoln has finally answered the text I sent him earlier.

Me: You know… you're the one Eddie is shooting off the road and trapping in burning buildings. Shouldn't you be the one with the bodyguards?

Lincoln: Whatever do you mean?

Me: Do not play dumb with me sir

Lincoln: Ooh sir. I kinda like that

Me: Don't try to get me all hot and bothered when I'm trying to yell at you

Lincoln: LOL but you're giving me Blanche vibes with 'hot and bothered' so now I'm really getting started

Me: Impossible man

Me: But seriously this is what I didn't want, Linc. To be a burden

Lincoln: Would you still feel like a burden if I told you this wasn't even my idea? That the guys insisted on doing this when I told them I was confident he was here

Me: It would depend

Lincoln: On?

Me: On if that's true or just bullshit so I won't yell at you

Lincoln: I don't bullshit, Angel. Everyone loves you as much as I do. They wanted to do this.

Lincoln: Don't worry, Dom is never far from me on shift so I've got a bodyguard too.

Ummm, record scratch. What? Did he just tell me he loves me in a text? Should I… should I address that?

Me: I…I have short-circuited

Lincoln: Do you need a factory reset?

Me: Ha! I think so

Does he not realize he said it?!

Me: Ummm welp okay then. Are you coming to Sasha's soon?

I decide that I will not address this over text. This requires a face-to-face conversation. He's fucking good. I'm so twisted up over him mentioning the word love that I forgot to be mad about the bodyguard thing.

Lincoln: Yep. Shift change is in a few minutes. I'll shower and head over.

Me: See you soon

I toss my phone face down on the table, still baffled.

Thirty minutes later, he walks into Sasha's and flashes me that damn smile that makes me want to rip all his clothes off. What an ass. I swear I'm going to make him buy me my panties from now on since he insists on making me soak through mine every day. He raises his brow at me, and I know he's asking if I need a refill. I told myself I had enough caffeine today, but if I'm going to sit here with him and not address the "love" comment, I think I need a fix. I nod yes, and he goes up to Sasha to order. Two hours later, Carter comes in to pick Nevaeh up for her karate class, and she's sad to see her babysitting duties come to an end, but I promise her she'll have another shift soon. Now that I only have one Cole family member to entertain I can go back to my writing. Lincoln doesn't mind just sitting with me while I get my work done.

Lincoln is rubbing my shoulders when we hear glass shatter. Everything happens in slow motion. Lincoln's head snaps to the source of the noise as he grabs me and rolls us to the floor, managing to cover me completely without crushing me under his body weight. He yells for Sasha as a few patrons behind us scream and take cover. Lincoln takes off to see if he can catch the violator or at least get a direct visual. I run over to Sasha to make sure she's okay. Her phone is poised to call the police, but her hand is shaking. I offer my hand in comfort which seems to ground her enough to connect the call.

Lincoln returns a minute later and eyes the brick that was thrown through the window before making eye contact with me. I can feel the anger radiating off of him, but his eyes are soft with worry. He stalks over to me and I crash into his arms.

"You okay?"

"Yeah, I'm fine."

"Sasha, you okay?"

"I'm good. Police are on their way." She looks over at the brick and lets out a deep sigh. She's probably thanking the heavens that Nevaeh wasn't here to witness that.

The police arrive to take pictures and bag up the brick for evidence. I've been chomping at the bit to see the brick because I could see there was a note attached to it, but we refused to touch it in the hopes that Eddie left fingerprints behind. I'm not holding my breath on that though, considering he's never left them behind before. The cop on the scene turns over the brick so I can see what message Eddie's left for me this time. **"The time is coming. Hope you're ready."**

Looks like he's growing tired of this game he's forced me into. *Good, I've been tired.* I just want this to finally be over.

Isaiah and their dad show up to board up Sasha's windows while Lincoln and I sweep up the broken glass and help straighten up. She's going to remain closed until her window is completely fixed, and I feel horrible that I'm costing her business. I take a moment to remind myself not to be selfish and take everyone's choices away from them. They told me they wanted to stand by me and asked me not to push them away. I'm trying to honor that, but alarms are going off in my head, telling me we are in no way ready for what's coming.

"Ciara." Lincoln calls my name, and my attention snaps back to him. We're standing in front of my door. I don't even remember leaving Sasha's. *Fuck, I can't afford to zone out like that. Stay vigilant.* Lincoln covers my hands with his own, and I realize my hands are shaking too hard to put the key in the door. He grabs them from me and leads me inside to the couch before going through my security checks. Every time he does that for me, another piece of my heart becomes his. The pieces are falling so rapidly that his name is the only one my heart knows now.

"Everything is going to be okay," he exhales as he sits down by me, and I can't tell if he's trying to convince me or himself.

"You can't promise that, Linc."

"There is no other option."

I don't know what to say to that, so I decide to move on to the other elephant in the room. Jesus, was it just earlier today that he implied he loves me in a text? It feels like years have been shaved off my life since then. "So umm…we should probably talk. About what you said earlier."

He seems grateful for the subject change. I'm glad I'm not the only one. "What did I say?" he asks.

"You know, when we were texting."

"Oh, when you were getting all hot and bothered?"

"After that."

"When I told you the whole bodyguard thing was the group's idea?"

"After that."

"When your brain short-circuited?" Oh, so we're playing games now, I see.

"Before that."

"No idea what you're talking about."

I roll my eyes and move to stand up when he grabs my wrist, rubbing his thumb over my pulse point.

"Ciara?"

"Yes?"

"I know what I said." He pauses. "And I meant it."

My breath rushes out of me. And again because Mama ain't raise no fool, I need further clarification. "And just so we're both on the same page here, what exactly did you say?"

He chuckles. "I love you. I think loving you was inevitable. I didn't want it to be, but my soul recognized its match in you the moment you jumped in front of that car. It forced my heart to start beating again, just to answer your siren call." My breath hitches as his words etch themselves onto my soul. "I'm not telling you this so you'll say it back. It's okay if you're not there with me. I know life is complicated right now, and you may not be ready to hear this but I don't want to go another day without telling you how I feel. Your courage feeds the piece of me that's been hiding beneath the ashes of my life. Your selflessness calls out to my soul that's been drifting away so slowly I didn't even recognize it at first. I feel like myself again with you. You set me free, Angel. So I don't care if you're never ready to say the words back to me. I will always be yours." He doesn't even wait for me to respond. He just kisses the top of my head and then goes to the kitchen to make dinner.

Well…fuck.

Later that night, we're lying in bed and I can't bring myself to sleep. Every fiber of my being is pushing me to tell Lincoln how I feel, but the idea that I may not survive this is cutting the words short. I thought I had come so far, but I'm still letting Eddie control me. I'm still letting my fear stop me from living.

Lincoln has been through a lot. He was made to believe he wasn't worthy of love because of his need to serve his community, and he fought through that to fall for me anyway. Me. The girl whose life is in shambles. The girl whose heart is covered in scars. Without even trying, he's been soothing those scars away since the day I met him. He told me I set him free, and I think if I don't make it out of this, my biggest regret in life will be not telling him he set me free too. He deserves to know that he's more than worthy of love and he *is* loved. If I can't keep him safe, I can at least give him that.

"Hey, Linc?"

He opens one eye and wrinkles his brow. "Yeah?"

"I love you."

He opens his other eye, smiles brightly, and pulls me into his chest. "Good night, Angel."

I drift off to sleep in his arms and dream of a future where life is fair and two people who are meant to be together can actually keep each other.

CHAPTER
Twenty-Eight

Eddie

D O YOU SEE WHAT YOU'VE MADE ME DO, DOLL?

You make it so easy.

I could've picked you off on your way to the airport with those idiots, but I decided to follow your firefighter instead. I could've easily ended him with one bullet to the head. He's lucky I went for the tire.

I've grown tired of our game, doll. You're not taking me seriously enough. Do you know how it makes my blood boil watching all these fucking assholes march into that coffee shop to "protect" you from me? How fucking ridiculous. There's the firefighter, the younger version of the firefighter, the Magnum P.I. wannabe, the suit, and the burly angry one. Then there's the bartender, the coffee shop owner, and even her fucking daughter. They all waltz in there every day just to keep you in their sights. They're worse than the bitches you left at home.

How does it feel? To know that you've put these people you claim to care about in my crosshairs. You sit on your high horse, but you're the most selfish person I've ever encountered. I told you what would happen if your friends got in my way. And look at you now. Your circle's even larger now. Their blood will be on your hands. I hope you choke on it.

I hope you read the message I left for you. Our time is coming.

CHAPTER
Twenty-Nine

Lincoln

I'M NOT NAIVE ENOUGH TO THINK THAT BECAUSE CIARA AND I HAVE confessed our true feelings for each other that everything will work out in the end, but I have been riding a high the last few days knowing we're on the same page. It's still surreal exchanging "I love yous" regularly now.

I pull out my phone to call Sasha. She's opening the cafe back up today, and I know the brick incident got to her more than she let on.

"Hey, Linc," she answers on a sigh.

"Hey sis. How's today going?"

"Good, I've got my little helper today. We're getting everything ready to open." To anyone else, she would sound confident, but I hear the slight shake in her voice. She's nervous.

"Are you ready to reopen?"

"Yeah. I mean the window has been fixed. I've just been taking a few 'me days' but my baby needs me. No, not you, baby. The store. Well yes, I know you need me too but I meant…ugh, you're too grown." I laugh as I listen to Nevaeh give Sasha shit on the other end of the line. "Your niece is too much. Do you know she asked me if she was going to get paid for help-ing me today? I almost whooped her right there."

"Stop the cap. You have never whooped Nevaeh a day in her life."

"I know, I know. Doesn't mean I haven't thought about it. I just don't need it. I've got the look."

The fucking look. It's a look all the women in my family have perfected that tells their kids they've pushed the limits too far. When you get the look, you know you've fucked up and you better run as far and as fast as you can and don't come back until you've gotten your shit together.

"You do have the look down."

"Hey, is Ciara avoiding me? We've been texting like normal, but when I asked her if she's coming to the store to write today, she said she had other stuff going on. How much of that is bullshit?"

I asked Ciara if she was heading to Sasha's at some point, and she was adamant she wanted to just stay home today. I think she's feeling guilty for the damage done to Sasha's store, and she knows Sasha was freaked out by the whole thing. I hate the idea of her being vulnerable at home alone, but I can't force her to go. But regardless, what I won't do is throw Ciara under the bus. Sister or not.

"Nah, I think she actually had some errands to run."

Sasha is silent for a moment. "Hmm, okay, good answer."

"Why do you say it like that?" I'm not sure why I even ask because I'm pretty sure I don't want the answer.

"Because I know you're full of shit. But we raised you right, you took your woman's side. Good. I'll just harass her ass later."

I couldn't help but laugh at that, and the laugh became louder when Sasha once again shut down Nevaeh's request for a swear jar. We've been having this talk since we were teenagers. "Sasha, you're only one year older than me. You did not raise me."

"You keep telling yourself that, but it took a village for us to keep you and Izzy in line."

"You know he hates when you call him that."

"Oh, I know. Alright, let me go. I've gotta finish getting everything together."

I'm still not convinced she's okay enough to handle this. "Okay, sis. But Sasha?"

"Yes?"

"You're sure you're okay. After…everything?"

"Oh my gosh. Yes, Linc. I'm fine. I was freaked out when a brick came sailing through my window, yes, but I'm over it now. My main concern was Nevaeh, and she wasn't even there to see it so we're good. If anything, it made me respect Ciara even more because she's been dealing with shit like that for the past two years. You got a good one, Linc."

Don't I know it. "I know."

"Okay, get off my phone."

"Bye, sis."

"Bye."

I put my phone away and go back to creating the shift schedule at work when the alarm rings, signaling it's time for the real work.

False alarm.

The call we responded to was a false alarm.

I don't mind a false alarm because it means no one is in danger, even if it's a pain in the ass to process, but something in my gut is telling me that something is wrong. The guys and I get back to the station, and I check my phone and find ten missed calls from Sasha and four from Ciara. The hairs on the back of my neck stand up. Whatever the fuck is going on is not good. I decide to call Sasha back first.

"Lincoln, Nevaeh is gone!" Sasha screams into the phone the minute the call connects.

I still. "What do you mean she's gone?"

"I went into the back room to grab something, and when I came back out, she was gone! I don't know where she went. She wouldn't just go off on her own, Lincoln. She knows better. Something happened." Sasha speaks a mile a minute.

I give my captain the bare minimum of information and get the fuck out of there. "Sasha, I'm on my way. Did you call the police?"

"Yeah, they're here asking questions. Ciara is here too." Good, at least she and Sasha have eyes on each other.

"I'm on my way, just hold on for me." I can hear her hyperventilating, and suddenly Ciara is speaking to me.

"Linc."

Her voice calms me, but I'm still dangling on the edge. "Are you okay?"

"I...fuck. Just get here."

"I'm coming." We hang up, and I speed the whole way there, praying I'm not too late.

When I get there, Ciara has her arms around Sasha, and it seems like she's the only thing keeping Sasha standing. The police are looking around for evidence while one officer asks Sasha questions that I don't even think are registering. When they look up to see I've joined them, Ciara supports Sasha until she can transfer her into my arms.

"We're gonna find her." I look over to Ciara, but her eyes are completely vacant. She's shutting down before my very eyes.

"Okay ma'am, can you tell me again what Nevaeh was doing when you went into the back room?" the officer inquires.

"She was sitting at a hightop with her tablet. We were the only ones here at the time, so I stepped into the back to grab clean mugs for the front."

Ciara reminds the officer that this could be connected to her situation with Eddie. Her voice is so cold and distant, I don't even recognize her.

I turn back to Sasha. "You gonna be okay here? I wanna go out on my own to look for her."

"Yeah, yeah."

I look up at Ciara and tilt my head toward the door, silently asking if she wants to come with me. She nods, rubs Sasha's arm, and follows me to the door.

"Um, officer? Can I...?" She motions for the officer to meet us by the door. He comes over and waits for her to speak. "You need to have your guys checking obvious places near the shop. He probably didn't go far with her," she whispers. My heart breaks for her all over again. I know she's right back in that trunk right now. If this bastard shoved my niece in a trunk somewhere, he is going to beg for death by the time I'm finished with him.

Ciara and I climb into my car. Her knees are tapping hard, and she has one of her braids wrapped around her finger so tight I think she might rip it out. I place my hand on top of her thigh, and she jumps before relaxing and giving me a fake smile.

My eyes are zeroed in on the streets, looking for any sign of Nevaeh. Ciara suggests we park and walk around, listening for seemingly ordinary things that are out of place or off in any way. She pays special attention to the trunks of cars as we walk around, tapping them lightly to see if she gets a response.

We spend hours searching for Nevaeh with no luck. My fear and anger are catapulting to new heights with every failed search. We've been checking in on Sasha and Carter the whole time we've been out, and Sasha is falling apart at the seams. I can't imagine how she's feeling right now. Our parents, Nina, Logan, Jada, Reggie, Michael, Niecy, and Malcolm are all at the shop. Isaiah, Kai, Dom, and Shane are all out searching like Ciara and me.

When my phone buzzes with Carter calling me, I almost fumble the phone trying to answer. "Carter, what's up?"

"They found her. She's safe but shaken up. Get to the police station." I hang up, and Ciara and I rush to the station.

When we get there, Sasha is sobbing uncontrollably while hugging Nevaeh, and the family is crowded around them. Isaiah and Kai come in behind us, and Isaiah taps me on the back before we move up toward the commotion.

"We want to ask her some questions about what happened today. Do you want to come back to one of the interview rooms with your parents, sweetie?" A female police officer kneels down to Nevaeh's level. She nods silently and grabs one of Sasha's hands and one of Carter's. They follow the officer to the back, and the minute they're out of sight, the family explodes into chaos.

"How the fuck did he grab her so quickly?" Isaiah yells.

"Are we sure it was that guy?"

Isaiah looks at Reggie, bewildered. "Don't be a fucking lawyer right now, Reggie. Of course it was him, who else would do this?" Ciara shrinks into her chair at that. I wrap my arm around her shoulder and give Isaiah a hard glare. "I'm sorry, Ci. Didn't mean it to sound like that. This really isn't your fault. It's that sick fucker's fault."

Ciara shakes her head, but her eyes remain on the floor. "Doesn't matter. All that matters is Nevaeh."

Everyone continues talking, speculating about where he took Nevaeh when Sasha, Carter, and Nevaeh return to the lobby. Sasha bends down and whispers something to Nevaeh that makes her smile. Carter grabs her hand and leads her out of the building, waving goodbye to all of us on the way out.

"Umm, we're going to get Nevaeh some ice cream and take her home to watch movies and relax. Just let us have tonight—just the three of us—and then everyone can come visit her tomorrow. Okay?" Everyone nods in agreement.

"Did she say where he took her?" my mom asks. My dad nudges her, but she dismisses him.

"She was in the park. She said she was so wrapped up in her tablet that she didn't even hear him come into the store, but he grabbed her around the mouth so tight she couldn't even scream." Mom gasps and turns into Dad's arms. Reggie hugs Malcolm and Niecy extra hard. Isaiah curses and slams his fist into the seat in front of him. I'm clenching my jaw as tight as possible, but I'm barely holding it in.

"She said he threw her in a car and tied her arms behind her back. Then he drove her to the park and tied her to a tree. A hiker found her and ungagged her. She said she was crying so hard and repeating that she wanted to go home that the woman just took her to the police station instead of waiting for police to arrive."

"Fuck." Is the only word spoken for a moment.

"Did he…did he touch her?" Dad asks. Mom cries harder into his shoulder.

Everyone freezes with rapt attention, but Sasha puts us out of our misery quickly. "No, he just tied her up and dragged her through the trees. She said he never even spoke to her. She didn't see his face, but she said he had really bad scars on his hands. That's all she got." I turn to Ciara, and her entire face has gone gray.

"Why the hell would he do this? What's the purpose?" Reggie wonders, and I think she's more trying to piece it together herself than actually asking.

"I don't know. Listen, I gotta go. Today has been too much, and I don't want to spend anymore time tonight without my eyes on my baby. She's surprisingly okay as she can be after everything, but I am far from it. Thank you all for coming to help. We appreciate it. I love you." She rushes off, leaving the rest of us to try to collect ourselves. After saying our quick goodbyes, we all go our separate ways.

On the car ride back to Ciara's, you can cut the tension with a knife. Nervous energy is flying off of Ciara, and I'm not sure how I can help her get through this. I reach for her hand, and she hesitates but she takes it. She doesn't hold it tight though.

Walking to her door, I feel like I'm walking to a firing squad. Ciara takes off to do her security checks and I get the message loud and clear—she needs to do it herself tonight. When she comes back to the living room, she makes no move to sit down.

"It's been a long day. What do you want to eat?"

Her head snaps up at my words. "Lincoln," she sighs. "I'm tired. I think it would be best if I just spend the night by myself tonight."

No. "No." It comes out louder and firmer than I mean it to, but I don't take it back.

"No?"

"No. Do you really think I'm okay with leaving you home alone after everything that happened today?"

Her fists clench at her sides. I welcome the anger. I would rather us duke it out right now than her shut down on me. "You're not my babysitter."

"No, but I love you and I would feel much better if we were together tonight."

Her fists unclench and I think she's softening on me, but her next words deliver a crucial blow. "I can't do this."

"Can't do what?"

"This, Lincoln. This whole fucking thing. This is out of control now. We tried it your way, and now we're doing it mine."

Jesus. My brain is barely functioning after today. I can't even begin to process what she's saying right now. "What is your way?"

"I need to leave."

Suddenly I'm transported back to that dream where Ciara told me Erica was right. That we'd never work out.

Fuck that. She's mine. I made my choice. I choose my future and that's Ciara, and I don't accept her telling me otherwise.

"Ciara. We talked about this. You promised to stay, to give me a chance."

"This is not about you being able to protect me, Linc," she insists. "This is beyond you now. You can't be everywhere at once. Up until now, he's threatened the people I care about, but he's never touched them, and now he's grabbing Nevaeh?! She's a fucking child!"

Like I don't fucking know that. Like I don't want to rip him apart even more now because he had his filthy hands on my niece. "I know that. But you can't just run away. That doesn't solve anything."

"It solves everything. With me gone, he'll come after me and leave you all alone."

Jesus. "I'm sorry. Are we back to you being the fucking martyr now? You want to act as bait so he can kill you, and I'm just supposed to accept that?" Our voices are at a ten right now, but neither one of us is backing down.

"Would you rather everyone you care about die?! Who's next? You want to wait until he grabs Malcolm and Niecy too? Want to wait until he actually kills somebody? Until he picks you all off until he gets tired and kills me anyway? What's the point of that? Just let me leave and end this once and for all."

"I'm not letting you go, Angel. I'm not." I step toward her, and she steps backward, putting her hand out.

"Enough. You need to stop thinking with your dick and start thinking with your head!"

What the fuck?

"My dick? You think that's the only part of me that doesn't want to lose you?"

She sighs deeply. "It doesn't matter. This has gone too far. Why don't you ask Sasha and Carter how they feel about me leaving town? I bet they'd be all for it considering they could've lost everything today because of me."

No. What's going too far is implying that I only think with my dick when it comes to her. This woman owns me—mind, body, and soul. Doesn't she realize that?

I'm seconds away from punching a hole in the nearest wall. "Jesus. That's not fucking true. No one wants you to sacrifice yourself. We can fix this together."

"There is no together! You're insane if you think you can make a difference at this point. He apparently can't be caught. The police don't give a fuck because they can't prove anything. What's another dead black woman on their doorstep? You can't protect me. Just. Let. Me. Go."

"No!" *I'm not doing this. I refuse to lose another person I love.* Ciara scoffs. I don't care. I keep pushing. "He wants you to do this. He wants you to isolate yourself away from everyone. This is all a game to him."

"Yeah, well, he's winning."

I open my mouth to say something when she throws her hand up. "I need you to leave, Lincoln."

"What happened to I have you and you have me?" I'm grasping at straws trying to hold on to her.

Her eyes soften. "I love you, Lincoln. I really do. I can't bring myself to regret our time together right now, but I will if this goes any further. If something happens to your family. I love you for accepting me, and I love you for giving me your heart despite what you've been through. I'm just sorry I'm too much of a disaster to hold on to it. I can't, Lincoln. Please." She moves to her door and opens it without looking at me.

I move to the door and stand there, imploring her to look at me.

When she finally does, I speak. "I don't regret anything, Angel. I meant what I said. I will always be yours." I caress her face, and she lets a tear fall before her face hardens again.

I head out to my car, but I don't leave. I stay parked, watching her building for the rest of the night, my heart cracking with every moment that passes.

CHAPTER
Thirty

Eddie

Y OU'RE WEAK, DOLL.

I know you better than you know yourself. I knew the moment I laid a finger on that little brat that you'd play right into my hand.

Kids really ought to pay more attention. She was so wrapped up in her tablet that she didn't even notice me walk in and sidle up to her. Pathetic.

She put up a good fight once I grabbed her. Not as good as you that day outside of your job but decent. That was a fun game we played that day, right? I enjoyed it. I think the little shit enjoyed it too. No wonder you like her so much.

Fuck, I could barely hear myself think over her incessant whimpering. That's one point I'll give you. You didn't cry like that when we played this game. You slept peacefully through most of it. As soon as I pulled my knife out, she was quiet though. I guess she's not as dumb as she looks.

I don't even know why she cried so much though. She was tied to a tree in a park. Big fucking deal. When I was her age I had been tied to many things—chairs, radiators, steering wheels. I'd be left there for hours. No food, no water, sitting in my own piss and shit. I had to learn to free myself. I bet the little brat won't do that though. She'll just cry until she's found.

Weak. All of you women are weak.

I've changed the game, doll. So what are you going to do now? Try to outrun me? Try to lure me away from your friends to some other bumfuck city? I think not. I still have one more trick up my sleeve.

CHAPTER
Thirty-One

Ciara

I've been packing for the last hour, but it's taking longer than it should because I can't see past my stupid tears.

I can't believe I allowed this to happen. I knew it wasn't smart. I knew I should've kept my distance from these people, but I let them capture my heart anyway, and now I'm even more lost than I was when I first got here. When Sasha called me frantic that Nevaeh was missing, my heart sank imagining her trapped in a trunk or worse just because Eddie wanted to fuck with me. Every tear that fell down Sasha's face cut me deeply until I emotionally bled out. He's escalating because I had the audacity to live my life. He wants my attention. He's got it. I can't let this go any further.

I don't even know how he found me, but it doesn't matter. He'll find me again, and this time I want him to. I want him to find me as far away as possible from Lincoln and everyone else I love.

I promised Simone that I wouldn't keep her and the girls out of the loop anymore, so I pick up my phone and start a video chat.

"Hey, what's wrong? Have you been crying?" Brittany immediately asks.

"He found me."

"What?" Sarah shrieks.

"Tell us what happened," Simone demands.

I fill them in on the situation with Nevaeh yesterday and how I've decided to move again.

"Wait. Why would you leave? You're safest there with them." All of their eyes are wide with a mix of concern and anger, but I didn't call to get their opinion. I called to say goodbye.

"Yeah, and they're safest without me."

"We're back to this shit? Fine, then come home." I don't have the heart to tell her that Baltimore hasn't been my home since this shit began.

"I'm not coming back, Simone. I'm sorry."

"Ciara! You can't go off on your own. He'll find you again and he'll…" Brittany can't even bring herself to finish that sentence.

"Where are you going to go?" Sarah cries.

"I don't know yet. I'll figure it out on the way. I love you guys."

"Don't you dare hang up!" I hang up and block their numbers. I hate myself for it. But by the time they hop on a plane and come here, I'll be long gone. I want to say goodbye to Nina and Sasha, but I'm too much of a coward to call them because they could actually get to me before I take off, so I settle for a text.

Me: I love you guys. Just wanted to say that

Sasha doesn't respond, but Nina responds right away.

Nina: I knew it!

Nina: Lol love you too girl. You okay?

No.

Me: I will be

I see Nina is typing another message, but I exit out of the conversation and call my mom.

"Hi, sweetie."

"Hi, Mom." I choke on the last word but I hope she doesn't notice.

"What's going on?"

"Nothing, Mom, I just wanted to call and say hi and I love you."

"I love you more. How's everything? How's Lincoln?"

I clear my throat, but my mouth is dry and I feel like I'm swallowing rocks.

"He's fine."

She's quiet for a moment. "That sounds like bullshit." I let out what I hope is a convincing laugh.

"Really, he's fine. We're fine. Everyone's fine. I'm just really tired and needed to hear your voice."

"You know, I really am so proud of you. I don't know if I tell you that enough."

I am hanging on by a fucking thread. I can't get into this with her right now. "You tell me all the time, Mom."

"But do you hear me and receive what I'm saying?"

Fuck. Me. "I hear you."

"You are so strong, baby. Oh hey, Brittany is calling me."

Fuck. She's calling to tell her what I said.

"Okay, well, I have to go anyway. Tell her I said hi. I love you, Mom. Thank you for all you've done for me."

"Umm, okay, baby. I love you more. I'll call you back soon?"

"Sure." I hang up and block her number too. *Fuck,* I'm now on the run from my mom too, because when she realizes I didn't tell her what was going on AND that I blocked her number, there will be hell to pay. Look at me finding the bright side to running. I can almost smile about it. I roll my eyes at my own blatant lie and go back to packing.

My phone rings, and it's Lincoln. I almost don't answer, but I owe him this.

"Hi."

"Hi, Angel. I gave us the night to feel all of our emotions, but we need to really talk about this now." I love this man more than I ever thought possible. He listens to me. He doesn't dismiss how I'm feeling. I know he would do anything for me. This is just not something I'm comfortable asking him to do.

"Yeah. Listen, Linc. You of all people should understand my need to make sacrifices for the greater good."

"Ciara," he says on a sigh. "I do understand that. But do you honestly think this is for the greater good? Do you think the world would be better off without you in it? Because I'll tell you it won't. Your light shines brighter than all the stars in the sky. I can guarantee that my life, my family's lives, are infinitely better because you're in it. Do you know why I call you Angel?"

No, and I have a feeling I don't want to hear it because it may break me. "No," I croak.

"Because your very existence is proof that angels exist. I knew the moment I laid eyes on you that my life had forever changed. For the better. I didn't recognize it at first. I tried to fight it. I tried to keep my heart locked up, but your beauty, your compassion, your strength, your smart-ass mouth, and your love were stronger than any chain I could wrap around it. This guy, whose name I won't even say because he's not worth the time, wants to snuff that out. He wants to take all the magic that is you and deprive the world of it. Don't let him." So as I said, I didn't want to hear this. I try to stop the sob from escaping my lips, but it's too late. "Angel."

I cut him off. I really can't handle this. I can't. I can't even hear that nickname right now after what he just told me. "Aren't you supposed to be at work?"

"I will call out."

"No, please don't. I can't have anything else on my conscience right now."

"I can't just leave this like this."

"Just please go to work. Call me tomorrow and we can talk about it face-to-face. I can't promise I'll change my mind, but we can talk."

"You promise?"

Shit. "Yes."

"Okay. I love you."

"I love you too, Lincoln." We hang up and I hate myself even more. I hope he can forgive me for lying to him. I hope he can forget me eventually.

I'll never forget him for as long as I live, but that's my penance to pay. He deserves better than that.

My phone rings again but I don't have the emotional capacity to handle another fucking phone call. It's Sasha. Shit. I can't ignore Sasha's call. After everything that happened with Nevaeh, I owe her one last call. I steel my voice because I can't risk her seeing right through me.

"Sasha, hey."

"Hello there, old friend." My blood runs cold at the sound of that voice.

"What the fuck do you want? Why do you have her phone?"

"Oh, I'm just making friends. You seem to be so good at it. I thought I'd give it a try."

I hate him. I hate him with every fiber of my being. "What do you want me to do, Eddie? Whatever you want, I'll do it. Just don't hurt her."

"How amenable of you. I think it's time we have a talk face-to-face. What do you think? Why don't you come join your friend and me at this coffee shop of hers, and I'll consider letting her live."

There's a beast inside me, begging to come out. I'm ready for whatever comes next. "I'm on my way."

"Good. And Ciara?"

"Yes?"

"I would advise you to come alone. Don't call the police or anyone else. If you want her to survive, that is."

He hangs up on me. *Hang on, Sasha. I'm coming.* It's time to end this once and for all.

I run out my door, but at the last moment I leave it slightly cracked. Even though Lincoln is at work, I'm ninety-nine percent sure he's going to send one of the guys to check on me. I'm hoping my door being open will let them know something is wrong, and they'll get in touch with him.

Please catch my meaning, Linc. Your sister needs you.

CHAPTER
Thirty-Two

Lincoln

I KNOW CIARA BETTER THAN SHE APPARENTLY THINKS I DO BECAUSE I know she's bullshitting me about waiting until I get off shift to leave. She's convinced that the only way out of this is to give Eddie what he wants, and I refuse to accept that.

"Hey, man, what's up?" Kai answers my call immediately.

"Hey, man. I'm sorry to bother you on your day off, but can you do me a huge favor? Can you go by Ciara's place? I think she's gonna try to leave while I'm at work, and I just wanna hold her off."

Kai knows about my fight with Ciara last night. He was the one I called to talk me down while I was sitting in my car watching her building.

"Yeah, yeah. Of course. I'll sweet talk her into hanging out until you get off. Shit, if she tries to take off I'll just jump in her car with her and keep you posted." And this is why I called him.

"Thanks, man, I really appreciate it." I gear myself up to make my next call.

"Lincoln, hi. I've been freaking out all morning. I didn't even think to

"Flights?"

"Down to you guys. Brittany called me to tell me Ciara told the girls Eddie found her again and she was leaving town. She blocked all of our numbers so we can't reach her. And let me tell you, when I see that girl again she is getting her ass beat." She tries to put humor in her voice, but it falls flat. There's nothing but worry there. "Lincoln, please don't let her leave."

"I'm doing everything I can, Ms. Angela. I think she's going to need you though."

"The girls and I booked a flight, so we'll be there soon. Thank you for calling me. You're a good man."

I don't feel like a good man. A good man would be able to save Ciara. "Thank you."

To make matters fucking worse, my crew is called to a parking lot that is full of vehicles on fire. We're told after the fires are out that they appeared to explode from a remote detonator. My mind immediately goes to Eddie. Did he do this? Why? It makes no sense.

Unless...

Is he trying to make sure I'm out of the way, occupied by a fire, so that I can't be there when Ciara needs me? My captain is on scene with us today, so he's handling command of the crew. He's currently giving a brief statement to the news crew who, of course, showed up to ask questions about the cars that were blown up. I step away and grab my phone, finding a few missed calls from Kai. A pain in the pit of my stomach forms as I call him back.

"Linc, something's wrong."

I fucking knew it. Every nerve ending in my body is on fire. "What do you mean?"

"When I got here, Ciara's door was open. I stepped in and nothing seems to be out of place, but she wouldn't just leave her door open for no reason. She does have a bag packed, but it's here and she's not so something's off. I called Nina and Sasha. Nina said she hasn't heard from Ciara since this morning, and Sasha isn't answering. I'm sorry, man. What do you want me to do?"

Alarm bells go off at that. "Sasha's not answering?"

"Nah, I called a few times."

What the fuck? Sasha wouldn't not answer or call back if Kai called multiple times. With everything that happened with Nevaeh, she's hyper-sensitive to this whole situation. Could Eddie have grabbed both of them?

"Stay there. Call me if she comes back."

"You got it." Right as I hang up with Kai, I call Carter.

He barely says hello before I start talking. "Carter, has Sasha called you?"

"No. I haven't heard from her since she left this morning. I was gonna call her soon actually. Why, what's wrong?"

Fuck. "Can't reach her. Ciara is missing."

"Let me call her." Carter hangs up without another word. I don't even wait for him to call me back. I leave the scene and head to Sasha's. I know something's wrong, and my gut is telling me to start there.

I'm coming. Please don't let me be too late.

CHAPTER
Thirty-Three

Eddie

I'M ALMOST SAD TO SEE OUR GAME COMING TO AN END.

I blew up a few cars today. Yet another fire you've made me set. You know, toys are supposed to be played with. They're not supposed to be doing the playing. Let's see how long it takes your little boyfriend to realize it was me behind it. He'll come running like the hero you want him to be so badly, but he'll be too late. His bitch of a sister will be dead. And you? You'll be right where you belong. With me.

I could keep the game going a little longer, but I've decided you need to be punished for your insubordinance. It'll crush you to watch the coffee-shop bitch die. And it'll absolutely kill you to watch the false hero die. Maybe then your little bodyguards will realize that I'm not fucking around, and they'll do what they should've done from the very beginning. They'll shun you. And then you'll be all alone. Well almost. You'll still have me, doll. Always.

I'll take good care of you.

See you soon.

CHAPTER
Thirty-Four

Ciara

THE "CLOSED" SIGN IS ON AT SASHA'S, BUT THE DOOR IS OPEN. I STUMBLE in and rush to the back room since no one is out front.

There he is.

The source of my nightmares.

Eddie is positioned against the back wall with a gun pointed at Sasha, who is standing perfectly still in the corner. She refuses to show Eddie fear, and I love her so much for that.

I decide to take a page out of Sasha's book, and I square my shoulders before looking into his soulless eyes.

"This is between you and me, Eddie. She doesn't need to be here."

"You're wrong. You involved her when you thought you could run away from me. I told you I'd never let you go. But you thought you'd run away and find a new group of fools to protect you. Did you really think I wouldn't threaten them like I did your friends back home? All of this is your fault." His words cut, but I won't let him know that. He laughs cruelly. "You thought you'd get yourself a hero boyfriend and he could save you from me? Laughable. You and I are inevitable, doll. Nothing can keep you from me."

I still don't understand his obsession with me. Is this all just a game to him? I don't want to agitate him, but I do want to keep him talking until I figure out what the hell to do. "What's so special about me?"

He glares at me and regards me from head to toe, never releasing his aim from Sasha. "I lost my job, my license, my livelihood. All because of that damn accident. All because of you. I wanted to see the scum who stripped me of everything I had. That's why I came to see you in the hospital. But when I saw you in that hospital bed, all broken, I knew. I knew I had stumbled upon something better than a job. You were my new favorite toy. My purpose."

"You lost your job and your license because you got behind the wheel drunk and high." His jaw clenches. So much for not trying to agitate him. I might as well dive in. "How did you even find me?" His scowl turns back up into a grin. I look away from his face, down to his scarred hands, to try to stop the shiver threatening to run down my spine.

"You're not understanding me. Nothing could've kept you from me. I would've found you no matter what. But your incessant need to talk out your feelings certainly sped up the process."

"What do you mean?"

"You'd be surprised how easy it is to find the weakest link in a therapist's office. All you have to do is pay them and threaten their family, and they'll willingly break into their boss's files and give you information on any client of your choosing."

Holy shit. This sick fuck had been getting information on me...from me. My desire to cope with the shit he put me through in a healthy way led to my downfall. How poetic.

"Does Dr. Goodwin know?"

He scoffs. "No, your beloved therapist didn't betray you. She just hires easily corruptible people." He moves his hand to point the gun at me instead of Sasha, and I release a faint breath of relief. "Does that hurt? Does knowing your own emotions brought us back together give you goosebumps?"

"What do you want from me?"

"Your precious family would've led me to you eventually. If I had gone to them and sliced them from their cunts to their throats, I bet you would've come out from hiding. But what fun would that be? If I were gonna kill them I'd want to make you watch every moment of it. All I wanted was to have some fun. You're the most fun to play with when you're broken. More moldable. I wanted to see how far I could bend you beneath my hold before you shattered into a million ugly pieces. But quite frankly, I've grown tired of this little game. I've turned into a goddam arsonist because of you." He looks truly disgusted with me over his own actions, and that clues me in to just how demented he really is. "You felt the need to try to hide behind the people in this fucking city to protect you. You thought you could replace me with a…public servant. I had to set quite a few fires just to make sure he was indisposed when I needed him to be. I've never set a fire in my life. Just one of the many ways you've ruined me, doll."

This man is delusional. He truly thinks I owe him something. That I bring out the worst in him. That he owns me and I'm his to do with what he pleases.

"So it was you who set the fire that day Lincoln was trapped in the building. It was you who trapped him in there." It's a statement, not a question. I don't need a confirmation—I've known since the moment Lincoln told me. He seems to recognize that I don't need a response. He just sets his mouth in a hard line. I subtly motion for Sasha to move closer to the door. He has his gun and focus pointed at me, exactly what I want. If I play this right, I can at least get her out of here. I take a quick look next to Eddie, to the door that leads to the roof. Maybe I can lead him up there and give Sasha even more time. Sasha takes a tentative side step closer to the door. He doesn't seem to notice. I try to get him talking again. "How long have you been here watching me?"

"Long enough. Long enough to see you wedge your way into this god-forsaken community. Long enough to see you draw that idiot into your web. Long enough to realize that you think I'm stupid. I even visited you in your apartment one night. I could've ended you right then and there. But I wasn't ready to end our game."

"So what, you're ready to end it now? What changed?"

"I told you. I've grown bored. I'm tired of watching you walk around here like you're above me. Like you've outrun me. Like you've won. It's time you truly learned your lesson."

I resist the urge to laugh. He obviously hasn't been paying as close attention to me as he claims if he doesn't realize I've allowed him to completely control my life. That I've been operating under the assumption that I'd never outrun him.

"When those obnoxious friends of yours formed a twenty-four-hour circle around you to 'protect you,' I told you then that I'd kill every single one of them to get to you. So you thought you'd run away to a different state and get new so-called bodyguards and I'd sit around with my dick in my hands? You must've thought I was a fucking joke. You. Are. Mine. You belong to me. I own you. You stole my life from me so I stole yours from you and yet you think you have the power to change that. So it's time you pay the consequences. I'm going to kill your friend here and make you watch as she bleeds out. Then we'll call your...boyfriend to come over here, and I'll make you watch him die too. After they die, maybe I'll finally be satisfied enough to put an end to your misery. Or maybe I'll let you drown in your grief while I slowly pick off everyone you care about."

My self-control is hanging on by a thread. I'm trying to keep my eyes on Eddie while making sure Sasha is continuing her advance to the door, but his words threaten to consume me. He won't be satisfied with just my life anymore. He's determined to punish me, and now everyone is going to pay the price for my life. I've had enough. I won't let this end this way.

"You don't own me." I grit out.

"I'll kill everyone you come into contact with. The mailman. The cashier at the goddamn grocery store. Every patron that walks into this pitiful coffee shop. Although who knows what it'll be once your friend here is gone. And just think, all that blood will be on your hands." He's preying on the fears I divulged to Dr. Goodwin. I'm working at a disadvantage because he knows all my deepest darkest secrets and fears, and I have no idea what makes him tick. He's obsessed with me and wants to make me pay for my imagined betrayal, but I don't understand why. I decide to go for straight agitation. Disobedience. If I can make him angry enough maybe he'll forget his plan and attack me head-on, and I can fight back long enough for Sasha to run for help.

"You know what I think, Eddie?" I ask, giving Sasha a slight nod. He doesn't even answer, he just tilts his head to the side. "I think you're pathetic. I don't owe you a goddamn thing. Not my time and definitely not my life. I didn't make you get in that truck that day. I didn't move away to run away from you. I've forgotten about you. You don't matter to me." His jaw clenches. It's working. "You're delusional. I'm not afraid of you. I wouldn't waste a single emotion on you." I keep my eye on the gun in his hand. This plan of mine only works if I can get to him before he fires that gun. I'm not bulletproof.

"You want to claim you don't fear me now, doll? Fine. We'll see how you feel when this is all over." He barely finishes his sentence before he redirects his aim right at Sasha.

"No!" I lunge in front of Sasha as she screams and Eddie pulls the trigger. I don't register any pain so he must've missed. I take a split second to notice Sasha is still standing before I lunge for Eddie. He tries to fire off another shot, but I'm on him before he gets the chance. We wrestle each other to the ground, and I manage to hold my own. I vaguely hear Sasha on the phone with the police, but I can't hear her words I'm so focused on getting Eddie incapacitated.

Eddie gets out of my hold and yanks us both up, but as he takes a step forward, I shove him hard so that he loses balance and stumbles back into the backroom shelves. I take that opportunity to run through the door and up the stairs to the roof. It's a risk. He still has the gun and my back is to him, vulnerable. Plus Sasha's still down there. He could decide to go after her instead of me, but I feel like I know him well enough to know that he's not about to let me run away from him. He talked a good game in there, but his focus is squarely back on me now. Where it belongs. I hear his growl and loud footsteps clamoring up the steps.

The door to the roof gives way and I glance around quickly. There's nothing for cover up here. I can hear people living their lives below me, completely unaware that there's a battle for a person's next breath happening above them. I'm cornered up here. I may not make it back down. But if I don't, then at least Sasha got away and she won't have to deal with the trauma of cleaning my blood out of her shop. I steel my nerves and stand by the side of the door, waiting for my moment.

Eddie bursts through the door, and I pounce. I land a blow to his stomach and he folds over briefly, but that grip on the gun remains ironclad. My fist goes flying toward his face, but he dodges at the last second. His cold eyes are alive and manic now. He's practically salivating over this. It makes him happy that I'm putting up a fight so he can enjoy snuffing me out that much more. Fine by me. If he wants me dead, he'll have to earn it. He wraps his pale, leathery hands around my throat, but before he can tighten his grip I drive my knee up into his groin. He releases me with a grunt right as I wind my fist up and pummel it into the left side of his face.

Finally, the gun gives way and falls out of Eddie's hand as he slumps to the ground. I jump on top of him and punch him in the face repeatedly. My hands are already sore from the sheer force I'm unleashing, but if I let up he'll get the upper hand again. He intercepts my last punch and bends my wrist to an unnatural position. He moves to stand to his full height above me, still holding my wrist, but he loosens his grip for a split second. It's enough for me to kick at his leg and scramble away, closer to the gun. When I look up, the look in his eye is pure evil. He looks completely deranged. He advances toward me, and I grab the gun and point it at him. I hear the door open and I know Sasha's here, but I can't afford to take my eyes off of Eddie. Dammit, Sasha. You were supposed to get far away from here. He smirks, like he doesn't think I have the balls to pull the trigger. I know in this moment it's him or me and everyone I love. He lunges at me, and my choice is made. I pull the trigger.

His body lands with a thud an inch away from me. I don't have to check. I know he's gone.

"Ciara!" Sasha runs over to me. The adrenaline is wearing off, and I feel tired and weak.

"Are you okay?" I ask Sasha. She looks me up and down, and her eyes freeze on my chest. Her face goes pale.

"What?"

"Ciara, you've been shot." I look down at my chest and see the blood pooling there. Adrenaline is a powerful drug. I now understand how anime characters keep talking long after a hole has been blown through their stomach. It's as if my brain didn't register that I'm hurt until I physically saw it. I feel myself going down, but Sasha catches me. I hear voices yelling in the background, and even in my haze I know he's here.

I turn my head to look at him one last time, and I hope he can see the apology in my eyes before the darkness overtakes me.

CHAPTER
Thirty-Five

Lincoln

SHE CAN'T DIE. SHE CAN'T DIE.

I can't believe I was too late again.

No.

I can't think like that. She's going to make it. I won't accept any other outcome. She has to make it through this. And when she does, I am going to spend the rest of my life making sure she knows how much I treasure her. We wasted so much time fighting our feelings for each other. Our time can't be up.

When I got to the roof of Sasha's bakery and saw Ciara fall into Sasha's arms, my world stopped spinning. When I looked over and saw Eddie lying in a pool of his own blood, the only regret I had was that I wasn't the one to end him. Death was too kind for him, but I hope he's burning in hell right now.

I'm pacing back and forth in the waiting room of the hospital, irritated that I can't be with her. The doctors and nurses will bend the rules for me to go back to an exam room with her when she's conscious, but giving me her medical information when she's been shot is a step over the line.

My entire family is in the waiting room with me, anxiously waiting for

Ciara's mom's arrival so the doctors will tell us something. I left her mom a voicemail letting her know Ciara is in the hospital, but I know she and the girls are on a flight trying to get here. I can't take anymore waiting. I'm about to come out of my skin.

The police arrive to get Sasha's statement about the events. She asks them to allow her to give her statement in front of all of us so she won't have to repeat it again. Our eyes are glued to her while she gives us every painful detail of Eddie's delusion. How brave Ciara was, distracting Eddie so Sasha could edge closer and closer to safety. How he told Ciara he was going to kill every single member of our family and Ciara's before finally killing her. How he aimed his gun at Sasha before Ciara jumped in front of the bullet and fought him off. How Ciara fired the shot that killed him.

"When he fired, Ciara lunged in front of me, but she never stopped moving so I didn't even realize she was hit. I just thought he missed. I wanted to help her, but I knew the chances of me making everything worse with them wrestling over the gun were too high. After it was...after it was over, she... umm...she just wanted to make sure I was okay. She didn't even realize she'd been shot. I was the first one to notice." She struggles through her last sentence. I take a break from my pacing to hug her. My dad lays a hand on her shoulder. My mom rubs her back. Reggie grabs her hand. Isaiah reaches across and lays a hand on top of her thigh. I notice his other hand is holding Nina's, and he's rubbing circles on her palm. "I know she blamed herself for Nevaeh being grabbed. I didn't get a chance to tell her I didn't blame her. I didn't get to tell her it wasn't her fault. That I love her like a sister already. But she still protected me. She jumped in front of a bullet for me. I can never repay that. I didn't..." She chokes out a sob, and I hug her tighter.

"Shh, I know. She knows. She knows you didn't blame her." Despite what she said during our fight, I know she knows how much my family loves her. How much I love her. "She did what she did because she loves you too."

Ms. Angela, Brittany, Simone, and Sarah burst into the waiting room.

"Where is she?! Ciara Jeffries. Where is she?" Ms. Angela runs over to the information desk.

"Ms. Angela." I run over to join her, and she pulls me into a hug.

"Are you family?" a nurse asks.

"I'm her mother," she shrieks. The nurse nods and goes to get a doctor. "Lincoln. What happened to my daughter?" Sarah, Simone, and Brittany crowd around me, wondering the same thing. I decide it would be best to tell the story while we're a distance away from everyone else. I tell them everything Sasha just told us, and they all burst into tears.

"Fuck. I can't believe this," says Sarah.

Simone opens her mouth to say something, but a doctor comes out and she closes it again.

"Ms. Jeffries?"

"Yes." Ms. Angela places one hand in mine and the other in Brittany's. Simone and Sarah each put a hand on her shoulders.

"Your daughter is going to recover." We all release a collective breath. "She was shot in the chest. Three inches to the left and we'd be having a different conversation. She did lose a lot of blood. She's in the ICU, and she hasn't woken up yet, but she's stable."

"Can we see her?"

"She can have two visitors for now. I don't think she'll wake up while you're there, but you can see her."

I look at the girls and silently plead with them to let me be the one to go with her mom to her room.

"Go. We'll go fill your family in," Sarah concedes. I thank them and rush to catch up with Ms. Angela, who is following a nurse to Ciara's room.

"Fair warning, she's going to look rough when you go in. She's hooked up to a lot of machines, and she looks a little weak right now, but she's tough." Despite her warning, I'm still not prepared for what I see when we walk in. Ciara looks frail. She looks like she's barely breathing on her own. My knees almost give out at the sight of her.

Ms. Angela walks over and barely contains her sobs as she lowers herself into the chair by Ciara's bedside. I'm almost afraid to touch her for fear of disrupting her IV, but the thought of being near her and not touching her is too much. I gently lay my hand across hers.

"I'm so sorry." It's all I can manage to say. I am sorry. Sorry I couldn't prevent this. Sorry I let it get this far. "Ms. Angela…"

She cuts me off. "Lincoln. Do you love my daughter?"

"More than life itself," I answer with no hesitation.

"Then I think we can drop the Ms., don't you think?"

I give her a sad smile and nod. "I promised you that I would keep her safe. I promised her I would. I didn't do that. I'm so sorry."

"You did. You kept her heart safe. That's all she needed you to do. It was always meant to go this way. She needed to end this herself, or she'd never be able to move past it. I would prefer she not have ended up in this hospital bed to end it, but she's beaten death four times now. She's a fighter. This is not the end to her story. This is not the end of your story together. So what she needs from you now is for you to be positive and continue keeping her heart safe."

"She is my future."

Her lips curve up in a grin. "Well then, it's definitely time we drop the Ms." She goes back to holding Ciara's hand, and I release a breath I didn't even realize I was holding.

I leave Angela in Ciara's room and allow everyone else to take their turns visiting her. She doesn't wake up the entire time we're there, and though the doctor tells us that's normal, I'm still worried.

Four days go by and she still doesn't open her eyes. The doctor can't explain it. I feel helpless, and I'm growing angrier by the second. Angela and I have both been sleeping in the hospital, taking turns to go get food or go shower and change so that Ciara is never alone. She's shown no sign of waking up.

I pull up a chair to her bedside table and grab her hand, gently rubbing her pulse point. "Angel. I need you to show me those chocolate eyes, okay? I need you to come back to me. We're just getting started, you have to be here. I love you, Angel. Please."

She doesn't stir. The only sound in the room is the machines that tell me she's still in there somewhere.

CHAPTER
Thirty-Six

Ciara

I CAN HEAR THE BEEPS OF A MACHINE. I KNOW I'M IN A HOSPITAL BUT my eyes won't open. They're fighting me.

I slowly get my eyes to cooperate, but I wince once the light hits them and close them again.

"Ciara." I hear my mom's voice, and I want to follow her voice but it's too painful. "I turned the light down, sweetie. Can you open your eyes for me? I'm here." I slowly open my eyes again and allow them to readjust. Mom is standing over me, waiting for me to say something.

"I…" I immediately choke on my words. My throat is extremely dry. Mom grabs a cup of water and holds the straw up to my lips.

"Slow sips." I take a couple of sips before trying to readjust in my bed and wince from the movement. "I can call the nurse."

"No. Not yet." I clear my throat. "He's…dead."

Mom eyes me with sympathy. "Yeah, baby. He's dead." I took a life. I know I had to do it. I know he was going to kill me and Sasha if I didn't. I don't feel guilty at all. If there's anything to feel guilty about, it's the fact that he got to die a swift death instead of rotting in a prison cell. But I do feel un-settled by the fact that I actually killed someone. I push that aside for now.

"You gonna yell at me for blocking your number?"

She crosses her arms over her chest but smiles. "You're lucky you're in a weakened state right now or else I would put you over my knee for that. I suppose you're forgiven."

I laugh, but it fades into a cough. Mom gives me another few sips of water. "Thank you. I really thought I knew what was best. But honestly, I don't know shit."

"Finally, she gets it."

"Ha ha. Seriously. I did this all wrong. I was trying to save everyone, but I was only making it worse. And it was all for nothing because he was so unhinged he was never gonna give up anyway. I regret pushing everyone away. I'm so sorry, Mom. I really hope you can forgive me. I hope everyone can. I hope Lincoln still loves me."

"Girl, do you honestly think that boy doesn't love you?"

Then where is he?

"Where is he?"

"He just went down to the cafeteria to grab me some food. He'll be mad when he comes up and sees he wasn't here when you woke up."

He still loves me. I didn't push him too far. I didn't ruin us. Thank fuck.

"I guess I could pretend to still be sleeping but...I won't." We share a laugh, but the moment sobers when Mom speaks again.

"There is nothing to forgive, Ciara. Everyone knows your heart is too big and your mind is too stubborn to listen to reason. We all love you. I am so proud of you for fighting through this."

Lincoln enters the room, and his eyes immediately lock on me.

"Angel."

That name settles deep into the marrow of my bones. It feels so good to hear him call me that again. "Hi."

Mom grabs the food from Lincoln and steps out to give us a minute of privacy. Lincoln never takes his eyes off of me as he crosses the room and kisses my forehead.

"There are those eyes I love so much."

I clear my throat and gather strength for what I'm about to say. "I want to make something clear." He eyes me curiously. "I was an asshole. I didn't mean what I said about you only wanting me to stay because you were thinking with your dick. If you want me to, I'd like to do what I said I'd do in the first place. I'd like to stay."

He chuckles. "I mean, maybe I do think with my dick when it comes to you. That's just not the only part of me that stands at attention for you."

"This is becoming painfully cheesy now." I smile.

"Good. Of course I want you to stay, Ciara. I want you to stay forever." He shakes his head as if talking himself down from continuing our conversation on this path. "Besides, who's going to eat my flats if you leave?"

"Someone with some fucking sense, I guess." I roll my eyes. He just laughs and pulls me in for a kiss. He breathes life back into me with every second the kiss lasts until a throat clears behind us.

"You two lovebirds done? We'd like to love up on her now," Nina proclaims. Everyone files into my room. The nurses are probably going to lose their shit, but it's so good to see everyone.

"And now that you're awake, it should be noted that if you ever hang up on me and block my number again, I will drag you," Simone says with her finger pointed at me.

"Jesus, Simone." Sarah rolls her eyes. Simone shrugs and I laugh, thankful to have these people in my life.

Six weeks later, Lincoln and I are sitting in his condo. I still have my apartment, but I haven't spent a night there since coming home. Everything feels right here with him.

"Stop stressing about it, Ci." Lincoln flops down on the couch next to me, handing me the bowl of popcorn and M&M's.

"Of course I'm stressed about it, Lincoln. Christmas is in a couple of weeks, and I don't have all the gifts I need. I'm so behind." I made sure to get all of the kids' gifts, but I still have to get gifts for everyone else, and I'm running out of time. Being in the hospital really put a dent in my plans.

"Yeah, you're in recovery. No one is expecting anything." He slides his hand up my thigh, and my core is on fire. We haven't had sex in six weeks, doctor's orders. You'd think I'd have better composure considering I went through a two-year drought before Lincoln, but I am unraveling, and if his hands aren't on me tonight, I'm going to snap. Better yet, I'm going to get Lincoln to snap. He's been so gentle with me since everything happened and that's so sweet. Really. But I want the toss me around, rip my clothes off, up against the wall Lincoln back. He tilts his head at me, and I realize I haven't answered him.

"Yeah, it's just that you all made Thanksgiving so special for me. I want to make Christmas special for you." I was still in recovery during Thanksgiving so both families brought dinner to Lincoln's. Lincoln's mom taught me how to make both jollof rice and egusi soup, as much as she could while I had to sit down often. The guys served me all night long. My mom extended our tradition of watching *Soul Food* and one cringey Hallmark movie to Lincoln's family. It was beautiful watching both families come together. "Anyway, everyone is getting gifts. It's going to happen. I got this shit." I turn back to my laptop to continue my Amazon search. I mean, if I'm going to get everything in time it's probably best to stick with Amazon Prime.

"I only want one gift from you this year, Angel."

"What's that?" I ask without looking up from my computer.

"For you to say yes."

"Yes to what?" I gasp when I look up and Lincoln is holding a velvet box in his hands. He gets down on one knee and opens the box, revealing a gorgeous solitaire diamond ring. "Lincoln," I rasp.

"Here's what I know. I know you have the biggest heart of anyone I've ever met. Your selflessness knows no bounds. I know you have the insane ability to make me laugh one moment and make my dick twitch in the next. I know you make me happier than I've ever been, and I breathe easier when you're near. I don't need to wait any longer to see if we're right for each other. Our love story was written in the stars the moment I held you in my arms.

I don't want to waste time. I want to start the rest of our lives right now. So question time, Angel. Don't think, just answer. Will you marry me?"

"Yes!" I yell, tackling him to the floor. I kiss him all over his face, and he slides the ring on my finger. I kiss him again and slide my tongue across his bottom lip. He opens for me, and I deepen the kiss until he groans and pulls away.

"You're supposed to be taking it easy." *Ha!* If he thinks we're not about to consummate this engagement he's lost his mind.

"Doctor said I could start mild activities again. We can go slow. I promise." I drag out the word slow as I slide my tongue from his ear down his neck. His grip on my hips tightens.

"Bull. Shit."

It absolutely is. I mean, we'll start slow, but we won't end that way and we both know it.

"I've never had husband-to-be dick before. Are you really going to rob me of the experience?"

He throws his head back and laughs. "You're ridiculous. Technically, every time we have sex from now until we get married will be husband-to-be dick."

"Okay, but are you really going to make me tell all my friends that after you proposed you gave me a sweet kiss and we went to bed? Or are you going to ravage me and make Nina and Simone proud?"

"I absolutely do not want to talk about Simone or Nina when I'm hard beneath you."

I wiggle in his lap, and he groans again. "So let's not waste it."

He pins me with a serious gaze. "Are you sure?"

"I've never been more sure of anything in my life." He makes quick work of my shirt and our pants before sliding me down his shaft, so painstakingly slow. We moan into each other's mouths.

"Forever starts now, Angel."

I can't wait for every moment.

Epilogue

Lincoln
8 months later

"**S**TOP FIDGETING, ASSHOLE. YOU'RE MAKING ME NERVOUS."

Dom stops messing with his cufflinks to flip Isaiah off. "Shut up, asshole. I'm just straightening them out."

"What do either of you dumb shits have to be nervous about? Are you getting married?"

"Just tell me the truth. How long until you tell her the story? I need to be prepared for my future sister-in-law to give me shit for the rest of my life."

This damn fool.

"I'm not gonna tell her the story of how this band of idiots came to be. We made a deal. She knows that and judges me mercilessly for it. But some poor unfortunate souls have to settle for you jackasses for the story to come out."

"Good, so it's never coming out then," Shane adds.

"That was the plan. Now back to important shit. You ready for today, man?" Kai asks.

The moment my mom and Angela heard we were engaged, they went into wedding planning mode. It's been exhausting. I had no idea there were so many options for centerpieces. Ciara and I almost ran away to elope, but neither of us wanted to suffer through the shit storm our families would rain down on us for that.

I would take the craziness of the past eight months over the months of Eddie's bullshit any day though.

We've come a long way in the past eight months. Ciara released her debut novel, and it was a huge hit. Sales definitely increased even more when a news article connected her with the story about Eddie Brighton. At first, she shied away from making any statements to the public about it. She wanted to move on with her life, but then she realized that there are probably a ton of women and men out there who are suffering at the hands of unstable psychopaths like him, and she wanted to help them in any way she could. I've never been prouder of her.

The man who gave Ciara's therapy file to Eddie was arrested. Ciara still admires Dr. Goodwin and would recommend her to anyone, but after everything that happened, she felt more comfortable finding a local therapist here to start over with. She still had a lot to work out with her need for control and feeling unworthy of saving. She also had to cope with the fact that she killed Eddie. I felt no remorse whatsoever for the fact that he was dead, and I know she didn't either, but she struggled with the fact that she was responsible for a loss of life. She's come a long way in that regard, and her nightmares are almost non-existent at this point.

I started seeing a therapist myself. I needed to speak to a professional about my guilt over everything with Erica. A lot of my insecurities about that situation came back with a vengeance when I almost lost Ciara. The guys all supported me in my journey with therapy, another reason why I'm proud to have all of them stand by me today.

Michael and Carter make their way into the room. They were wrangling the kids together for their duties. Nevaeh insisted on being the flower girl, as if there was another option. Malcolm and Niecy are the ushers, and they are taking their roles very seriously.

"Okay, everyone's set," Michael tells me as he adjusts his tie.

"Let's go get me married."

"You nervous?" Isaiah asks, standing by my side as my best man.

"Not at all." It's the truth. I'm excited to see Ciara walk toward me, but I'm not nervous at all. I'm just ready to get started with the rest of our lives.

Nevaeh skips down the aisle, making a show of tossing the white flowers on the ground. She almost manages to steal the show, and I have the biggest smile on my face as she skips toward me. She stops in front of me and motions for me to bend down to her level. I do and she plants a big kiss on my cheek.

"I love you, Linky. I can't wait for Ciara to be my auntie."

"I can't wait either, Short Stack." She bounces off to her seat.

Ciara's bridesmaids make their way down the aisle, one by one. Reggie, Nina, Sasha, Simone, Sarah, and Brittany last. Ciara refused to decide who would be her maid of honor so she told them they had to decide amongst themselves. They decided to have a battle of movie knowledge—Nina's idea. Brittany won, and on a Harry Potter question no less. I'd expect nothing less from my beautiful bride and her band of misfits.

Finally, Ciara steps out arm in arm with her mom, and I'm stunned speechless. She looks absolutely stunning. Her dress has a V-neck cut that exposes the curves of her breasts. The top of her dress hugs to her body perfectly before fanning out to a floor length gown, covered in lace that makes her look like a goddess. I'm a lucky-ass man.

She makes it to me and grabs my hand. Angela kisses one of my cheeks and pats the other one with her hand before turning to hug Ciara and sitting in her seat by Nevaeh.

"Hi."

"Hi."

"You look beautiful." Her brown cheeks blush.

My dad is officiating the wedding for us. He was ordained online and is very proud of himself for doing so. He takes us through the ceremony and then, just like that, we're married.

When it's time to kiss the bride, I take full advantage. There are cheers everywhere, and I keep going until Nevaeh yells that we're gross. I laugh and pull away.

"You're starting off this marriage by being extra, I see," Ciara smiles.

"I'm just starting it the way I want it to last, Mrs. Cole."

"I do like the sound of that."

Ciara

Holy. Shit. I am a married woman. If you would've told me a year ago I'd be celebrating my wedding right now, I'd have told you you were crazy.

As much as the entire wedding planning process overwhelmed me, I have to say the moms did their thing. Everything is so gorgeous, and I'm honored to be here with these people who own my heart and this man who owns my soul.

The moms set up a cocktail hour just for Lincoln and me so that we could eat in peace before having to mingle all night long. We used that time to do umm…other things. So now I'm starving, but I'm in too good of a mood to be hangry.

I spot Nina across the room, checking in on Jada and Logan. I turn to Lincoln and kiss him on the cheek. "I'll be back."

A lot has happened over the last eight months. I'm an actual published author now. My mom moved to Austin to be closer to me and her "future grandkids," who don't exist. Not that we don't want them. We talked about it and we definitely want kids, but now that we're not living in fear anymore we want to just enjoy each other, drama free, for a little bit.

A lot of good has happened, but a lot of sad too. Both of Nina's parents tragically passed away in a train accident on their way to New Orleans. Nina became the sole guardian of Logan and Jada, and it's been a tough adjustment for all of them so far.

I can't imagine what they're going through. I know they all held resentment for their parents for being gone so often, but now that they're not coming back, I'm sure they have no idea how to feel. Nina does a good job at putting on a tough front for the kids, but she is stressed beyond belief. Logan has become even quieter than he was before. It's like he thinks if he just blends in with the wall and doesn't cause trouble, nothing else bad can happen. Jada never wants Nina to leave her sight.

"Hey, gorgeous." Nina turns around and hugs me. I ask Logan and Jada if they'd be okay if Nina steps outside with me for a minute. Logan just nods, and Jada looks worried, but she says it's okay.

We step out onto the venue's patio, admiring the gorgeous flower wall the moms had put together. "How are you doing?"

She shakes her head and wags her finger at me, rejecting my concern. "Uh-uh. No you don't. Today is your day—you don't need to check on me."

"You are my sister, Nina. I don't just push you to the side."

"I'm fine, really."

She's not fine. She's absolutely not fine. But I won't completely call her out on it right now. I've been where she is. I've been the one carrying the weight of the world on my shoulders, refusing to share any of the burden with anyone else. "Okay, sure. But I have a surprise for you anyway." Her brows rise in question. "Sasha is going to keep Logan and Jada for the weekend so that you can have some time to decompress."

"What? No. No. I can't do that. Jada will freak out."

I grab her hands in mine. "We talked it through with her earlier today, and she's excited to hang out with Nevaeh. Reggie and Michael are gonna bring Malcolm and Niecy by, too, so I think she'll be distracted enough. If it gets to be too much for her, you can cut your weekend short, but you deserve to try. We are going to get you all through this. Together. Take the break, Nina."

I won't take no for an answer, but I do give her the time to process the idea. She sighs and looks away wearily. She makes eye contact with someone across the room, and the look on her face has me turning to see who she's looking at. I turn in time to see Isaiah break eye contact with her and walk away. Hmm. The tension between those two is bound to come to a head. If anyone can pull her from the brink of despair, I think Isaiah and his joker personality might be the one. But she's not ready to hear that so I leave it. Baby steps.

"Okay, okay. I'll do it. Thank you, Ci. Really." She squeezes my shoulder and heads back inside.

When I come back inside I see Lincoln dancing with his mom, and the sight puts a smile on my face. He sees me and whispers something to his mom before heading over to me. He holds out a hand, and I grab it to join him on the dance floor.

"So. This is our life now," he says.

"Yep. What do you think so far?"

"I think this has been the best ride of my life, and I can't wait for the next wave, Angel."

"Good answer."

"I thought so."

I lift my head from his shoulder and stare into those warm brown eyes. "Thank you."

"For what?"

"For loving me when I didn't love myself enough. For setting me free. For being my home." I realize that I was beyond lost when I left Baltimore. I was wandering without a home. I found my true home here, not just in Austin, but in Lincoln. As long as I have him, I'll never be lost again.

"Always, Angel," he promises.

I seal that promise with a kiss.

The end

Preview of
WHERE WE FOUND OUR
Heart

CHAPTER
One

Nina

LOOK AROUND THE WEDDING VENUE AND I FEEL A SENSE OF CALM FOR the first time in months. Everything has come together beautifully. The color theme is white and gold. It's both whimsical and regal at the same time. White draping across the entire ceiling makes the venue seem endless. Centerpieces of hydrangeas at each table stand tall and command attention. The gold accents are subtle, not ostentatious at all, yet emit power all the same.

The bride, my best friend Ciara, is wearing a gorgeous A-line floor-length gown. The V-neck bodice fits her like a glove while the bottom flares out a bit to give a princess vibe. The whole dress is covered in stunning gold lace. The intricate details of her bright red phoenix tattoo, spanning the entire length of her arm, accentuate her beauty and make her dress pop against her almond-colored skin.

I remember being with her, her mom, and our friends when she found the dress. We all cried at how beautiful she looked. Until today, that was the last time I cried tears of joy. The tears I cried that day were beautiful. I was proud to let them fall and give them over to Ciara's happiness. The tears I cried mere weeks later and every day after were ugly and angry. Full of pain and loss. If I could go back to Ciara's wedding dress shopping day, I'd appreciate those tears a hell of a lot more. We knew her soon to be husband, Lincoln, would lose his shit when he saw her in it, and he did. The look on his face when he saw her walking toward him was enough to bring anyone to their knees. The look of the man behind him, watching his brother with pride, is one I tried and failed to ignore.

I'm staring out at the dessert table when I feel a tiny hand tap on my shoulder. I turn around and look at my sister, Jada. She looks adorable in her light pink floor-length dress. She insisted on getting a long dress to match me. She's tripped over it four times tonight, but she's so damn cute. She looks so much like our mom—it's why I call her Mini—it almost hurts to look at her.

"Nina, ShaSha said CiCi and Linc are going on a honeymoon. What's that?" I laugh every time she calls my other best friend, Sasha, "ShaSha" because she can't seem to pronounce Sasha.

"A honeymoon is a trip that couples take to celebrate their wedding alone." Her face drops at the word "trip" and I curse myself.

"Are they going to take a train?" she asks, frantic.

"No, Mini. They're going to take a plane, but they'll be okay, I promise." It's a tricky thing. Because I can't actually promise that. I shouldn't say that. But I have to give this innocent little girl some peace of mind.

"Okay, if you're sure." I look up at my brother, Logan, and though he's looking down at his lap I know it pains him to listen to our conversation right now. It's been four months, and I still don't know how to properly explain to her that a vacation doesn't mean a death sentence.

Our parents were on their way to New Orleans for an anniversary trip when their train derailed, and they were killed in the crash. Now I'm the sole guardian to my fourteen-year-old brother and six-year-old sister, and I have no idea what I'm doing. I used to babysit my siblings a lot because my parents often acted like they didn't have minors to raise and took off on vacations frequently. But babysitting for a few days and being completely responsible for shaping them into well-rounded people ready to enter the world are two completely different things. And let's face it, I have an uphill battle here. I'm left trying to undo the damage our parents have caused while trying not to fuck them up any more. Thanks, Mom and Dad. I hope you're having a great permanent vacation wherever the fuck you are. Ugh. I don't want to be mad at them. That's not fair or right.

I'm pulled back to reality when Ciara approaches our table.

"Hey, gorgeous." I turn around and give her a huge hug. She asks Logan and Jada if they'd be okay if I step outside with her for a minute. Jada looks nervous at the thought of me being out of her sight. She's become a permanent attachment at my side since our parents passed. I know it's not healthy, but honestly I think the only reason I haven't had a mental breakdown yet is because she's always with me. Logan just nods, and I drown in his silence. I miss my brother. He's always been quiet, but he's always had a charming personality to the people he loves the most. That boy is nowhere to be found right now.

I follow Ciara out to the venue's patio, and she wastes no time diving in. "How are you doing?"

Nope. Not going there. Not today. Not tomorrow. Maybe not ever. "Uh-uh. No, you don't. Today is your day—you don't need to check on me."

She levels me with a hard stare. "You are my sister, Nina. I don't just push you to the side." And this is why I love her. We've only known each other for a year and a half but I've never met anyone as selfless as her. She's always putting everyone above herself, but she's done enough of that for a lifetime. She's earned the right to be blissed out of her mind with happiness today. I'm not going to drag her down with me. My misery does not want company.

"I'm fine, really."

"Okay, sure. But I have a surprise for you anyway." Who gets someone else a surprise on their wedding day? I don't respond, but just raise my brows in question. "Sasha is going to keep Logan and Jada for the weekend so that you can have some time to decompress."

"What? No. No. I can't do that. Jada will freak out."

She shakes her head adamantly. "We talked it through with her earlier today, and she's excited to hang out with Nevaeh. Reggie and Michael are gonna bring Malcolm and Niecy by too, so I think she'll be distracted enough. If it gets to be too much for her, you can cut your weekend short, but you deserve to try. We are going to get you all through this. Together. Take the break, Nina." Nevaeh is Sasha's daughter. She's Jada's age, and they always have a good time whenever they hang out. Reggie is Sasha's sister. Her and Michael's kids, Malcolm and Niecy, are older than Jada and Nevaeh. Niecy is thirteen and Malcolm is ten, so they'll probably spend most of their time with Logan, if he doesn't crawl deep inside a book and shut out the world.

The idea of having a weekend to myself sounds nice. I'm a speeding car headed straight for a brick wall. I just need someone to hit the brakes for a moment. But can I do that? What would I even do with a weekend to myself? I've been part of a trio every day for four months. I don't understand the meaning of privacy anymore.

I feel him before I see him. I look up and there he is. Isaiah Cole. He's the guy I want nothing to do with and yet I can't seem to stop thinking about him. He also happens to be Ciara's brother-in-law now. He's looking right at me, and I can't tell what he's thinking but I don't have time to decipher his mood today. He's so hot and cold, I can't get comfortable. But part of me just wants to take a bite out of him. *Jesus.*

I realize too late that Ciara has seen the exchange between him and me. I'm not stepping on that landmine yet, so I give her the answer she's looking for instead. "Okay, okay. I'll do it. Thank you, Ci. Really." I squeeze her shoulder and head back inside.

* * *

Long after the wedding is over and the kids are with Sasha and Carter, I'm sitting on my couch wondering what the fuck I'm going to do with this weekend of newfound freedom. I've been forbidden from seeing the kids—unless Jada can't cope—and from going to the bar I manage, Neon Nights. Who the fuck am I if I'm not watching the kids or running that bar?

You're a woman with needs that haven't been met in quite some time.

I feel like that meme of Kermit with the hoodie on.

The non-hoodie version of me is saying, "Spend the weekend coping with your feelings. There's plenty of housework you can do. There are a lot of healthy ways you can spend your time."

While the hoodie version of me is screaming, "Sex is healthy. Go to Isaiah's place in this sexy-ass bridesmaid dress and fuck his brains out like you've wanted to do for over a year."

I look myself over in the mirror. This dress really is beautiful. It's gold and looks amazing against my chestnut skin. It's mermaid style and hugs to my round hips like a second skin. I know I saw Isaiah checking out my ass at least once tonight. And he looked like a damn GQ model in his suit. Part of me knew I was going to do this. It's why I haven't taken the dress off yet. Yeah, okay. Decision made. I strap my heels back on and head out before rational thought can take over.

The whole ride over to Isaiah's is a hot mess. I debate turning around three different times, but the hoodie version of me keeps her foot firmly planted on the gas. I've been to Isaiah's house exactly three times before. I dropped Sasha off there once after we'd gone to brunch because she didn't want Carter to see how drunk she'd gotten and tease her. He hosted Nevaeh's birthday party last year. It was not adorable at all. My ovaries did not almost explode. Nope, not at all. And Ciara and Lincoln's engagement party was held at Isaiah's house. I never understood why a single man in his twenties chose to buy a single-family home in the burbs. To each his own, I guess. I loved my apartment in the city, but now that I've got two kids to raise, I'm a fellow suburbanite.

I spend an embarrassing amount of time outside his door debating how many knocks makes me look casual and not like I'm desperate for sex. Even though I'm very desperate for sex. Three knocks then silence. That's my limit. I won't knock again. It seems three is the magic number because it doesn't take long to hear the lock to the door clicking.

This man has the audacity to answer the door in the men's equivalent of lingerie—grey sweatpants and no shirt. I do what I hope to God is a subtle drool check, because I am Nina Fucking Williams and I'll be damned if I let a man see me drooling over him. Even if he is too sexy to be real.

He leans against his door with a knowing smirk, and I make it my mission to wipe it right off his face. "How you doing, Nina?"

Okay, we're off to a good start. Since I met Isaiah he's given me whiplash. One minute he flirts with me and gives me all his attention, the next he barely acknowledges my existence. And having a serious conversation without him defaulting to flirtation or jokes is like pulling teeth. I have no time for games, which is why I said I'd never date him, but I'm not exactly here to date him, now am I? He's starting off by addressing me like Joey from *Friends*, so I'm guessing he's in a flirty mood.

"Am I Rachel or Phoebe?" He just smiles and steps aside so I can come in.

"Definitely Phoebe. That fits you. Kind of like how that dress fits you."

"Perfectly, you mean?"

That gets a real laugh out of him. "I always love your modesty."

"Modesty is overrated. We both know I look fine as fuck in this dress." His eyes trail down my body, and I resist the urge to shiver under his gaze. I wait for his eyes to lock with mine and when they do, I hold my stare, daring him to make the next move.

"You do. It would probably look even better on the floor." Now he's speaking my language.

"My thoughts exactly." His eyebrows rise at that. Yeah, I'm not here to play games tonight.

"Shit, I've never loved weddings more than I do in this moment."

"Look, you and I have been doing this dance for too long now. The kids are at Sasha's for the weekend against my will, so I can do anything I want to do—and I want to do you." His eyes soften at the mention of my siblings. That's exactly what I don't want. I need to lock up the sympathy and get the heat back in his eyes. I mean, Jesus, didn't he hear the part where I said I wanted to do him? Focus, man. I swish my hips as I get closer to him, and his eyes follow the movement.

Bingo.

"Nina, you don't have to explain. If you have needs, I'm more than capable of taking care of them for you."

"Then stop talking and get over here." He closes the distance between us in a second and pulls me in for a heated kiss. This kiss is full of passion and promises of what's to come, and I immediately feel the heat in my core. I want to lift my leg up to his waist, but this damn dress is preventing that. I did not think this through well enough. He reads my mind though and spins me around to unzip the dress, following the zipper with his tongue. Holy shit. I step out of the dress and his eyes are hooded with desire, staring at me in nothing but my sheer bra, panties, and garters.

"Fuck. You are gorgeous."

His words have me feeling bold. "Needy over here, Isaiah. What are you gonna do about it?" He growls and lifts me up with ease.

He follows me down to the bed before lifting my legs over his shoulders and kissing his way from my ankles to the place where I need him most. He blows a breath against my panties, and I'm already about to lose it.

I have dreamed of this moment several times. We've been treading the waters of this sexual tension for over a year now, and it's finally pulling us under its waves. I've never wanted to drown more in my life.

"Shit, Isaiah." He taps my hips, and I instantly lift so he can pull my panties down. He continues kissing my inner thighs. A bite here, a nibble there. He's teasing me, but never giving me the pressure I need. I'm going to kill him.

"Isaiah?"

"Yes?" He drags out the word.

"If you don't eat my pussy soon, I'm gonna finish without you."

He throws his head back in laughter. "Hmm, I'm tempted to keep teasing you until you beg for it."

Ha! Yeah, okay. That's not even in my vocabulary. I glide my hand down my chest until I reach my folds. I want him to touch me, but watching him as he watches me touch myself is getting me going all the same. I make a show of pleasuring myself until I hear him curse and slap my hand away.

"That's what I thought." I feel vindicated until he finally licks up my center and then all thoughts leave me. His tongue is the stuff dreams are made of. All his teasing is over with. He dips two fingers inside of me, spreading me wider. His free hand squeezes my ass, pulling me closer to his mouth. I moan his name loudly when he thrusts his fingers deeper inside me. He sucks my clit so hard I don't even have a moment to breathe before my orgasm hits me like a freight train.

What. The. Fuck? I may not have been fully prepared for Isaiah Cole but damn if I'm turning back now.

My legs are shaking, and he caresses them while climbing up my body to reach my lips. He crushes his mouth to mine, and I taste myself on his tongue. I grab the band of his sweatpants and pull him down to completely cover me. He leans back up to pull his pants and briefs down. His erection bobs free…and holy shit.

I should've known. I should've seen this coming, but I really was not prepared for this man tonight.

That thing is a weapon.

A weapon of mass orgasms.

He has what I like to call "special occasion dick." A dick so big it's not meant to be experienced on a regular basis because it will rearrange your fucking organs. I've only experienced it once in my lifetime. You don't find them in the wild, otherwise known as the streets of Austin, often. It's only meant to be enjoyed for a special occasion like a birthday, or a promotion, or a recovery from a shitty breakup, or your parents dying and your first weekend alone without your siblings. *Eew.* That's incredibly morbid. Buck the fuck up, Nina.

I hear the crinkle of a condom wrapper and watch as he sheaths himself, never taking his eyes off of me.

"I've been waiting a long time for this moment," he confesses. He leans down and bites my neck, then immediately cools it with his tongue. He continues that trail down to my shoulder, making it impossible to think straight.

"You're the one who's been playing games for the last year. You're so hot and cold I can't tell which way is up." He sobers for a moment at that statement but immediately morphs his face back into that schoolboy smirk.

He starts singing, well it's more like talking in a slightly higher pitch but I can tell it's supposed to resemble singing, something. I recognize the lyrics but I can't quite make out the song. Hot? Cold? Up? Down? What? Wait, is that… "Are…are you singing Katy Perry at me?" That is definitely Katy Perry that I just heard. He's full of all kinds of surprises.

"I didn't turn any music on, so I thought I'd set the mood." I look back down at that fucking python between his legs, and I don't know if I want to laugh at his dumbass behavior or yelp in anticipation. He kisses me breathless before entering me in one hard thrust, and the yelp wins.

"Are you okay?"

My pussy clenches at his words, and I feel him shudder inside me. "Yes. Move." He thrusts again and I match his pace.

He continues singing about wrong and right and black and white.

I let out some mix between a laugh and a moan. "Are you seriously still singing that fucking song?"

He seems to come out of a daze in that moment, shaking his head slightly. "It honestly just slipped out. You feel so good, I'm trying to focus on not coming early."

He lifts one of my legs so he's stroking me deeper. He's devouring me with his eyes. My back is arched, my hands tracing my puckered nipples. I take a moment to admire the body of this man. He's got the body of a swimmer. His shoulders are broad. The veins in his forearms stand out. The abs on his torso are defined, hard-earned. The deep V at his hips is begging for my tongue. There's a sheen of sweat covering his chest. My eyes follow the path of a bead from the top of his strong pec all the way down to the place where our bodies become one. I never want this to end.

I wrap my arms around his neck and pull him down to me for another kiss. I push my hips upward and place my hand on his chest until he falls back. Grabbing his shoulders, I force him to sit against his headboard. I straddle his hips, and he lines himself up to my entrance. I slowly sink back down his shaft, and it draws a guttural groan from the both of us.

"Fuuuuuck," he cries out.

I rock my hips forward, taking what I need from him. His lips are parted, and his breath is shaky. He's watching me with fire in his eyes. I feel powerful under his gaze. He grips my hips so tight it may leave a bruise, but I don't care. I need it all. He thrusts forward, hitting me right where I need him. I can't hold eye contact anymore. I throw my head back and moan. He takes advantage of my exposed throat and licks a trail from the swells of my breasts to the erogenous zone behind my ear.

"Oh fuck, I'm coming," I announce before I come apart.

"Thank fuck," he cries out before pumping another two times and spilling his release.

I let out a deep exhale. "Holy shit. S.O.D. for the win."

His eyes crinkle with amusement and confusion. "What the hell is S.O.D.?" he asks.

"Special Occasion Dick." I explain to him what the term means, and he lets out a deep bark of laughter that's like music to my ears. He kisses my forehead before going to the bathroom to dispose of the condom.

I'm on cloud nine right now, but I also have no idea what comes next. I don't want a perfect night to be ruined by him awkwardly trying to get rid of me when he comes back. I got what I came here for, so it's time to get the fuck out. Maybe now I can focus on housework.

"Where are you going?" he asks when he sees me snapping my bra back into place.

"Umm...I was just going to—"

He cuts me off. "I don't think so, Phoebe. That was just a warm-up. Tonight's still a special occasion, isn't it?"

Welp. That housework can go fuck itself. I unclasp my bra again.

The next morning, I am deliciously sore. This was exactly what I needed. Isaiah is back in his room getting dressed while I'm in his kitchen making coffee.

Even though most of our hours were spent exploring each other's bodies, we also spent a lot of time talking and laughing. It's hard to reconcile the Isaiah who doesn't take shit seriously with the Isaiah who senses exactly what you need and delivers. I feel like I can finally catch my breath when I'm with him. That's a dangerous feeling. I don't want to accept this ventilator I've been given, because when I'm forced to breathe on my own I may fail.

The handle on Isaiah's door turns, and my head snaps in that direction wondering who the hell is about to walk in here. I'm dressed, so I'm not worried about that. Albeit in my bridesmaid dress from last night so there will be no mistaking what went down here. A gorgeous black girl walks in and stares at me like I've broken into her home.

She can't be taller than five feet four inches, and I'm five feet eight inches—six feet with my heels on—but she sizes me up in a way that makes me feel more naked in my dress than I was with Isaiah last night.

"Hi. You're cute. I guess you're why Isaiah didn't answer my call last night. Figures. You done yet?" Her tone is so flippant like she and Isaiah have some sort of open relationship while he has a revolving door of women coming out of his house.

I'm not foolish enough to think that just because we had sex that means we were going to be anything serious, but damn, I just feel cheap now.

I chug the rest of my coffee because I'm not one to waste caffeine. I leave the mug on the counter because fuck him, and I walk toward the woman who brought my fantasy crashing down around me.

"Yeah, I'm beyond done. Have fun." I walk out with what's left of my dignity and run home to lick yet another wound.

Acknowledgements

To my mama—You were my very first friend in this world and you'll be my best friend until my last breath. You have always believed in me, even when I didn't believe in myself. If I had listened to you and pursued writing when I was younger who knows where I'd be now, but I wouldn't trade this journey for anything, and I'm so grateful to have you by my side while I do it. Thank you for always being my biggest cheerleader and the greatest example of a boss-ass bitch. You are strong, kind, wise, and a total badass. My main goal in life is to be half the woman you are. I love you with all my heart.

To Brad, the pillow to my blanket—You won't read my stuff but you'll promote the shit out of it, and that's why I keep you around. Seriously, you always let me know how proud you are of me. In the words of Queen Bee, you always make me feel fine as hell. My personal hype man. Even though you're highly annoying, you rarely let me write in peace, and we almost came to blows over MY writing table, I can't think of a better duo than us.

To Krissi, mah pooks—Thank you for always being down for a drink and an adventure when I need it. Where would I be if you hadn't bullied me into eating lunch with you all those years ago? Probably a lot less drunk but also a lot less happy. I couldn't ask for a better friend than you. You may be older than I am, but you keep me young. When I get lost in my head, you always get me to chill the hell out and relax. You drag me out of the house when I become antisocial, but you're also down to stay in and binge-watch *90 Day* and *To All the Boys* with me. Balance is key. It's an honor to call you a sister. I love you more than words can say. Always.

To Jasmine, my soul sister—I am so incredibly proud of both of us for starting the next phase of our lives. Watching your growth with every new release is an honor. And when we start our haunted house specials, the world won't know what hit them! Thank you for always giving me that extra push when I need it. There's no one I'd rather get advice from than you. I forced a friendship with you over food neither one of us can eat anymore, but it was one of the best decisions I ever made. If I tell you I love you then it will be in print forever and you'll never let me forget it so I'll just say…you know things about me sure. #IYKYK

To Auntie—Your love of romance novels is partly what inspired me to try my hand at this genre. I know my books are in a different lane than what you're used to, but I hope I made you proud.

To Linda—From our first phone conversation, I knew you were who I needed on my side to get me through the crazy world of self-publishing. I was, and still am, a complete deer in headlights when it comes to figuring all this stuff out, and you make it make sense. You're always there when I have a million questions, which is all the time. Thank you for believing in me!

To my betas, Tricia, Eliza, and Meghan—Thank you for reading my little story and pushing me to make it the best version of itself. Your feedback was life-changing. Us Harlot Authors gotta stick together!

To my boo, Andrea—You were my first friend in the book community and girl, you give me life! You showed me that I can still be authentically me and still be successful. You are a dope-ass queen and because of you I know even more dope-ass queens in Romancelandia, and I could not be more grateful.

To Melanie Harlow—If it wasn't for you and the Harlot Authors group I may not have had the confidence to keep going. Thank you so much for being willing to share your insights with so many people. You are a gift.

To Shari—You were a complete lifesaver with my website. I know as a millennial I'm supposed to be good with all things technology, but I'm low-key trash with all of it so you are a rockstar for helping my vision come to life!

To my editors, the Happily Editing Anns—You ladies are the best. You took my little book baby and helped me turn it into the best version of itself. Your ideas completely transformed this book into a version I never saw coming but am so unbelievably happy with. It's such a joy to work with the two of you. I can't wait to keep this train moving. Thank you for your guidance!

To my cover designer, Stacey Blake—You absolutely killed it! I am so in love with the cover of this book and that's all thanks to you dealing with my fifty million changes. Thank you for making my vision come to life.

To my pup, Nisa—You're a dog so unless you have some secret abilities I don't know about, you're not going to read this, but I'm obsessed with you, so you better believe you're getting a shout out in my acknowledgements. When my characters aren't cooperating and I need cuddles only you can provide, you tolerate me while I hug you for too long. It doesn't get much better than that. Mama loves you!

To the readers who took a chance on a black romance writer from Baltimore, thank you. Thank you, thank you, thank you. Your support means everything to me, and I can't wait to continue on this ride with you.

ABOUT
the Author

Natasha is an indie contemporary romance author living in Baltimore, MD with her family and fur baby.

She likes to write about everyday heroes who are a bit haunted and heroines who are sweet, sassy, and a little badass-y.

When she's not writing, she's usually reading, obsessively binge-watching TV, playing with her adorable dog, or hunting down delicious gluten free snacks.

Made in the USA
Middletown, DE
26 August 2021